Postmarked Calexico

Postmarked
Calexico

a novel

by Jim Davidson

Western Eye Press
2010

POSTMARKED CALEXICO
is published by Western Eye Press,
a small independent publisher
(very small, and very independent)
with a home base in the Colorado Rockies
and an office in Sedona Arizona,
Postmarked Calexico is also available
in various eBook formats.

Western Eye Press
P. O. Box 1008
Sedona, Arizona 86339
1 800 333 5178
www.WesternEyePress.com

First softbound edition, 2010.
ISBN13: 978-0-941283-24-3
First electronic edition, 2010.
ISBN13: 978-0-941283-23-6

This book is set in
Garamond Premier Pro
Adobe's OpenType revival
of classic old style typefaces
first cut by Claude Garamond
and Robert Granjon
in the middle of the 16th century.
Designed by Lito Tejada-Flores.
Cover photo by the author.

Contents

Jackson

Notes to Myself I

ALL THINGS LEFT BEHIND WOULD BE LOST, but that was the price of escape. Part rebirth, part death.

For three days, the two of them walked north beside the Sea of Cortez, keeping to the water's edge, allowing the tides and winds to sweep their tracks away. Mexican soldiers, they knew, controlled the roads, and moving on foot among the shorebirds looked to be the safest way.

They passed two small fishing villages, and the young Mexican woman, Lucia, bought fresh water, tortillas, and beans at each, slipping into the little camps only after the sun had faded into the western desert. At night, they slept further back in the dunes, looking always for embankments high enough to protect them from the wind and to hide small cooking fires, thin of smoke.

Each carried a loose shoulder bag and wore a floppy Mexican hat, and seen from a distance, the pair looked no different from the dozens of goatherds who worked the ragged jungles stretching from one village to the next.

They spoke very little and strained their eyes against the glare of the sun, stopping, waiting, sometimes pulling back into the jungle if they saw other figures, silhouettes, anywhere near the water's edge.

Each morning began with a fresh set of tracks.

I don't know that it happened exactly this way. But they left a hint behind, so I do know what they were running from—and why. To them, the sea was life, the inland desert, death.

If you've been there, you know it's true.

"Do you deserve this, being hunted, chased?" Lucia asked as they sat beside *their little fire sipping tea. The moon was just a sliver in the southern sky. "Who can say?" he answered after a while. "You do the best you can. Even when you see it's all an illusion, you keep on chasing it anyway. Am I a fool? Probably. So maybe I deserve to be hauled off in chains, just for that alone."*

For a long while, she watched the flicker of light. Then she asked another question.

"Do they know Señor Abeyta is dead, you think?"

He broke a stick of driftwood across his knee and just sat there, half in each hand.

"Stories like that travel fast. Maybe you should ask your father, the treacherous son of a bitch."

Lucia had come to Obregón, down the rough back road, to warn him and Señor Abeyta that her father had betrayed them, sold what he knew, what he thought he knew and maybe a lie or two to the Mexican and American police.

"They're not coming on the run," she'd said that day. "Not today anyway, but they'll be here soon."

On the beach, the two of them said nothing and sat watching the flames lick through the small pieces of sea-worn wood.

"But what difference does it make," he asked, "whether I deserve it or not? Does a cripple, too old to run, deserve to be pulled down by a pack of hungry dogs? Sometimes. Right and wrong are just words."

He stirred the coals with a piece of rusted pipe.

"I never expected to live very long anyway."

The dialogue is imaginary, but the sentiment is not. I heard those same words from the same man in an earlier time, a safer place. The images are faded now, but still I trust in them, because I know the man. Once, I thought he had ruined my life.

About noon on the third day, they climbed to the top of an outcropping of rock that stretched its long gray fingers well out into the sea, and stopped to study the shoreline that swept away toward the north.

"It's not far now," Lucia said. "Two miles, maybe three."

They were looking for a battered old trailer, a palapa*, a sun-bleached truck that marked the campo of a man the villagers called El Brujo, the old wizard. He was a friend of hers, she'd said, but a strange man who had, through many years, grown large in the eyes of the villagers, like a cross between a powerful shaman and a whiskey priest.*

"He can get us mules," she'd said.

From there, they could cross into the Cataviña Desert, a vast expanse of twisted cactus and giant boulders, fabled by the local Indians as the place where their earliest forefathers had long ago disappeared.

"Even the army stays out of the boojum," she'd said.

But for now they saw nothing. The serpentine sand and smooth, almost soundless, surf bled off into the horizon like faded paper, and the sun was just a white hole in the midday sky.

This, too, is a guess. They were headed north, but not to cross the border. He'd already explained to me why he might never be going home. So they must have been trying to flank the Vizcaino Mountains, trying to find a route across to the western, the Pacific, side.

After that, I don't know. His plans, like his life, seemed to move in distinct chapters. The future, like the past, he once told me, was an error of imagination.

Daylight had nearly drifted out to sea, redrawing the faces of the dunes and painting the old metal trailer in shades of gray. The old man was standing ankle deep in the surf, watching a flock of floating birds. His white hair blew wildly in the wind, and a loose baggy white shirt flapped around him like a robe.

He turned slowly to watch the two people walk his way, studying them, showing them the same steady interest he'd allowed the feeding birds. But when Lucia pushed her hat back and let it hang from the string around her neck, when he could see her face, he stepped forward and smiled and reached out to take her hands.

"Lucia," he said. "It's been a long time."

She stepped back, smiled , and seemed to be squinting little tears out of the corners of her eyes.

"We used to meet in the park on Sundays," she said, talking to her traveling companion but still looking at the old wizard. "Before things got bad. He was teaching me how to play the Indian flute."

"So long ago," El Brujo said, smiling again, but more in pain, in remembering things lost.

Then he turned his eyes to the man in the floppy hat, the man with small glasses and a short-cropped gray beard.

For a moment, he said nothing, as though sorting through, collecting, weighing words.

"Let me guess," he said then. "You are the one everybody seeks, but no one ever really finds. The one they call Isaac Po.

PART ONE

Unfinished Business

Whitewater was still two hours away, and the weather was rough. Snow swept across the highway in thick horizontal sheets, and Jackson could barely see the centerline and the edges of the road. The lights of oncoming cars flickered and flashed through a boiling cloud and then were gone. Their taillights, like red fireflies, disappeared in the trailing wake.

The hour was only about six in the evening, and his gas tank was still half full. But his wipers were icing badly, dragging streaks across the glass, and his eyes were starting to throb and burn.

On the west edge of River Bend, the big lights and signs of a truck stop floated up out of the storm, and he pulled off the highway. A snowplow was working the parking lot, crawling around a dozen or so semis that had pulled in to wait out the blow. He sat inside his vehicle with the engine running while a boy in a heavy coat, a scarf tied around his head like a turban with a Texaco star ran the iced-over pump and stared at the slow-moving numbers, as though waiting for three cherries or four gold bars and the sound of silver dollars spilling onto the frozen ground.

As Jackson waited, an old truck pulled almost alongside, between the highway and his car, and sat with lights on, idling. When Jackson climbed out to take care of business, he could see behind the truck a long trailer piled high with bales of straw. Then the driver stepped out of the cab, slammed the door, and almost like comrades-in-vodka, the two men ducked and leaned and stumbled against the wind, toward the wall of glass and light.

At the doorway, the truck driver stepped back, giving way, and in that moment of clear, clean light, Jackson could see his face. It was a face—the high forehead, short-cropped beard, hair pulled back in a ragged ponytail, long and straight nose—he had looked for, in crowds, down dark alleys, for just over twenty years.

The truck driver was Isaac Po.

Those years, weathering, the grind of wind and rain, had been no more or less kind to Isaac Po than they had been to Jackson: hair streaked with gray, a face thinned and wrinkled a bit, skin grown leathery and parched. And he wore small round glasses now.

"Isaac."

The other man's hand, reaching to grab the edge of the door, fell back to his side, and he took a step back and squinted, unsure. They stood there, locked inside three or four long seconds, before Jackson spoke again.

"It's Jackson."

"I'll be go to hell." A half smile creased the other man's face. "So it is." He paused and ran his hand through his hair. "Just like that."

"Like what?"

"We're older."

"What did you expect?"

"The end of a canyon, maybe. A campfire and a bottle of bad rum. Coyotes. Not a shithole truck stop in the eye of a blizzard."

"Does it matter?"

"It does to me."

"Why?"

"Fucking winter."

The door closed behind them, and with a thud, the whistle of the wind was gone. The world smelled like motor oil and wet gloves and stale tobacco. Pools of water stood on the floor, floating technicolor slicks of grease. Heat roared down from a hot grill bracketed high upon the wall.

"How long has it been?" Jackson asked. He himself knew, within a few months either way. But did Isaac Po know? Did Isaac Po ever reach back for any of it, ever try to find a focus in the fog?

"I can't count backward anymore. A year passes, ten years pass, it's too blurry for me. It's all just yesterday."

Just yesterday, just like that.

"Twenty years," Jackson said.

No answer.

"You never think back on those days?"

The other man paused.

"Some," he said, and he paused, and in that moment, a hard look, a look of defiance, crossed his eyes, like he'd been nicked or jabbed or burned. "But only when they sneak up on me." He paused again. "Like right now."

Jackson turned to pay for gas, and when he turned back, Isaac Po was gone. At the counter and in the booths, big men in caps and bib overalls slouched in ones and twos, staring at their hands, smoking, coughing, and Isaac Po had faded away. Then Jackson saw him come out of the men's room and stop to fill a styrofoam coffee cup. He moved alongside and filled one for himself.

"You probably don't know," Jackson said.

Isaac Po stared at him blankly. He plainly didn't understand. And why should he understand a frameless question like that?

"About Corinne. She died last month."

The other man looked down and took a wooden spoon and stirred his coffee, thoroughly, as though he'd put something into it.

"I'm sorry to hear," he said.

"Her funeral, it was three weeks ago."

"I see."

Jackson poured and stirred sugar into his own cup.

He was stung by his own poor manners.

Why do I have to begin with this? Why not ask where him where he's been all this time, what he's been doing, if life is good? Hell, twenty years, eighty seasons, too many days and nights to even count have gotten away.

What's wrong with five minutes worth of civility?

Still, we're little more than strangers to each other now, strangers who might never pass this way again. And like strangers everywhere, don't we have to fall back on a language we can both understand?

Corinne is dead, but what does that mean? Nothing, except that she was there in those other days, alive, a symbol of the years when nights were drunk and funny and Bob Dylan was just a background noise, singing through his nose.

And then you were gone, Isaac, and she was a big part of that, too. You walked away and nothing was ever quite that funny again, and nobody seemed to want to dance.

Her name, her memory, her tombstone, bring back old questions, that's all. Why did you slip off into the night, Isaac? Where did you go?

Why did you leave with nothing to say to me?

His old friend stood at the counter paying for coffee.

"I got that one, too," he said to the kinky-haired clerk when Jackson walked over, and she punched the cash register a second time.

She was middle-aged and stiff and her eyes were dull, and Jackson wondered if, on slow nights, she just sat there and stared at her own reflection in the streaked glass, seeing the girl she probably had never been.

"Where are you living now?"

They were walking back toward the outside door.

"About four hours east."

And? Jackson waited for the rest, waited for some tightening of that arc. Four hours east took in a large portion of a couple of states. Not much useful information there. But nothing else came.

"You mean, around—"

"Look, I apologize, Jackson. I mean it. I know we ought to stand and talk. But this storm has me in a real bind. If I don't get over the divide in the next couple of hours, I might well end up with that trailer wrapped around my ass. Sorry, but I've got to get back on the road."

He opened the door and walked out against the whistling wind. Jackson followed, and Isaac Po turned halfway back and used his free hand to protect his ear from the blowing snow.

"Goddammit," Jackson shouted, "you can't just turn and walk away."

"What do you want from me, Jackson? What do you want?"

His voice, loud against the storm, was a shout of its own.

"The truth would be a good place to start."

"Look, Jackson, I guess you think I owe you," he said, stuffing his hands into the pockets of his coat. "Maybe I do, maybe I don't. We can sort that out. But not on a horseshit day like this."

Then he walked away, out into the slashing and swirling storm, out into the black and white night.

When, Isaac? When we run into each other again, in another snowstorm, another twenty years from today?

Thirty miles east of River Bend, the storm petered out. For a while, wind sent squalls of snow spinning down the pavement, then nothing. The centerlines came up out of the gloom like paper tickets out of some vending machine, popping into view, then diving away under the fender of the car.

Suddenly, it was a quiet night.

The lights of Cordova. Past the gas stations and bars and cafés there, and on into the darkness. Spitting snow again. Another fifty miles to go.

Fate.

If LaDonna had been with me tonight, we would not have stopped in River Bend for gas, or we would have been there later. My wife would have wanted coffee in Eagle, would have had to pee in Glenwood. We would have been late getting out of Denver.

But she'd stayed behind.

A cottontail rabbit ran out into the road, stared, then turned and hopped back. Maybe it was a game.

I myself might have stopped sooner or simply paid the kid at the pump without getting out from behind the wheel.

A small moon broke out from behind a gray-edged cloud.

But instead, I stumbled across Isaac Po.

Gaining altitude then, and patches of ice and packed snow were taking over sections of the road.

Fate.

Some games are meant to be played out to the end, even if twenty years have to pass while one player paces the universe and the other sits at the table and waits.

Jackson, just before midnight.

"This is not my house."

He sat in a chair next to a bay window in the library, drinking scotch and staring out at dark peaks and dark spruce he couldn't really see. Ice rattled in his glass and an old railroad clock ticked and those were the only sounds. The moon scurried around behind ragged clouds.

He was talking to an old photograph he held loosely in his hand. In the picture, a younger Jackson and a younger Isaac Po stood side by side, leaning against the bleached wall of an old mine shack, each squinting a little into the sun.

Photo by Corinne, probably. If not Corinne, then who?

He'd run across the yellowed photo a couple of years earlier, when it had fallen out of a book. He'd set it aside, to look at and think about, because of a strange sadness in Isaac Po's eyes. He guessed that the photo might have been the last taken of the two of them.

"Not my house," he said again.

Enough rock and timber, two-story glass, imported tile to build a small hotel. The place had been built by her then-husband, a big player in the early days of the ski town. But that was BSB: before the snow bunnies, before getting caught with his pecker in the wrong hands, before he'd turned his wife into a public fool, and she, in turn, had turned him into a financial skeleton.

He was glad the house was dead quiet. No wars to discuss. No terror. No tax cuts. No social events. No return on invested capital. Perhaps she was lying in bed, naked, in a Denver hotel, explaining the fine points of all of this to her broker, her banker, her candlestick maker.

It didn't matter.

He'd stumbled across Isaac Po, and, though he tried to think about tomorrow and the dawning of another day, he could not. There was only yesterday. No tomorrow, no tonight. Only yesterday.

"Dammit, Isaac, how we owned those long, dark nights. Or did they own us? The ladies played the music boxes and we were the monkeys that danced. How we worked the alleys, inside the shadows, outside the lights. How we lived, how we found a way to live."

He rattled the ice in his glass.

"And how, maybe, we knew all along it was never going to last."

"Leo Tolstoy tried to give away everything he owned and live like a monk," Isaac Po said late one night after they'd been drinking rum and soda since the sun had gone down. They'd helped a friend move out of some woman's frigid trailer and into another woman's warmer arms. Work worthy of rum, they told themselves.

It was one of those memories that had kept its edge and shape through the years.

"Tried to run away from his money but he got too late a start. Died in a train station out in the middle of far eastern Shitskistan."

Tolstoy had been a minor character in Isaac Po's first and best book, Sorry, Sold Out.

"That's what we need to do, Jackson."

"Die in a train station?"

"No. Run for it."

"I thought we already had."

Whitewater's standard bar talk: escape.

"No train stations," Jackson said. "Too cold, too dark."

"We remember him for the way he died."

"What good does that do him?"

"What are they going to remember you for? Me?"

"Living well is the best revenge. Thoreau said that."

"No he didn't."

Thoreau had appeared in Isaac's book, too. Like Tolstoy, he had been a talking face on a new kind of paper money, given away only to the very wise and to the very poor.

"We have to do something, you know. Something much bigger than this."

Jackson had no answer.

"Otherwise, all we get is a tombstone that says Rest in Peace. And what's that? Greek for he never really amounted to shit anyway."

So now he's driving an old truck through a snowstorm, pulling a trailer filled with bales of straw. Are those the trappings, the pleasures, of a noble end? Feeding cows? Bedding horses? Smelling vaguely of steaming dung and the piss of stable stock?

No, he'd seen anger in Isaac Po's eyes. Or was it simply fear, of the known and unknown both?

Maybe Tolstoy was wrong. Maybe Isaac Po found out that sacrifice turned out to be just sacrifice. And the end turned out to be just another cold railway station where we all huddled in the dim light and waited for the whistle of a never-coming train.

Jackson thought he heard a sound, like someone driving up the steep gravel driveway cut through the heavy spruce.

Tossing off his drink, he walked to the front door and turned on the outside light. No one was there, but he could see the source of the sounds. A squall of sleet had blown in from the north and was sweeping that side of the house with pebbles of soft ice.

He opened the door, walked out into it, standing just on the edge of the light, and let the beads of sleet pepper his face and gather in his hair. Off to the south, the moon was still skipping across openings in the pale clouds.

How long since I've just stood outside and felt the storm? How long since I've walked away from the light and stumbled around in the dark, in the shadows, in the trees?

He couldn't remember.

How long since I've heard an old owl, trying to scare up supper, or the rattle of the creek, late in the fall, just before it goes dry?

Other memories, faded and fondled and mutilated and gone.

"My hands and ass are soft," he said aloud, unsteady on his feet, talking into the unsettled night. "I can barely swing an ax. I doubt that I could still gut a deer. For Christ sakes, give me some raw smoke rolling off a piñon fire and a pot of bad coffee and a bed on the rocky ground."

He stopped to wipe the sleet from his eyes.

"See? I live inside a mothball, a Tampax box, a plastic Easter egg.

"Goddamn it, this is not my house."

In the Company of Goats

Late March.

The sun was still almost an hour short of breaking fully over the high peaks to the east as Noche slipped on her heavy jacket and walked out of the house, carrying a bucket of warm water and a rag. She stepped into the shed and came out with two milking buckets, then stopped to look at the herd of goats, as though she'd forgotten they were around.

She counted, just as she did every morning of every week. Twelve does in the main pen, and twenty-two kids in the weaning pen. After she finished milking, the kids would be let in to nurse. But not for long. Once they were weaned onto hay and grain, they'd be sold off, raising just enough money to help her limp through the rest of the year.

She poured oats into the little rusted tub next to the milking stanchion, led Angelina, the bell doe, over and fixed her head through the slats, locked the stanchion loosely, then wiped the goat's udder tenderly with the rag and warm water.

Then she began to milk.

And, as she did some days at dawn, she began to sing an old hymn, circa 1922.

> *"Morning has broken, like the first morning.*
> *Blackbird has spoken, like the first bird.*
> *Praise for the singing, praise for the morning,*
> *Praise for them springing fresh from the Word."*

And then she chanted: "Om. Mani. Padme. Hum." After, sometimes, she wept, and she had to stop herself before her tears dripped from her cheeks and rolled across her bare wrists and contaminated the milk.

The valley was land in need of water.

Few called it desert, but neither did they have a better name for it. A mixture of sparse grasses and sage, of chamisa and yucca, spread over the rolling sand from the low foothills on the east to the low foothills on the west. Scattered clumps of cottonwoods provided the only breaks in a flat but layered landscape.

To the east, the towering, steep peaks of the Sangre de Cristos cut a jagged line into the sky and seemed to rise from the valley floor like cliffs from a long-dead sea. Much further away, the more gradual San Juan Mountains closed the valley on the western side. To the north, the two ranges converged in a low easy pass. Only toward the south did the valley seem to fall away and open into a broad and endless sky.

The house sat back about a hundred and fifty yards from the gravel road, behind a metal gate, next to a half-dozen gnarled old trees. Simple, long and low, it might have been built a century before, with a long face toward the south and a short porch on the west. The wood was old and weathered gray, and the roof was covered with wooden shingles, some broken, some gone.

To the east of the house, another rougher building that was both a feed shed and a barn for her goats was flanked on two sides by a series of pens and, beyond that, fenced land ran a quarter-mile toward the mountain range. Other outbuildings, indistinguishable one from another, at least at first glance, were scattered here and there.

After the kids had finished nursing, she put them back in the weaning pen and let the does out into the fenced pasture to graze. They bleated and grunted and wandered away until all she could hear was the sound of Angelina's bell.

Life was much tougher, now. Noche didn't like to admit it or want to think about it, but it was true. Before, Isaac Po had tended the goats and she had made the cheese. He had tended the garden and she had canned and sold the vegetables. He had taken care of firewood and coal, and she had sold her weavings and took odd jobs when it came down to that.

But now he was gone: no explanation, no timetable, no map. In simple terms, life had been divided by two, but deep inside, it seemed to have broken apart into little fragments, some of which she could salvage and reglue, others of which were left to blow away in the wind.

So now she sold the milk to a friend in town and mourned each time she let go of a pail of it. She had loved mixing the rennet with the milk, separating the curds from the whey, feeding the whey to the does, and forming the cheese into shapes.

But that's what you did, she thought. You sold off pieces of yourself, like cheese, as time ran out.

Just at sundown, she returned to the goat pens. And except for letting the kids in to nurse, she did it all again. She milked, cooled the buckets in a tub of cold water, then fired up her old jeep and hauled the precious cargo into town.

By dark, she had a fire going in her old cook stove, and she drank wine and watched the day melt away and wondered when things would change.

Or if they ever would.

He had left before, once. But that absence had its boundaries: she knew where he had gone and why, and knew, within a space of months, when he would be back.

This time, she knew nothing. And although she lived her life as though he might appear by her bedside at any given dawn, she sometimes believed otherwise. She sometimes believed in the darkest part of tomorrow that she would never see him again.

Still, she sensed a kind of harsh magic in the way she lived her life, even if she was the only one privy to the mystery, the only one willing and able to see the show.

Each day, each night, she would go on.

To Your Health and Wealth

JACKSON SAT IN HIS SECOND-STORY OFFICE in town, in front of a window that framed high jagged peaks, and he did nothing that would pass as anything.

He'd sold his newspaper two years before, and now, dependable as a molting rooster, he migrated into his little rented space five days a week and scratched and clucked his way through what he still sarcastically called his "business hours."

He made telephone calls, fiddled with a computer he'd never really learned to use, and kept a muted television tuned to a business channel just so he could occasionally see a stock symbol he recognized crawl across the bottom of the screen. Sometimes those little Wall Street runes made him feel richer, sometimes poorer, but never by enough to keep him from his afternoon nap.

Some days, he played golf, and bought lunch for a handful of his old friends. Other days, he sat and watched the traffic below and felt the skin on the backs of his hands grow brittle and mottled and dry.

He looked down on the street and wished for a fireball, a wall of water, Chinese troops, anything that might sweep away the sameness and change the color and order of things. The future lurked down there, and it would probably replay itself in an endless, numbing loop: the same goofy costumes, the same coddled dogs, the same carefully tended designer garbage cans.

Most days he accomplished nothing. Tomorrow, he often said to himself. Tomorrow. But enough tomorrows stacked end to end would become a funeral procession. They'd beat the drums slowly, play the fife lowly, and the vultures would have to fight over his yesterdays.

The Main Vein Saloon.

He sat there nursing a beer and watching strangers, and he could look at the shapeless backs and butts on bar stools and remember himself and recall bits and pieces of Isaac Po.

He hadn't been in the old tavern more than a handful of times in the past ten years. And most of those nights he'd walked out early, with the sad feeling that the true soul of the old town had been pushed out the back door, left to rot in the alley like the old and yellowed photos some careless fool had ripped off the walls. He mourned. After all, they had once lived, in the sense of a place being hardwired into their souls, in that bar.

In the beginning, it had been a watering hole for miners, and little more. The plank floor had been gouged and burned, the tables and chairs wired together and mismatched, and the mirror over the back bar cracked and scratched. The brass rail had been scuffed and nicked by ten thousand old boots. The toilet had been cramped, one stall with a urinal that gurgled like a boiling radiator and smelled rank, like a pisser in such a place ought to smell.

Now it was Just Another Quaint Bar: polished, padded, purified, smelling vaguely like the inside of an old lady's purse.

In those good old days, the saloon had been the magnetic core of Whitewater. Some stopped there every night after work, others just a few nights a week. Carpenters and miners, lift operators and hotel owners, English teachers and bankers' wives—sooner or later they all got caught with their flannels unbuttoned in the Main Vein Saloon.

Hank, the guy who owned the joint, sometimes tended bar, and when he did, he gave too much away and drank too much of his own goods. And one night, well after midnight, he'd tried to climb the stairs to his apartment over the bar with the cash register drawer in his hand

and he'd fallen down and spilled money everywhere and his wife had come down in her nightgown and beaten him over the head with the metal drawer until he'd needed a dozen or so stitches.

Hank, for Christ sakes, where have you gone?

"I once went to a party where a woman, a math teacher I think she was, came over to me and said she understood I was a writer and my name was Po."

Isaac Po was telling a story about himself, something he very rarely did.

"'I've read your work,' she said, and I asked her if 'quoth the raven nevermore' was part of it, and she said, 'yes, yes, it was,' and she liked it so very much.

"'I just finished another one,' I said, 'called "The Cask of Amontillado." Perhaps you'll come across it. You'll like that one, too.'"

He'd shown up in Whitewater, driving a car with Michigan plates, and he might well have moved on had he not been trapped and taken to a rumpled bed by Betsy, the redheaded divorcée behind the bar. The Main Vein had spoken to him, not just in the raw vocabulary of Betsy the Beast, but in a raspy, simple other kind of tongue. In a matter of days, he'd learned the drill—where to sit, when it might be his turn to slip a few quarters into the jukebox below the Coors sign, who underneath the curtain of suggestive bullshit was in play and who was not. He liked Bob Dylan, and he liked the seat at the north end of the bar, farthest from the door.

But he wasn't cut from the same wood as most of the rest of them and he didn't try to pass himself off that way. He'd written two novels—titled Sorry, Sold Out and Nasty Water, Damaged Goods—that had been praised and quoted by people who often feasted on authors' bones, and a third book was set for publication a few months down the road. He was at rest from that third book, and he'd come to Whitewater to visit his sister, a high school teacher, and to breathe the clean air and to sample Whitewater, where duct tape was the answer, whether the question was one of broken windows or fractured expectations.

Isaac Po the novel writer and Jackson the newspaper writer had become natural friends.

When winter ended and the warmer sun brought streets running red with snowmelt and mud, Isaac Po was still there. He never said he'd stayed because of vicious reviews of that third book, and with it, lousy sales. But now and then he did ridicule the outside world and Edgar Allen what's-his-name and stayed on through a full winter and then another summer and well into that fall.

He took odd jobs in the warmer months, mostly on construction crews, because he said he was a farm boy at heart and never wanted to lose the ability to make things fit, to work with his hands. He lived alone in a little two-room shack down by the river, where the tables and chairs were piled high with books and where, sometimes, he would hole up and not be seen for days.

Through the first three or four seasons, he was there when the music played, putting in his regular shifts at the Main Vein and taking his turns dancing across the face of the full moons. When he felt like calling it forth, he had a poetic way with women, the eyes of the world-weary, an easy laugh—so where he slept, and how well, was generally one of his own choice.

But as the lushness of the last summer became the yellows and oranges of the last fall, he seemed to pull more deeply inside himself, and he spent more time alone. Although Isaac Po and Jackson still closed the saloon once in a while, still got together for beers after work, the writer drifted further and further toward the margins of the Main Vein world.

Then, one morning, he was gone. No handshakes, no good-byes, no forwarding address. Isaac Po, as it turned out, had left Whitewater forever.

Champagne, on ice.

When Jackson got home early that evening, LaDonna's silver wine bucket was sitting on the bar in the living room, and a bottle of good sparkling white was chilling in cracked ice. The cork had already been popped.

When she came downstairs, she was dressed to match the occasion, whatever that might turn out to be. She was a tall woman, full-breasted, with short hair graying at the temples and little else to give away her age. She worked tirelessly, almost daily, at the health club—aerobics and racquetball, and she swam. She tried to watch what she ate. She liked to see herself reflected in the admiring eyes of any man.

"Have I not been paying attention?" he asked, waving vaguely toward the bucket of ice.

"Have some."

"I've been drinking beer."

"Have some anyway."

He found a small tulip glass in the cupboard and filled it and waited. She would tell him, in time, when the stage was properly set.

"You know that Greystone condo that has been on the market for a year or so? I sold it today."

"Congratulations."

"Thank you."

"Done deal?"

"They were asking nine sixty-five and I took them an offer for nine and a quarter. They'll jump all over it."

"Nice job," he said and raised his glass.

She drank along with him, then took a seat on the couch.

"I'm taking the buyers out to dinner at La Pension. They're a great couple, from Houston. I want you to come along."

"No," he said. "I'd only be in the way."

"You would not."

"I spent a couple of hours at the Main Vein."

"I thought you hated that bar."

"I do."

"Well?"

"I was just there enjoying hating it, that's all. I have a lot of passion invested in that place."

She shook her head as though she didn't understand.

She didn't. She couldn't, and she never would. And as he stood there, he could almost feel another crack opening across the floor between them.

"Just take a shower."

"No, not tonight. I just don't have the appetite for it."

She sat her glass on the side table with a bang.

"Dammit, why is this so much to ask? This is how we live. This is what we do."

He shook his head.

"We don't," he said. "You do."

She eventually went without him, as he knew she would. She didn't need him in her show, any more than he needed the medallions of beef, the blue gin, the appetizers and desserts and brandy out of the proprietor's closet. She didn't need his opinions and companionship any more than he needed the small talk and forced laughs.

For years, he'd been happy enough in that game. But the stories and the evenings always ended the same way: *yes, so nice,* and *we must do this again, thank you very much,* and *next time you must come to our place,* and *how about tennis next week,* and *let me put you in touch with—*

Followed by sighs and silences on the long drive home.

Their shared interests, he thought at the end of those nights, had been winnowed down to just two: a good white wine and staying out of each other's way.

Time had borne him out.

The funeral had been a small one.

LaDonna had never known Jackson's first wife or any of her friends. The old days of abandon, of howling from the tops of roofs, had faded into a sort of secret background by the time LaDonna, then named Mrs. Alvin Teller, had come to Whitewater.

She'd heard only a few of the stories, and she would have felt out of place.

So he went alone, glad to be spared the history lesson, the way it had to be.

Most of those gathered around the grave were members of Corinne's family. Some he could recognize and call by name; some he could not. A few of her old friends still lived in Whitewater and had made the same drive he had made south to Santa Fe. A few others had been away for many years, but were, for the most part, easy enough to recall.

One of those was Adele, Isaac Po's sister.

"We didn't know if you would come," she said.

"Why would you doubt it?"

Services were over, and people had begun to file toward the cemetery gate.

"Well, you know."

They both stood there in their dark suits, scuffling dirt around with the toes of their polished shoes.

"She would have done the same for me," he said. But would she? He wasn't so sure.

"We appreciate it."

"It's all right."

They turned to walk along behind the others.

"How did you even get the word?"

"Funny, you know."

"What?"

"Somebody left me a message on my machine. I don't even know who it was."

Corinne had left Whitewater sixteen years before and had been living in Santa Fe for the past five. She'd been a painter of some talent and never strayed far from the towns and colonies where artists could find shelter and were reasonably well fed and watered.

They'd stayed in touch for a few years, but after that, he knew only what her friends were willing to pass along.

"Do you know a kid named Scottie, who waits tables at the Common Market?"

They were standing beside Adele's car after most of the funeral crowd had driven quietly away.

"I don't go there often. I have to take out a bank loan every time I do."

"I understand it's pricey," she said.

"Yes. Why?"

"That's my son."

"A lot of good-looking kids waiting tables in Whitewater these days."

"I suppose. Just thought I'd ask."

"I'll pay more attention next time. Make sure he's toeing the line."

"Right."

Adele started to turn away.

"Odd of me to ask, I guess," he said, "given the circumstances and all. But what the hell."

"What?"

"Isaac. Do you ever hear anything from him?"

She settled back against the side of her car again.

"I wasn't going to bring it up."

"I understand."

"Sometimes he writes, sometimes he doesn't. When he was, well, I mean, I haven't heard from him in quite a long time."

"Where is he?"

"Back down in the southern part of the state. The name of the town didn't ring a bell. I'd have to look for it."

"What is he doing?"

"Now, you mean? Probably what he did before. Growing vegetables. Odd construction jobs. You know, that kind of thing."

"Writing?"

"Probably. I mean he didn't say. But I don't think he ever stopped. He just stopped writing for other people's squinty eyes, as he used to put it."

"Okay, well. Anything you want me to tell your son?"

She smiled.

"Tell him to wash his hands after he uses the restroom. He was never very good about doing that."

Driving back toward Whitewater that afternoon, it occurred to Jackson that he'd failed to ask Adele where she lived now, what she was doing, those simple courtesies. More of his stock of manners that seemed to be drying up along with his scaly skin.

Isaac Po had been on his mind.

He'd heard an oddness, a kind of distance in the way she talked about her brother. Almost as if he was a foreign port, a place she'd read about, but otherwise could not find or describe.

Or perhaps she was just uncomfortable talking to him.

What do you say to a man when he asks about your brother? And that man was your brother's old friend? And your brother had run off with that man's wife, had disappeared in the night twenty years before?

Corinne had come back after a couple of weeks. Isaac Po never did.

The marriage ended after another two months.

"Rest in peace, Corinne. It's okay now. In fact, it always was."

Solitary Confinement

As the afternoon sun moved across a cloudless sky, drifting toward the peaks to the west, Noche struggled to move six portable greenhouse frames away from the cucumber beds. Made from old two-by-fours, sheep fence, and thick plastic, the greenhouses were heavy and clumsy, almost more than she could handle. But without them, the ground would not heat quickly enough in the spring, and there would be no protection in the fall, when a killing frost could sink down off the Sangres with no more warning than a change in the direction of the wind.

Then she pulled last year's vines out of the ground, dragged them away, and threw them into the pasture for the goats.

Most years, that work would have been done in the fall. By Isaac Po. But last year, as now, he had not been around.

The last time Isaac Po had left Noche and the valley for any length of time, he had gone in handcuffs.

The federal police, Patriot Defense Administration their business cards said, had come just at dawn when shapes and movement could barely be seen inside the fading shadows. They'd parked out by the gate and walked in, and six of them had surrounded the house.

Isaac Po was ready. He'd lain awake in the morning darkness for the fifth night in a row, knowing they would come, and he'd heard the far-off sounds of closing doors and felt the vibrations of heavy feet approaching the house.

He was dressed and had his belongings packed, so he simply shook Noche awake, kissed her forehead, and walked out into the growing light.

Four years later, he'd returned. That had been in late November, just four months before, long after the garden had disappeared beneath the early snows.

Four months ago, and now he was gone again.

If the goats represented half her life, in the summer months the garden took what was left.

For two years, before they had even planted a single seed, she and Isaac Po had worked the ground as methodically as ants, knowing the sandy soil under their feet, though rich in minerals, needed help. Day after day, they had driven their old truck into the higher country, mining the pine, spruce, and aspen stands for their centuries-old accumulations of decaying plants, never taking much from any one site, but still hauling home loads of thick, sweet, black soil.

To that, they added nearly as much cow and chicken manure, free for the taking from barns and fields and coops across the valley. Finally, adding a measure of chopped straw, they used long-bladed irrigation shovels to mix the sand and richer soil together, turning the layers, digging as deeply as they could.

Paradoxically, water came easily. Although the surface was sun-baked and dry, a plentiful aquifer lay less than a hundred feet below. With a hand pump, they could fill a pila, or storage tank, resting on a timber frame above the garden, and supply the plants from there.

Through the years, they'd learned to live according to one fundamental rule: they would put no serious time, money, or effort into any crop that could not be harvested in 70 days. Cold ground in the spring and killing frosts in June and September made longer-season crops a gamble they could never afford.

Along the random edges of the garden or in the sheltered corners, they played with squash, with tomatoes, with peppers. But that was a game, and the prize might be a half-ripened fruit or half-dozen little green chilies that had somehow managed to account for themselves just before the onslaught of the ice-snorting winds.

Most years, those plants struggled to become nothing at all.

Solanum tuberosam. The potato.

Red, gold, or white. Small and new, or big in an indefinable shape. Hidden all season like the end of an O. Henry tale, then as leaves turned brown, dug and laid out on the ground to dry and toughen the skins. A promise made and kept.

Although they might have picked thousands of potato beetles off the leaves in the course of a season, even though the leaves at times looked like lace doilies, the crop was the most dependable they put into the ground.

Every fall, they would carry basket after basket to the root cellar dug into a north-facing dune.

Every winter, they would remove them, two by two, and bake and fry them, and in that way, recapture some of the summer sun.

Every spring, they would let the little ones grow eyes, cut them into quarters and plant them in the ground and start all over again.

One pound planted + water + labor = 10 pounds of food.

Survival math.

She felt a chill as the sun dropped behind the peaks, and knew it was again time to tend the goats. She could hear Angelina's bell off toward the east, so she opened the pasture gate and headed off in that direction.

Noche awoke startled—to the sound of crying goats and the barking and growling of a dog.

At first she had trouble bringing herself around. Then she grabbed a lantern and walked out, away from the house, shining the light toward the pens. There, a single big shaggy dog was roaming the fences, driving the does and kids alike into frenzied and confused circles.

She watched for a couple of minutes, then slipped back inside and picked up a loaded .22 rifle. As the dog circled back around a corner of the fence, she held the lantern in the hand that propped the barrel of the rifle, and she could see him, and she shot. Again, and again, and then again.

Afterward, she dragged the body into a nearby arroyo, beyond where the goats could see it, and maybe forget about its smell.

"I'm sorry," she said, looking down upon the twisted carcass in the lantern light. "I'm so very sorry. I don't know who you are or where you've come from, but I can't let you do this to me."

Om. Mani. Padme. Hum.

Ties that Bind

THE HOUR WAS 11:20 P.M.

He was sitting on a bench in front of an art gallery, long since closed for the night. Cars and pickups glided slowly along the main street, and couples and small crowds moved from restaurant to bar and on into the flow beneath the flickering lights.

He was where he wanted to be.

The weekly poker game had folded early, short of players, and he'd closed the Elks Club card room and walked out into the night—out where twenty years had not really passed him by and he could believe that—as long as he didn't see himself reflected in a window or in some other person's eyes.

He'd looked in on the Main Vein and saw the fringes of LaDonna's polished crowd, the fifty-dollar haircuts, the three-hundred-dollar boots, and walked on. He'd taken one step inside another bar, one that served the condo cleaners and table waiters and bus drivers, with duct-taped jackets piled high on a table near the door. He'd stepped back outside again. The music was loud, and the women lined up at the bar were supple and young, bold and fearless.

He was slow and unsure and couldn't speak the language anymore.

So he sat on the street with his hands in his pockets and studied the night.

While he watched, a door opened across the street and a young girl stepped out onto the sidewalk. His eyes follow her as she waited for a car to pass, then another, and he watched as she moved across the street and stopped two feet in front of him.

"Your name Jackson?" she asked.

He guessed she was about fifteen. Her slender frame bore the hollowed look of someone who had dropped out of school and spent most of her waking hours hanging around alleys and the murky boundaries of parks.

How could she know his name?

He nodded, studying her, trying to understand.

"My grandma wants to talk to you," she said, half-turning and waving her hand vaguely toward a row of upper story windows across the street: cheap apartments, rented month-to-month, as they had been for at least fifteen years.

One was dimly lit, and he could see a silhouette, a head and shoulders, framed by the brickwork, the glass streaked with reflections of light from the street.

"There?" he asked, pointing.

"Yeah."

"Why?"

"I dunno."

"How did she know I was here?"

"She sits there all night. Got good eyes. Sees a lot of shit happenin'."

He followed the girl across the street and up a flight of wooden stairs poorly lit by a low-wattage bulb screwed into an old porcelain fixture bolted into the wall. The steps creaked and groaned.

At the top, she opened a door, let him pass by, then closed it behind him. He heard the thud of her heavy boots clomping back down the stairs.

Only a table lamp was lit, throwing long shadows across the floor and leaving the corners dark and unknowable. The air stank of a million cigarettes, stale, acid, rank, and he thought for a moment that he might choke on it and felt like he might have to swim through it in order to get further into the room.

The figure he had seen from the street turned away from the window, and as she did, he could see a wheelchair.

"Long time no see, Jackson."

The voice was raw and raspy.

"I spot you down there on the street now and then."

She laughed, a low and throaty smoker's growl.

"But you don't see me."

He'd expected the voice to be familiar, but if it was, it barely was, and it came back to him across such a wide gulf of years that he could only guess about it, unable to tie it to any name, any face.

"It's Velma," she said. "Velma Widell."

At least fifteen years, perhaps more, had passed since he'd last seen her. She'd been around, back in those strange old days, but on the fringe, slipping along on the edge of the tavern herd like the ghost of a wolf. She'd been older than the crowd by about ten years, the middle-aged widow of a miner who had been trapped and killed underground, but she'd learned how to play a survival game of her own. Just before the lights came up and the taverns closed down, after so many other, younger, softer possibilities had faded away, she would drift in out of the night and take a seat next to an empty-handed soul and have one drink and wait.

Some called her the Bird of Prey.

Few men who awoke in Velma's bed went back for a second night, not anytime soon, nor did they have much to say about it.

Jackson remembered the smell of incense there and oriental fabrics and black bedroom curtains that let no light in at all.

His eyes adjusted to the dim room, and he could see signs of hard times come and gone: a carpet worn through to the bare wooden floor, a cabinet held together with tape, stacks of old newspapers and magazines, more tape holding window glass together, rips in the discolored wallpaper.

He wondered how long she'd been there, whether she'd been sitting there through all those years gone by. He was tempted to say that he didn't know she was back in town. But he couldn't do that because he didn't know whether she'd ever left or just slid deeper and deeper into the townscape until she'd become a withered blade of grass.

"I had no idea you were still around," he said.

"I'm not," she answered.

He waited.

"I've been dead for two years now," she said. "This is just my otherness here, slow to leave. I had some debts to repay."

"I see you," he said. But did he really? She did seem thin, as though light might be passing through her body.

"No," she said. "You see what you remember. That's all."

The cigarette smoke was real. The shifting light from the street moved through changing layers of gray haze and caused the focus to fade in and out.

"Closer," she said. "The dead can speak, but they can't yell across the room."

He walked further in, into the arms of darkness, and had the sense of being inside a burned-over field of cardboard and fermented fruit. A cigarette smoldered in an ashtray on a table near the window, next to a glass of something he knew would be whiskey.

"Sit down," she said, and pointed to a chair partly covered with magazines. He moved the stack to the floor and sat there, waiting.

She said nothing, and in the silence he studied her face and could see how time had worn her down. Skin over angular bone. Her eyes were shapeless shadows, and her hair was gray and thin and lay flat against her skull.

"Why did you send the girl down to get me?"

"What's your hurry, Jackson? Too busy trying to get laid to talk to an old friend? I guess you haven't changed."

He started to argue the point, that he had not been out there on the rut, but he stopped, because from up there, her vision might be sharper than his idea of truth.

"No. It can wait."

She took a long drag on her smoke, and he could feel yet more oxygen being burned out the room.

He thought she might offer some of whatever she was drinking, but he didn't want it. The air itself was loaded enough to make his eyes burn and his head start to swim.

"So why?" he asked again.

She sat there without saying anything, making him wait, and from somewhere in another room, he could hear the ticking of a clock.

"I just thought we might talk, that's all. There's nothing wrong with a couple of old friends having a talk now is there? No, nothing at all."

"It's late."

"Late. No. I sit up here and watch these streets long after the lights have gone out. You'd be surprised who I see slipping along the alleys after the world has closed down for the night."

Was she trying to tell him something? Something she thought he didn't already know?

"It's late for me to be out."

"That's a whole different question."

She reached under the table and pulled out a half-empty bottle. From the square shape of it, he guessed Jim Beam.

"Here, it's good for the night vision. Glasses are in the sink, but you might have to wash one out. The weird granddaughter can't seem to do much work. She's down there on the street, like you, trying to get laid. Come to think of it, maybe you were meant for each other."

Then she laughed that sandpaper laugh again.

"There was a time, Jackson."

"No, thanks. It's too late."

"For the drink or the girl?"

"Both."

She took another sip of her drink and just sat there, staring at him.

"The times have passed us by."

"Maybe."

"We don't look the same, you and me, but we are the same. We sit and we watch, and the people and the years go by."

He didn't say anything, and for a while neither did she. They just sat there in the dim light, hearing voices and slamming doors and traffic moving along the street.

She sipped her drink again.

"Do you remember the night we got under the floor?"

He'd forgotten it, the way he'd managed to stuff the ugliest of those old nights back among the cobwebs and the dust. But she'd brought it up, and just by saying it, by giving it a sort of name, she caused him take it out and look at it again. And he was surprised how clear the image was, underneath the layered leaves of so many years.

It had been a Wednesday night. He'd just put that week's edition to bed, except for a couple of page negatives he would shoot early in the morning before the box went off to the printer. Corinne was out of town, something to do with her job with the ski company.

The night was a slow one, the way weeknights sometimes were in the middle of summer: no reason, just a worn-out feeling to the air. Isaac Po was chopping modern man into little pieces again, doing his best work on the very rich. He'd found a new hero in Somerset Maugham. He'd read The Razor's Edge three times, he said, and liked it better every time.

"'The sharp edge of a razor is difficult to pass over; thus the wise say the path to Salvation is hard.'"

"Whee."

"It's from the Upanishads."

"Didn't they do 'I Shot the Sheriff'?"

"Fucking dumb."

"But I did not shoot the deputy."

"I'm gonna shoot you. Right in the ass."

By 12:30 the bar had mostly emptied out, leaving only a handful of hard-core drinkers slumped around the bar like fish washed up on the beach.

Isaac Po was quoting the book, quoting Larry, the rich kid.

"'I can live on very little. I don't mind where I sleep and I'm quite satisfied with one meal a day; by the time I've seen all I want to of America,

I should have saved enough to buy a taxi and become a taxi cab driver.'"

By then Jackson had put away enough beer and bourbon, he was tired from a long day, and he had no interest whatsoever in driving a philosophical taxicab.

"Cab driver, take me home."

"Yeah," Isaac Po said, "I'm outta here, too."

Jackson stood, and the walls seemed to wobble a little, the floor seemed to be sloping away in every direction, and he watched his feet carefully as he headed for the door. But they couldn't get out, couldn't leave. Velma Widell, apparently on her way in, was blocking the doorway.

"Perfect," she said, drawing the word out, like the voice of a cartoon cat. "Just the two guys I needed to find."

Leaning against the doorframe, she talked. She was scared, a little, she said, and wondered if they would help her. She'd made the mistake of letting a man called Wiley, a married man, the night watchman at the ski area, stop by her house a few times when he quit work at 2 a.m. But he was a rough man, unpredictable, and she'd told him twice he wasn't welcome anymore.

"Just come to my house with me," she said. "When he sees you there, he'll get the drift. He'll know his little playhouse is closed for the season."

He could tell from the sloppy way she said the words that she herself was about a half-bottle away from a clear mind.

What could they say? Ah, go on home, and it will be all right? Or you can sleep on my couch? Or why not call the sheriff? It was easier, under an almost-full moon, to just go along with her game.

The shack was a small one, down by the old railroad depot, part of a collection of old miners' houses that had been thrown together sometime in the '30s or '40s. They were still owned by the mining company and maintained only enough to be rentable.

Velma unlocked the door, and they stepped into the inkiness of the inside. The air was stuffy with the smell of incense and cooking oils.

She turned on a light, and they could see clutter everywhere around them: a lifetime's collection of little statues, bolts of brightly colored cloth, rolled blankets and rugs, and books with covers showing pictures of old men in long gray beards. . He didn't know exactly how Velma thought or what she believed in, but the gods were many, and they went in for cotton and wool by the yard.

She started moving things around in a clumsy half-drunken series of pushes and shoves, then straightened herself.

"Hell no," she said. "I've got a better idea."

She kicked a rug back from the center of the floor and pointed to a metal ring inset into the wood.

"Pull that up."

And while Jackson was doing that, was opening a trapdoor that led into darkness under the house, Velma took two six-packs of beer out of her refrigerator.

"Wiley's. Last thing the sunuvabitch needs."

She handed the beer to Isaac Po, then took a big flashlight out of a cabinet and cast a beam down into the hole.

Jackson could see a three-rung rickety-looking wooden ladder leading down into a space no bigger than the inside of a small furnace room. Shelves sagged across one end, where canned vegetables might have one time been stored.

"G'won," she said, waving to them both.

Later he would ask himself why in the hell he would have even considered such a move. But that night, like a lot of nights, was just another adventure in the process of happening, and he was never one to walk out in the middle of anything unknown.

They sat there in the dirt, backs against the raw side of the cellar, drinking beer. Velma had turned out the light, and they were left with rustling sounds and smells of the close, rich musk of the underground, mixed with the different, sweeter ripeness of rotting wood.

"What are we doing?" Isaac Po asked.

"Shhhh."

Minutes passed, and nothing.

Then they heard the sound of a car pulling up in front of the house, the killing of the engine, the slamming of a door, heavy steps moving to the front of the house. Knocking. Then louder, a pounding.

"Velma?" said the hoarse voice. "Goddammit, let me in."

He waited for a minute.

"God damn you, open this sumbitchin' door."

More sound of heavy steps as he walked around to the side of the house.

Then he came back and pounded on the door again.

No answer.

"Shit."

Then the car started again, and he was gone.

For another five minutes, they sat silently in the darkness. Then Velma clicked her light on.

"Now," she said, and she reached across the top of a sagging floor joist next to her head and took down a small package wrapped in waxed paper. Inside, a piece of brown cardboard, a plastic straw, and a small envelope. She showed them the big spoonful of white powder inside the envelope, and he knew it was cocaine.

Wiley's, too? They didn't ask.

They took turns passing the cardboard and straw and envelope around until it was all gone. Then she turned the light out again.

But they were wide-awake now, alert, and had become new people, overflowing with insight and wisdom. No truth, no magic, no distant moon was beyond their grasp.

"You know," Isaac Po said, "this is how it's all going to end. People will live back in caves, sneaking out only after dark to eat shit from garbage cans and get their water from puddles of rain."

They'd been sitting in the darkness for several minutes, or many minutes, or hours, unable to see each other, hearing nothing but the sound of warm beer going down.

No one answered him.

He began to sing.

"We know for certain
On some lovely day
Someone will set the bomb off
And we will all be blown away."

Then quiet moments, long waves of quiet moments, hung over each of them like old drapes.

"I wonder what the last man on earth will do," Isaac Po asked, "just after he's swallowed the last bite of the next-to-last man on earth?"

Jackson had a vision of a lonely soul, walking slowly, leaving one set of tracks along the littered beach of a yellow-colored sea.

"What's that sound?"

"What?"

"Listen."

"Birds."

And then they could see it, light filtering in under the rotten skirting around the house, a dim glow that seemed to be coming at them from every direction, like fluorescent gas.

"It's morning."

"No."

"It sure as hell is."

"Can't be."

"Well, what do you think that light is then? Last call for alcohol at the Worm Shit Bar and Grill?"

They stood outside as gray turned to green, and the day came on. Dirt was smeared on their clothes and on their skin, and Jackson could see cobwebs in the hair of the other two and he could feel some on the back of his own neck. The eyes of the others had turned to shadows, and their faces were grim and pulled downward by the gravity of the night.

Robins were singing, and they seemed to be ganged up in every nearby tree.

Then, without a word, the three of them turned away from one another, and each walked a separate way, slowly, in measured steps, like weary soldiers marching home from an unwinnable war.

"Yes," he said. "I remember. Some nights are hard to forget."

They sat silently for a while. Below, the sounds of the evening had begun to temper, shrink, withdraw into the night. Fewer noises. Less light coming through the window.

"I saw him not long ago."

"Your old friend."

"Yes."

"No coincidence, these things," she said. "You may think so. But some of us know better."

"What do you mean?"

"That's why I sent the odd girl to fetch you."

Jackson watched and waited.

"No coincidence," she said again.

No answer.

"So you know where he lives?"

"No. Sort of. No, not really."

"But maybe."

"Maybe."

"You should find him."

"Why?"

She took a moment before she answered.

"I don't know the year, now. Maybe it was '78, I don't remember anymore. Anyway, the border patrol in Arizona stopped a car driven by a half-breed Navajo named Hosteen or Kokopelli or who the hell knows. His passenger was my only daughter. And when they pried open the trunk of the car, they found a half-dozen bags full of desert magic."

Desert magic? That sounded to him like some kind of sagebrush perfume.

"Peyote buttons. The half-breed's ass was hauled off to jail. And my lovely daughter, the little chickie who knew it all, was going to be right behind him if she didn't get some legal help."

A door slammed in the hallway, and he could hear the sound of heavy feet going down the stairs.

"Anyway, I was broke as a cheap drum. I was cleaning rooms, limping along on old Widell's disability. Like all of us, I guess, back then. Broke in one way or another."

She stopped and wiped her forehead with her sleeve and thought for a minute while she stubbed her cigarette out.

"But there was this mining claim. My old man had patented a little placer claim down along the river, and he'd found an ounce of gold, but not enough to make it worth a tinker's damn. A hillside and a sandbar. A miner's wet dream. They were all that way, all about to get rich. Anyway, I went to your old friend, whatshisname, and sold him the claim for three, I don't remember, four thousand dollars."

She smiled a little in the dim light.

"Boys from back east, they like gold mines, you know."

She sat back and sipped more of her drink.

"I'd forgot all about it. Then, about six months ago, maybe nine, could have been fifteen for all I remember, a man in a cowboy shirt showed up here and said he wanted to buy the claim. He wanted to build something down along the river, and he needed that land."

She smiled again, but in that flat, painful sort of way.

"I told him, nope, it's gone."

She paused.

"He said the courthouse records still show it in my name."

She tipped her drink back and forth in her hand. No rattle. If she'd once had ice, it had long ago gone to water.

"'Better look again,' I said. Maybe he never recorded the deed. Maybe you just missed it. Those old mining records are a helluva mess. Anyway, for a minute, I thought about it. Signing a deed that was no good, taking his money, and getting the hell out. But I knew better. All my luck has done come and gone."

She looked down at her legs.

"Somehow, they'd get me, lock me in the slammer, and let me shrivel up and die, and nobody would give a big rat's ass."

A shrug.

"I didn't have the guts to ask him how much it was worth. I probably don't want to know."

She looked back out toward the street or back toward what might have been.

"'Who did you sell it to,' he asked me. And you know what, I couldn't tell him. Goddammit, I couldn't remember his name. I could see his face. Well, maybe. I remembered that he wrote books. But I couldn't come up with a name."

"Isaac Po."

She thought for a moment.

"Po, Po, Po. Repo, creepo, cheapo. I shoulda had that tattooed on Widell's chest."

Then she dug around on the table next to her and held a piece of paper out to Jackson.

He saw that it was a whiskey-stained business card, embossed, nicely made.

Barry Halverson, the card said, with a name and phone number in Los Angeles.

He shut the door behind him and stepped out onto the street. Whitewater had already closed down for the night. Shops and taverns were dark, and only a few cars were still parked along the curb.

Except for two other people, walking together about a block away, the streets were deserted.

I came out looking for action tonight, and I found it. Not like waking up in some strange woman's bed, but not so different. Like waking up in some strange woman's life, and how is that not partly the same thing?

He fingered the wrinkled business card in his pocket.

Not a coincidence, the old lady said. She has good eyes, the young girl said. She sees a lot of things.

"Is your name Scottie"

It was four nights later, and he was sitting at the bar of the Common Market, sipping a brandy, waiting for a break in the action. The early crowd was finishing desert, and the late diners were just starting to filter in.

"Yes," the young waiter said.

"I know your mother."

"I don't hear that very often."

"No. Not around this crowd, anyway."

"I, uh, can't stand around here much. The boss wants footwork. Happy feet. Push those ten-dollar cocktails. Can I get you another brandy?"

"Yeah, sure."

In a few minutes, he was back with the drink.

"Is there something you wanted me to tell my mother?"

"No, not that. I just need her telephone number, that's all."

"I don't think the address I have is good anymore."

Adele, on the other end of the line.

"What do you mean?"

"I sent him a letter a couple of months ago, my first effort in more than two years, sad to say. It came back, no longer at this address, in some woman's hand. It's the one I've used since, well ..."

"What was the address?"

"Just a post office box in San Tomas in the Dry Mountain Valley."

"Where is that?"

"I don't know. I meant to look it up, but I never did. You can find it on the map."

"Okay."

"Wish I could give you more help."

"Well, maybe someone there will know where he is."

"Maybe."

"I can check it out."

"If you find him, give me a call someday, huh? I'd like to know what you think."

"About?"

"His life, whatever that means. How did he get so far away? Where has he gone?"

Straw Man

NOCHE KICKED A RUSTED MILK CAN ASIDE, moved the piece of flagstone under it, and uncovered a key buried in the sand. She then unlocked the padlock on the door and let herself inside the shed made from bales of straw.

It had taken a while, but the PDA, the federal police, had found the place, Isaac Po's writing and thinking space, and cleaned out most of its contents. Gone were many of his books, dozens of them, and the shelves on two walls were mostly empty. Gone also was his antique computer and printer, a stack of heavily-edited paper, and a pile of scribbled notes—all left there on purpose, meaningless, because he knew they would come.

She poured herself a glass of wine, then sat on the bed and watched the sun go down.

Nothing plucked the strings of her loneliness as much, but no place allowed her as much hope. The single room, still with bare straw walls, was heavy with his presence.

If he were to come back, he would come back to this.

Noche had met Isaac Po eight years before when he'd come to the valley to give a demonstration on building houses and sheds out of bales of straw. The building he had started that weekend, and subsequently finished over the summer, stood on a ranch belonging to an old man named Emilio Chavez. That fall, just as he was putting the last coat of dark brown stucco on the exterior straw bale walls, he bought the little ranch.

The bale building would become his writing space, his private world, and it stood north of the goat pens, almost out of sight from the house. Each year, he had intended to finish the interior walls, but that work had never gotten done.

She had moved down from her cabin—higher on the steep hillside in the heavy spruce and pines, a place she'd owned and lived in for several years. But the winters there were harsh. Once the churning clouds of snow began to settle inside the shadows of the thick trees, the world went to sleep under a blanket that grew ever thicker by the week. From November into April, no sign of life.

So she was grateful for his invitation, glad for his company and comforted to move down onto the lowlands where winter painted with a much finer, lighter brush.

She had wanted to be with him. The fire in his eyes, whether he was extolling the good or damning the bad, appealed to the deep inside of her and seemed to bring her, step by halting step, out of a numbness that had attached itself to her like the fungus on the outside of an aging aspen tree.

She wasn't expecting him to turn her life around, but she was expecting that he would see the strength and wisdom in what she had become, and that was all she'd ever asked from any man.

She kept the cabin and went there often in the brown and green parts of the year, just to be near the little creek and to be able to meditate among the silent towering blue spruce, inside the chatter of the robins and chickadees.

She felt empowered, somehow, knowing that she could move freely between two very different worlds.

When she left the straw bale shed, just as darkness was settling in, she took the lock and key with her. She needed it to lock the gate on the goat barn. During one night or another, she'd begun to worry about the safety of the goats. Perhaps she had heard a faint noise, or perhaps it was just a feeling. She couldn't truly account for her unease.

The lock was just a symbol, a gesture, and she understood that. If they wanted in, they would get in.

Perhaps she just wanted to comfort the goats.

Water Resources 101

IN 1941, WOODY GUTHRIE was hired to write a song a day for one month in support of a plan to build Grand Coulee Dam across the Columbia River. He wrote twenty-six songs and was paid $266.66. Some accounts indicate he was paid by the U.S. Department of the Interior, while others contend that his employer was the Bonneville Power Administration.

My eyes is crossed
My back is cramped
Trying to read the Bible
By the coal-oil lamp

A propaganda film extolling the virtues of the dam and using Guthrie's songs as a sound track was never released, and in 1953, the Eisenhower administration ordered all copies of the film destroyed because of Guthrie's known Communist leanings.

I'll turn my stone and till my land
Waiting for the big Bonneville Dam
That Bonneville Dam is a sight to see
Makes that e-lec-a-tric-i-ty
E-lec-a-tric-i-ty
Makes that e-lec-a-tric-i-ty.

A 1943 photograph of Guthrie shows a sticker on his guitar that read "This machine kills fascists."

After fifteen years of illness (Huntington's Chorea), he died penniless in a New York hospital. During his last years, Bob Dylan would often visit and sometimes sing for the dying man.

Meanwhile, the Bonneville hydro system continues to churn out some 5 billion kilowatt hours of power each year at a conservative value of $250 million per annum.

So the taxpayers got a fine return on their $300 million initial investment, farmers irrigated 500,000 acres with virtually free water and even the Native Americans eventually got paid off to the tune of $52 million.

And what did Woody get? $266.66.

PART TWO

Confluence

THE WOMAN BEHIND THE POST OFFICE COUNTER in San Tomas said she was new, and that she had never heard of a man named Isaac Po. Jackson asked her to check her records to see if he'd once had a box there, but she said she could not do that.

"Rules," she said. "Government security. You understand."

Next, he tried the little lumber and hardware operation, and they did know him there.

"But, hell, it's been three or more months since he's done any business here. Hard to say if he's still around these parts or not. Know where he lives? 'Fraid not. Somewhere out in the valley was all I ever knew."

Then he asked at the little grocery.

"Sorry, mister. Well, at least not by that name. We got a lot of customers here, names we never do get straight. Most pay cash. Might know the faces, but, hell, names. Nah. I don't know."

He was outside and about to get back into his car when a big man in bib overalls and a bushy black beard walked his way with his hand in the air, as though he wanted him to wait. So he stood there and leaned back against the door of the car.

"Say," the big man said, his voice a slow deep drawl. "I heard you askin' about Isaac Po. I do know the man. We do a little commerce from time to time. But to the best of my knowledge, he's been gone from here a while."

The man stepped back and hooked his thumbs in the straps of

his pants.

"But I saw Noche, the woman he lives with, that is, I mean when he's around, at the post office the other day. I'm pretty sure she'd still be livin' in their old ranch house, out on Vaca Road. I can tell you how to get there."

No one came out of the house when he slammed the car door and stood waiting. No dogs barked, and a pen full of brown goats chewed slowly and eyed him in silence. He waited for maybe five minutes, then walked to the door and knocked.

No answer.

He knocked again.

No answer.

The door latch opened freely, but he was hesitant to walk in. He was a stranger there, even if it was the right place, and nothing assured him of that, either.

Who has the right to walk in, unbidden, through the door of another man's house?

But he'd come a long way and meant no harm. At the very least, he could leave a message: *I'm looking for Isaac Po, an old friend, and I will come back toward evening. I hope this is not a problem for you. Jackson.*

So he walked in.

The floor was adobe, worn and polished to a rich burgundy patina, cracked in a few places from decades of use. The furnishings were made of simple, heavy wood with a homemade handcrafted look. The windowsills were tiled in blue and green, and filled with healthy plants.

In the center of the room stood a table unlike anything Jackson seen before. The base was made of rough timbers, and the top was a single slab of wood about five inches thick, three feet wide, five feet long. Scarred and gouged and burned in places, it looked as though it weighed as much as the old kitchen stove.

A smaller table in a far corner was covered with books and maybe, he thought, a pen and scrap of paper that would serve his needs. He took two steps in that direction, then stopped.

A woman was standing in a doorway that led off to another room.

She just stood there, watching, as though he was an experiment, an animal on the loose, and she wanted to see how far he would go and what he would do.

"I'm sorry," he said, feeling a little rush of guilt. "I knocked."

"What are you doing here?" Her voice was slow and soft, difficult to hear, not the sound of a woman who had been intruded upon but more like a woman talking to a hummingbird that had flown in through an open window.

"I knocked," he said again. "So I thought I'd leave a note. That's all."

"I was in the middle of something," she said. "I heard a sound, the rattling of wood. The wind, I thought, or maybe a ghost."

She was looking at him, yet she was not. She seemed to be seeing through him, or past him, and he fought the temptation to back toward a wall.

"I'm sorry."

"Yes," she said, "it's all right. All right now. But what do you want?"

Then she stepped forward a few steps into a ray of sunshine, and her long black hair glistened and danced in the brighter light.

"I'm looking for Isaac Po. I'm an old friend."

She smiled, not broadly, but patiently.

"An old friend. Yes, an old friend of a man who has no old friends."

"What do you mean?"

She just looked at him and didn't answer.

"Is he here?"

"No. No, he's not here."

Again, he felt as though he should bend forward to better hear her soft voice.

"You're too late. He's gone."

"What do you mean?"

"He's gone. You can see it for yourself."

"Where?"

Again, she didn't answer.

"Look. I'm an old friend. My name is Jackson. I'm not here to cause anyone any problems."

"Yes, I understand. But the truth is simple. Just before the equinox, he left in the night, and I don't know where he's gone. He did not offer, and that meant I couldn't really ask."

"I saw him not so long ago. Earlier in the spring. It was snowing. We ran across each other at a truck stop."

"What do you want with him?"

"I just wanted to find him again, to talk to him."

"And your name is Jackson?"

"Yes."

She walked over to the window and looked out . Absently, she reached down and picked a couple of dead and dried leaves from a plant and laid them on the windowsill.

"He mentioned you," she said. "Seeing you on the road. And maybe that's part of the reason why he's gone."

"What does that mean?"

"He doesn't like the past. He calls it the bastard child of yesterday."

He considered that for a moment.

"And I'm the past?"

"Perhaps."

She paused.

"If you are who you say you are."

"What is your name?" Jackson asked.

"Does it matter?"

"I thought maybe it would be—"

He stopped. It was Spanish, and the word had slipped away.

"Noche," she said. "The woman they call Noche."

She wore an old flannel shirt and loose Levi's, and her feet were bare. She looked to be neither thick nor thin, but strong. He wanted to see the shape of her, an old bad habit, a curiosity about breast and neck, but he could not.

Her skin was dark, and it was only when she'd turned toward the window, toward the light, that he could see the scar that ran from the outside corner of her left eye, across her cheek, ending just at the edge of her nose.

She was not as young as she had first appeared. As they talked, he could see strands of gray in her hair and small wrinkles at the corners of her mouth, others at the corners of her eyes, partly hidden by the long hair.

Her face was small with a Spanish look, and her eyes were large and blue, like lights beneath ice, and they made him feel transparent, something made of wrinkled rice paper.

"Noche. A very nice name."

"It means night," she said. "When I was small, my brothers and sisters said when I brushed this head of hair, night would come falling down upon our house."

The little story made him smile.

"Isaac doesn't know whether he likes it or not. He says only fools, owls, and demons are unafraid of the dark."

The words came out almost as a whisper.

She made a pot of tea, and they sat on a bench on the north side of the house, out of the sun. It was early afternoon and nearly hot, and crows and flies made the only movement across the vast open land.

"He could get no rest here. Not anymore. Everything around us has changed."

"What do you mean?"

For a minute, she said nothing. Then she looked at him, straight at him, holding him fixed with her eyes.

"Are you who you claim to be?" she asked. "Do you really know the man called Isaac Po?"

"Twenty years have passed. Who knows what anybody knows? Maybe it's all imagination."

"I have to be sure."

"I'm lost."

"You met in the spring. It was snowing, it was dark, you talked."

"About nothing. We talked about nothing."

"You're old friends."

"He didn't want to talk."

"To pull up the past."

"What else was there?"

She looked straight at him again and smiled as though she felt some serious urge toward sympathy.

"What do you say to an old friend, Mr. Jackson, when you do not tell lies, but you want to hide the truth? How strangely does the conversation twist and turn until, finally, you have no choice? What words do you choose to explain how, only two months before, you were shipped home on a bus from a federal prison?"

The story she told was a short and simple one, and it rang so clearly with the old hot notes of Isaac Po's passion that he had to fight back the temptation to finish her sentences for her.

This could have been written on a damp napkin in the Main Vein Saloon, he told himself. Maybe it was.

A company from Canada had proposed the reopening of a group of old gold mines at the headwaters of the main stream that ran through San Tomas and watered the valley. The company wanted to mound all the old waste dumps and tailings piles and use cyanide to leach out traces of gold left behind sixty years before. Isaac had studied the process and believed it would only be a matter of time before the acid got into the drinking water.

"'The snow piles up ten feet deep, and it rains too much that high,' he said, 'almost every damned day in the summer. And there's too much water flowing out of those old tunnels. They will never be able to keep it under control. They'll have a disaster on their hands.'"

Isaac Po had fought the plan in every hearing, before every agency, in every political way he could imagine. He'd written letters and newspaper pieces. He'd called meetings. He'd filed a lawsuit, which was thrown out of court. He'd tried to barricade the road to the mine. He'd filed appeals, and he'd made personal calls on anyone who would give him the time of day.

"Somehow, he seemed to know. It wasn't just the process, the chemistry of it. He knew all about that. But it was something else. It was like he knew the land could never gag down that kind of bitter pill. It was all poison of the very worst kind, and anything it touched would shrivel and die and slough off, like rattlesnake hide."

But he'd lost the battle. He'd lost every step of the way. And the project had moved ahead.

"At first, he had some faith in the government, in the difference between right and wrong. But he was fooling himself. Money was changing hands, large denominations, and the government was helping haul the bags."

He could hear something that hinted of bitterness building in her soft voice.

Then one day, somebody told Isaac Po about finding two dozen dead fish in the creek up toward the pass. The two of them had gone to look and found dead fish and birds everywhere. Isaac Po brooded over it for a week or so, pacing the fence line around the goat pens, taking long walks in the dark. Then, during the long Labor Day weekend, he went to the mine, broke in, and destroyed a bank of electronic equipment and burned file drawers full of records. Next, he drained a batch of the cyanide into five-gallon water bottles and flooded the offices with the acid.

Finally, the watchman happened by, and Isaac Po, by then almost frantic with rage, had taken the man's pistol away from him and herded him down to the creek.

"He made him take off his clothes and wade out into the water, naked," she said. "Then he made him take a drink."

She paused.

"That was what did it," she said. "What made them treat him so harshly. He'd taken one of their men, one of their mighty men, and made him whine and beg."

The watchman hadn't died, but for several days he had been very, very sick.

"Five days later, just before dawn, the federal police, the PDA, the Patriot Defense whatever, surrounded the house. Right out of a bad-boy movie. Isaac just got out of bed, kissed me good-bye, walked out, and he was gone."

"What about the trial?"

"Trial? No, not for Isaac Po. He's a subversive, you see. A threat to civilization as we know it today. A protestor. A writer of antisocial trash. Trial? Not for such a man."

For the first time, he noticed the ringing of a bell, coming from the pen full of goats, and he looked that way.

"Goats," she said.

"I saw them. How long was he gone?"

"Four years, almost to the day."

"That's a long time."

"Yes," she said, lifting her chin, looking toward the mountains. "That turns out to be quite a long, long time."

He stood, then carried their cups inside, leaving them on the heavy table. He sensed that she was ready for him to go.

Outside, she was standing, leaning easily against a porch post. Her eyes were fixed on the far horizon to the west.

"What did he do here?" he asked.

"What do you mean?"

"To live."

"We raise goats on this place and milk them, and we make and sell goat cheese. That keeps us alive. We sell some vegetables. I sell quilts, now and then. He worked off and on as a black-market plumber."

"Black market?"

"No license, no state credentials. Small jobs for people, and he showed them how to do that kind of work themselves. He charged them only what they could pay, pennies, old lumber, deer meat. That's just the way it is around here."

"Writing?"

"Oh yes. He never stopped writing. He just boxed it up and kept it for himself."

"What did he write about?"

"Life? Death? I wouldn't answer that question," she said, "even if I knew."

Jackson stood beside the truck, and Noche leaned against it, looking off in the distance again.

"I'm sorry you missed him," she said.

"When do you think he might be back?"

"Maybe never."

"You're serious."

"Oh yes. He lives his life in chapters. One ends, one begins. This chapter might very well have turned over its final page."

She said it as though she believed it, but he heard the sigh of hope in her quiet voice.

"One more question. Why didn't you go with him?"

She held out her hand and he took it and was surprised at the strength in her grip. And at the same time, there was a softness there, almost a holding on, and he felt, just for that moment, that she might be reading his mind through the palm of his hand.

"You already know more than you should," she said, smiling slightly. "You tricked me into talking about the past. The evil child that sneaks up on us from behind. Isaac would not be very pleased."

Driving higher, back toward the north, Jackson's mind was a confusion of prison gray, desert brown, and the intense blue of eyes. And he felt strangely lost, as though he might be rising up and out of a jungle village where the women could change the men into birds and strangers were sometimes never heard from again. What was real? What was true?

You show me yours and I'll show you mine.

He hadn't told her about Isaac Po's mining claim, and he understood himself perfectly well. She had endless answers, countless facts, and he had but one. He could not do the trade until the scales tipped a little more toward level, even, fair.

The drive back to Whitewater was a six-hour trip over a couple of low passes and a lot of flat ground, leaving him with plenty of time to think about his day in the valley. Traffic was light, and the road in good condition. He didn't have to pay much attention. All he had to do was drive.

What does she really know? Much more than she is telling, without doubt. As it should be. Who, after all, am I, but another unknown, another set of questions that she is probably already sick of answering? Somehow, I wouldn't expect her to lie, but I do expect her to keep me, any stranger, well outside the compound walls.

The sun was dipping down toward the top of the peaks and he still had almost a hundred miles to go. He wouldn't make it back by dark, but so what? White lines and green-and-white highway signs. Cordova 25. Whitewater 75. He was getting tired.

How did anyone simply disappear, anyway? In a time when we were all tagged and traced like migrating ducks, no man, no woman, was free to walk off into the night?

He pulled off onto the shoulder and got out for a breath of air.

What it would be like to come awake every morning in that stark valley? To milk goats and work with old tools and watch the seasons pass? To make love to the sound of cottonwood branches scraping against old tin backed by a thin chorus of goats with hollow-sounding bells?

High and Dry

He quit going to his office in Whitewater.

For almost three months after his encounter with Isaac Po, he'd lived on the sweet drift of memory, letting the daylight hours slip silently past while he stared down at the street and tried to undo time, like taking apart a string of necklace beads. Nights, he'd drift off to a quiet chair in a darkened room and think about old songs and sweet lies and the best parts of getting lost. And, always, there was Isaac Po.

But then the trip to San Tomas had snapped him out of his reverie and reminded him that life had not ended twenty years ago, and though he might have slept through the second act, the drama had still not played itself fatally, finally, out.

Instead of driving down into town, he made pots of coffee in the mornings and sat outside in the warm sun, watching and listening to the birds that nested in the spruce and aspen behind the house. Jays, robins, chickadees, juncos, sparrows, flickers—some would stay the winter, but most would begin to disappear as the fall winds turned cold.

He realized that years had passed since he'd really listened to the songs and thought about the color and pattern of the notes. Rarely, in all that time, had he stopped long enough to truly see the birds, some bright, some drab, as they'd worked their territories, tree to tree, sky to ground, limb to limb.

But he knew the birds had been there all along, gathering at the break of dawn and singing every morning, to the sunrise, and to his empty chair.

LaDonna was away, gone to Denver for two weeks of real estate classes, and he lost track of her. He wouldn't try to find her, to call her, particularly after the sun had gone down.

Three times, he went back into Whitewater after dark and walked the streets, not certain what he might be looking for, but still pulled out into the nighttime by a vague need to let himself be seen, if not touched. He bought a drink in the Main Vein each time, then moved on, stopping to look into store windows, watching the reflections of people behind him, seeing only blank stares and blank faces, moving on.

Twice he sat on the bench across the street from Velma Widell's rooms and could see a dim light in the window.

But he never saw the woman again.

Sometimes he wondered if he ever really had.

"What are you doing?"

"Packing some food."

"I see that. For what?"

"I'm going to the desert for a while."

"Interesting day."

"I thought we agreed she would never come back here to live again. But what do I hear on the answering machine?"

"Farkus and Littlejohn are going to subdivide a big ranch on Horsetail Mesa. They want me to sell it."

"Last time was the last time. We agreed."

"I'm her mother, for Christ sakes. What do you expect me to do? Anyway, it's fourteen hundred acres. Helluva nice piece of raw ground."

"She doesn't need a mother. She needs a warden."

"You're an ass. Anyway, they want me to invest in the deal, too. Be a limited partner."

"Save your money. She'll need it for her nose candy."

"What's wrong with you?"

"Nothing that a year or so in the desert won't cure."

"I was going to ask you to ride up there with me to look at it."

"Your word is not worth much, is it?"

"You know, Jackson, you're just so cute when you get pissed off."

He stared at her.

"When are you coming back?"

"Don't worry, I won't sneak up on you. After all these years, I wouldn't do that to myself."

Alone.

Perched on a rock at the top of a sheer cliff, Jackson watched the last of the day's sun fade from the desert floor far below. First, the reds and browns of the rolling sand mellowed and softened and gave way to long brush strokes of smeared charcoal. Then the line between sun and shadow moved up the redrock spires like mercury in a dime store thermometer. Next, just enough light was left to cap the highest buttes with bands of orange, red, yellow. Then it was gone.

A raven called twice to the departed sun, then sailed out over the long empty space and turned invisible.

Caw, caw. An echo: caaaawww, caaaawww.

A small wind lifted off the cooling rock.

Behind him, thirty feet away, a fresh fire of dead piñon branches burned small but hot, sending a plume of colorless vapor into the sky.

The fire was not meant to drive away the chill. Nights were still warm that time of year. It was the light, the sense of being able to pile on more piñon and keep the edge of the canyon, the maw, the dark and empty air, out there where it belonged.

Uneasy, no, but not ready for the nighttime, either. He needed company, the ragged old song and dance of a decent flame.

The only color left in the desert country was a faint blue that lingered in the sky behind the high plateau to the west. All else was in shadow.

He sat there, drinking a beer and watching the flame, holding a dog-eared old paperback—one of dozens, hundreds, Isaac Po had left in his wake.

It was Quentin Behr's classic desert journal *Three Summers of My Discontent*.

Jackson's thoughts: *So this is it. This, right down to rocks the color of blood, to scorpions that breathe fire, to canyons where all the world's missing souls are dried and stacked, is that empty and promised land.*

Piñon, pack rats, and blood-red rock.

Quentin Behr's country.

Mid-October, years past.

The two of them had climbed well above timberline, in that exposed terrain where only low brush and lichens could grow, crossing over a high ridge that was mostly rock. They were bound for Long Lake, a cirque lake that was hard to get to, but one that often yielded a good catch of cutthroat trout. They'd climbed for three hours until, below them, the ruins of the old Mason Mine had just come into sight.

Then the weather changed.

First came the rain. With surprising speed, dark gray clouds boiled over the ridge to the north, lightning began to crack off the cliffs, and thunder rumbled around them like the heavy guns of war. In a matter of minutes, they felt the first of it; in a few minutes more, they were soaked, and nothing short of stopping to pitch a tent could have protected them. But the hillside was too steep for that.

Then the rain turned to sleet and then to a wet snow that stuck in their hair and coated the tops of their packs. Suddenly, they could see nothing. The peaks above had slipped into the cloud, and brush and rocks twenty feet ahead had turned to gauzy shifting shapes.

Both had begun to shiver. Isaac Po had fallen twice, once hard.

"We could be in deep shit here, pardner," Jackson said. "I can't take too much more of this."

"Me neither. What are our choices?"

"Not many."

"Get us out of here, Jackson. For Christ sakes, you drew up this plan."

"There's an old shack at the mine. Climbers keep the roof patched.

Let's drop down and hope we haven't already passed too far to the east."

His hands were turning numb.

The climbers had also kept a rusted woodstove in decent condition, and the stovepipe was wired tight to keep heavy snows from tearing it off the roof. By hauling armloads of broken board from beneath the collapsed walls of the mill, Jackson and Isaac Po were able to get a fire going. They hung their sleeping bags and clothes on a rope to dry.

The afternoon was wearing on, and the snow had faded into little more than windblown squalls, leaving patches of white scattered across the ground and little drifts pushed against the sharp-sided rocks.

The idea of restuffing the packs, of booting up, and marching on through the cold wind had not even been discussed. They'd lost far too much time.

They stoked the fire as hot they dared, aware that an overheated stovepipe could burn the shack to the ground, and waited for the night. Jackson made a pot of tea and added a dollop of 151-proof rum from a pint bottle out of Isaac Po's pack.

That's when the well-worn copy of Behr's Three Summers of My Discontent had come out.

"This is good stuff," Isaac Po said.

"'In such heat, the concept of snow, of ice, cannot exist. Walking among rocks too hot to touch, no man can remember winter, or even believe in it. No man can even imagine how water poured from a bucket could reach the ground before evaporating. Yes, the desert can turn bitterly cold in winter, but in the prime of summer, snow and ice simply fail to exist. Shimmering heat waves dance off the scalding sandstone and wash all the winter dreams away.'"

Jackson said nothing.

"Makes me feel warmer already," Isaac Po said.

"It's the rum."

"Man should always carry a book about the desert when he climbs above timberline."

"Why?"

"You can just feel the heat."

"You need a girlfriend."

"'Man cannot colonize the desert, although he may think otherwise. He may pave over patches of sand and red rock, he may dig long ditches and canals to carry water, he may even grow some of his own food. But, in the end, the very forces that shaped the desert will prove to be too much.

"'Skeletons of real estate developers will be scattered around like tamarisk leaves, bleaching in the sun. Pack rats will leave huge mounds of convoluted dung in the bottoms of bone-dry swimming pools. The more stubborn may take to their guns and fight for the last little drops of water, but it will soon be gone. Then what? Slow burial, caskets of drifting sand.'"

"I take it your man Behr is not a heavy investor in desertly paradise."

"Probably not. According to his gospel, the money would be better spent on good whiskey and bad women, since the coyotes are going to end up eating us all anyway."

"The last supper."

"Quentin Behr's idea of a fairy-tale ending."

On the mesa, Jackson added more wood to the fire.

In the fading light, he read about Everett Ruess, the kid poet who had walked the Utah desert alone for two summers until he simply vanished from sight. He'd been but twenty years old.

Disappear, reappear, or stay gone forever. Maybe out there somewhere, in that strange and empty land, Isaac Po has built his own piñon fire and he sits, waiting and watching, for the first coyote of the night.

Maybe, if we both build our fires higher and stronger, we can see each other across a hundred miles of thin air, of sand and sage and rock. Or maybe he is closer, maybe dug in somewhere down along the desert floor.

He stood and tossed his empty beer can aside. Then he walked over to the edge of the cliff, as close as he dared, wavering, not trusting his feet.

"Issssaaaacccc," he yelled out into the darkness. "Ssaaacc" came back to him from the cliff across the canyon.

"Wherrrrre arrrrre yooooouuuu?"

"Arrreeeyoouuuu?" The echo seemed to stretch the words.

"Asssshoooll."

"Sssshhhhoooooooooll."

He walked back to the fire and sat down against a rock. Then he picked up the battered old paperback and carefully tore out the sixty-three pages he'd just read and tossed them into the fire and watched them burn.

"That's how it works," he said aloud. "You're right, Isaac. Turn the pages, burn the pages. There's no going back."

Then he sat silently and watched as the nighttime clamped down harder on the canyons until only his thinning shadow and the little fire were left alive to soften the moonlight and the loneliness of the rocks.

Keeper of the Flame

LIKE THE AIR that hung over the Sonoran Desert, the sky over the valley was high and white with a distant haze that might have been dust or might have been the last molecules of moisture sucked out of the sand. No wind blew, none, and in the dead middle of the day, shadows were short and stayed bunched around the bottoms of fence posts.

Jackson was confident of his memory, certain that he could drive right back to the same green metal gate, drive in on the same road, approach the same house. But when he got there, he felt strangely lost. Some things appeared to be right. He could see goat pens and small sheds. The view, the distance to the mountains, seemed the same.

But there was no house. No one was living there.

As he passed through the gate and got closer, he understood. Mounds of black were scattered among the clumps of spare brush: ashes, black snags of board and metal angling into the air, and blackened adobe bricks.

The house was gone, charred, burned to the ground, and the air carried the slightly bitter smell of cremated wood.

Signs of life.

The goats stood in their pen, all facing him, jaws working slowly, and their big brown eyes followed him as he walked, as though he was part of a smoky drama that was still playing itself out. He walked back to the little sheds, little barns, and saw fresh straw scattered around and fresh water in the stock tank.

Ashes drifting in the wind, the soft clank of a goat bell, the faraway bark of a dog. Nothing about it felt real.

Where should I look, and what can I expect to find? Nothing holds its shape here; nothing can be counted upon except for its capacity to deceive.

He walked further, to the most distant building, and was surprised to see how much more solidly than the others it was built. Each wall had a single window sitting deeply back in its opening, and a single doorway faced east.

He knocked, as he'd done once before. No answer, but the homemade wooden latch opened easily, and he took one step in. The walls, a surprise to him, were made of bales of raw straw.

Otherwise: a wooden plank floor, a single table, two chairs, a small sheepherder's camp stove, and a low cot covered in Navajo blankets—disconnected, like the soft stares of the goats, from the ruin outside.

The table was part of an earlier memory: the massive dark and rectangular slab of wood he'd seen in the main house during his first visit. Except for the black-haired woman named Noche, no image from that morning had remained clearer, more defining of the place itself.

Two similar tables, maybe? If one, why not two?

He closed the door and stepped further inside.

Four tiers of shelves, partly filled with books, ran across two walls, but there were many vacant slots, suggesting the removal of much that had been there. He walked over to the north wall and ran his hand over the empty end of a shelf. No dust.

On the table, a pottery coffee mug a quarter full, no flies, no soot.

The stove felt cold, but it was not the season for fires anyway.

A cardboard box was stuffed partly under the cot, and he pulled it out and saw folded flannel shirts and sweatshirts and faded denims. He lifted the one and held it to his nose and inhaled the fresh smell of sun-dried cotton. No smell of smoke. He put it back, turned, and left the building.

The dozen goats stood in the pen, watching him watching them, dull-eyed, twitching their ears now and then to dislodge flies. Then one started gnawing at the hay again, and when she dropped her head, a rusty metal bell clanked a couple of times, dully, and that was the only sound. As he walked back toward the remains of the house, one by one the goats lowered their heads and began to eat.

The walls and roof had burned, and window glass was shattered and scattered across the sandy ground. Around the edges of the burn, amid the ashes and half-charred skeletons of sage, a partly melted refrigerator and stove and a soot-blackened sink. Further on, the remains of a bathroom.

The adobe floor had been cracked and blackened and broken by the heat and by the falling timbers. In that place of wreckage where the table would have stood, no trace—no partially burned legs or top or cross braces.

What has been saved, and what is gone? Whose hands have been at work?

Then his eyes focused tighter, closer to the ground. Lodged here and there under chunks of partly burned wood, small pieces of paper with blackened edges. One read, in the smudge of typewriter print, "never enough time."

On another, "sandhill cranes" and part of another word.

A third asked part of a question: "the death chant of a Tibetan monk?"

The remains of Isaac Po's last years.

The county sheriff knew a few things about the fire. Eight days before, local fire trucks had been called out about 7:45 p.m. to fight the blaze. By the time they'd arrived, the house was totally gone, and the best the firemen could do was save the outbuildings. The call, wherever it had come from, had come too late.

Were the goats in their pens?

He didn't know. He hadn't gone over there himself, it was his day off, see, and he hadn't come across anything written up about that, either way.

Nothing about the fire was under investigation, he said.

"As far as I know, it wasn't insured, so no insurance company is involved, and so nobody seems to give a damn and it all looks like an accident to me, anyway."

What had become of the woman who lived there?

The sheriff didn't know. He didn't even know her name.

Jackson asked around town, at the grocery store and at the post office. She was still around, three people said. But nobody knew for sure where she might be spending her nights.

"But," a girl in the post office, a white girl in an Afro hairdo, said, "somebody has to be milking those goats."

Sundown, waiting, a couple of hundred yards along the road to the west of the gate. Although the valley floor was softening into shadow, the high peaks of the Sangre de Cristos were pure flame, the tangerine colors of the fading day.

Then, in a cloud of dust and rattles, an old jeep with no top and fenders bent and rusted rumbled down the road from the east and stopped at the turn. Noche got out, opened the gate, drove on through, and left the fence open.

Jackson waited five or so minutes, feeling like the unexpected and probably unwanted guest, then drove in behind her. She was standing next to the goat pens, watching, holding an empty milk bucket in each hand.

"Hello again."

She didn't answer.

"I had unfinished business."

"You're wasting your time, Jackson." Her voice was still soft, but the tone had gone flat, like the moan of a faraway train. "Still. He's not here. He hasn't been here since the last time you came around."

He looked back toward the ruins of the house.

"What happened there?"

She shook her head.

"Be wise," she said. "Be kind. This has nothing to do with you. Turn around, leave us all alone, go home."

A plea or command? It was a fine line.

"Why do you say that?"

She didn't answer. Instead, she opened a small gate and closed it behind her. She led a goat into the milking frame, locked its head in place, knelt stiffly on the ground and began to milk. The stream of milk rattled against the bottom of the galvanized bucket.

The line of departing sun pushed closer to the tops of the peaks, and a suddenly cool layer of air settled down across the valley. A little breeze ruffled the cottonwood leaves.

He turned away, walked about ten feet, and stopped.

Noche was still bent over her work.

The sound of closing doors and gates meant, he thought, that she had finished her work in the pens. The sun had slipped off the peaks and faded into the sky, and darkness was sliding in behind.

He sat at the table in the straw bale shack, listening to the popping and cracking of a fire he'd put together in the sheepherder's stove. He'd borrowed a half-dozen pieces of dried juniper from a good stash he'd found in one of the other old wooden sheds, and now the room was warming quickly.

I'm trespassing, and she can't just leave without saying something, ordering me out, yelling at me, going for a shotgun she has wrapped in a blanket somewhere in one of the old sheds. Something. Something angry or apologetic or unpredictable.

She can't just drive away and leave me sitting here.

"You shouldn't be in this place."

She was standing in the doorway, and her voice had gone more flat and sounded tired.

"I'm not staying."

"You made a fire."

"I though maybe you could use it. Thought maybe you might be getting a little chilly out there."

"I'm used to it."

"Still."

She didn't say anything. Instead, she closed the door behind her, and stood there leaning on it.

"What happened here?"

"A fire. A quick, hot fire."

"I can see. How did it start?"

"How do fires ever start? An old wire maybe. Rotten stove pipe."

"Did you have a fire in the stove?"

"What is this, the inquisition? Twenty Questions? What is it that you want?"

"I don't know that I want anything. I'm just trying to understand."

"Understand? Well, understand this: the house burned down. Isaac is gone. And unless you know how to milk goats, there is not a helluva lot you or anyone else can do to improve the situation as it stands here and now."

"All right. Get me a bucket. I'll figure it out."

She walked closer and put her free hand on the table, bracing herself, looking down at him, pinning him to his chair with her eyes.

"Look, my friend. Are you a friend? Does it even matter anymore? Anyway, there is really nothing you can do to help. Okay?"

He looked away, toward the fire, letting the silence build, partly because he had no real answer for her, partly because he wanted to force her to talk her way beyond her anger, beyond her distrust.

"Two days after it happened," she said finally, "the PDA was here again. How did they know? And then the questions started again. Where is he? What burned? How did it happen? Where was I at the time? And they dug through the ashes. Then they questioned me again."

She paused and looked at him, and he could see exhaustion in her eyes.

"I'm sick of it."

She took three deep breaths.

"I can only tell you what I told them. What you see is what there is.

All you see is all there is."

Then she walked over to the cot, sat down, and for several minutes did nothing but stare at her clasped hands, as though she had willed herself away into a slow orbit around another moon.

"I had just pulled all the beets in the garden that day," she said finally. "There were too many of them, and they were turning scabby and about to go to the worms. A few had already gotten hard. So I decided to can them, to put them up, as everybody's mother used to say."

She'd taken the other chair, sitting at the far end of the table.

"I built a fire in the old kitchen stove, a big fire. I put two of my big canning kettles on, put water in and filled them with beets. Then I realized I didn't have any jar lids, so I went into the store, but they were out. I stopped to see a friend, and talked for awhile, and borrowed lids from her."

She paused.

"I had plenty of time. It takes a long while to cook beets."

Now and then, she looked past him, like she was telling her story to an audience neither of them could see.

"I remember the wind. Right after sundown, I felt a wind I hadn't noticed before. Somehow, I felt like it was the wind that did it, that somehow caused the fire to explode. When I got back here, the house was mostly gone."

She locked onto his eyes again.

"There was nothing I could do."

He added a little more wood to this smaller and different fire, and for a few minutes, nothing more was said.

A coyote howled, then a second, and maybe a third. The direction of the barks and howls seemed to be shifting.

"Tell me about this table."

"What about it?"

"It's a great piece of work. That's all."

They sat sipping tea, laced with a little brandy, designed to drive away a darkness that had settled over the land, a darkness that had nothing to do with the sun going down.

He'd pulled his truck closer to the straw shed and brought in a kettle and another cup, a jug of water, a box of tea, and a fifth of cheap brandy.

For a while, she didn't answer. Instead, she unlaced her heavy boots, pulled them off, and moved back over to bed and sat with her feet under her, as though they were cold.

"A couple of years ago, Isaac salvaged on old blacksmith shop. He made the table out of the old workbench."

"The top must be five inches thick."

"It's heavy."

"It might not have even burned, dense as it is."

She looked away, not saying anything.

"If it had been in the house. But it wasn't."

"No."

"So I'm just wondering."

"What?"

"What else did you manage to save?"

She looked at him steadily for a half minute, then sipped her tea, and looked back at him again.

"You're like a coyote, circling, lurking," she said. "What is it you think you smell?"

"The table. Those clothes under the bed. I'm just wondering if you might have known. If you might have been at work, moving things around, even before the fire started to burn."

For a minute, she said nothing. Then she asked if she might have a bit more of the brandy, and he walked over and poured about an inch into her cup and sat back down at the table again.

Another couple of minutes passed before she spoke.

"You should have driven on out of here while the gates were still open."

The federal men had been coming around more and more often, she said, asking about Isaac Po, asking the same questions over and over again, waiting to catch her in a lie, trying to get her to tell more than she could.

"They'd say they were parole officers. But they were not. Next time, it would be something else."

"Who were they?"

She shook her head and shrugged.

"PDA, I guess. Who else?"

She rubbed her eyes, as though she was tired.

"Then they started asking about his writings. They said he was a writer, they knew that, and they figured he must have left some of his work behind."

She stopped, and the clanging of the goat's bell replaced her voice. Far off toward the mountains, a dog barked, followed by the answer of the coyotes.

"Then I came home one night, and I could tell someone had been in the house."

Her words came at him like the opening paragraph of a story he wasn't ready for, one he might not want to read.

"I'd arranged a few books, their spines perfectly even with the back edge of a little table. Just an idea I had. And that night, for some reason I thought the house smelled different inside. The brushings of different skin. The scent of a different animal. And then I saw that the books had been moved. Not much, but moved, all the same."

The old wood popping inside the little stove sounded like a cap pistol going off. The room had gotten warm.

"I told Isaac when he called three or four nights later."

"He called?"

The pitch of his voice gave away his surprise. Somehow, he'd been quietly able to believe that Isaac Po was really, if not finally, gone.

"Not here. He wouldn't call here. He called a friend of ours and asked her to tell me that he'd call there again in two nights. And he did. And when I told him how the investigators had come again and again, he got very upset. He said I should burn all of his papers, his writing, and he told me where he had hidden them."

"Where was he?"

She looked at him with that same look he'd seen that first day, the look with the intensity of a desperate truth.

"You know, Jackson, I'd tell you if I knew. But I do not. He's not willing to do that to me."

She left no room for suspicion. She didn't know what she didn't know, and he had to believe that.

"It was all out here," he said, meaning the straw bale room where we sat.

"Yes. This was where he worked."

"They didn't get in here?"

"Oh sure. They had already taken a lot of his stuff—books, computer, papers. But he'd left that all out there as bait. The rest, he had well hidden away."

"Where?"

She didn't answer.

She was standing at the window, looking out into the night. From where he sat, she was just a silhouette against the mirror of the glass.

"He told me to burn his work and let them know that it was gone. Maybe then they would stop coming around."

She shook her head.

"How? I asked. How would they know? I couldn't just do it and then tell them about it. I didn't want to be hauled off on some pretense I couldn't understand, accessory to something they'd just made up. He thought about it for a little while. Then he said I should burn the house."

"Why?"

"He wanted to leave them with nothing and make it look like an accident. Maybe he meant that I should burn this building, too, and the rest. I don't know."

"But how? How could he expect you to do that? You live here."

"I don't have to. I still have my own place. A little cabin on Spanish Creek I've had for a long time. I don't live down here as much when he's not around."

She paused.

"Sometimes I just come down to water the garden and tend the goats."

She turned back from the window.

"So I took all the stuff he wanted burned and stacked it in the kitchen. I built a fire and put the pots on. Then I pulled the stovepipe loose right at the stove, so flames could lick out. Then I scattered his stuff everywhere, making sure all the pages were loose, so they'd burn. I even wadded a bunch of it and stuffed it high, behind the stove, just to be sure."

She paused.

"Then I crammed the stove full of pitchy wood and went into town."

She looked out the window again, remembering.

"When they came around two days later, I saw them in the ashes, picking up little scraps of paper, putting them in a box. I showed them the stove. The pots were still sitting there. The beets were just shriveled, charred little globs. What could they say? I'd lost it all."

She turned back, leaning against the windowsill with her arms crossed.

"It must have worked," she said. "I haven't seen them since."

"So that's it? It's all gone?"

"Don't ask me any more questions."

"What else did you save?"

"You asked me that."

"I'm not asking where."

"That makes no difference."

"Why?"

"I'm not telling you. That's all."

"Why won't you trust me?"

"Put yourself in my place."

"I try."

"I don't know you."

"A little."

"And even if I did."

"Even?"

"I do as I'm asked."

"What if you never hear from him again?"

"What if anything, Jackson? We can't live on what ifs. We live on what we make and what we grow. On good work, good intentions. On the hard truth that today, here, right now, might well be the best it will ever be again. That's all we can do."

From that moment on, he trusted her. He knew, at the end of some tough day, the end of some long night, he would get all from her that could ever be had.

"You can stay here for the night, if you like. But I took the bedding home and washed it and forgot to bring it back."

She'd stood and re-laced her boots, and was standing by the door.

"I have my gear."

"I figured as much," she said, looking toward the smoke-blackened kettle pushed over to one side on top of the little stove. "Your truck has sagebrush wedged in the radiator. Mud caked in your wheel wells."

They stepped outside. Darkness had settled deeply in, and the night seemed to be without a moon. He heard the clatter of the same goat bell a time or two and a creaking of one of the older cottonwood trees. The air was still and cool.

"Good night," she said and stepped farther into the shadows.

"Are you going to be around tomorrow?"

"Probably."

"I have something important I want to talk to you about."

"What?"

"It'll keep. I just wanted to make sure you would be around."

"I don't get too far away from my goats."

Then she was gone, and he watched first her headlights and then her taillights trail off into the darkness.

The valley was such a strange and open and silent place, he thought, standing there alone. To the south, such a wide-open sky. So much space, so many stars.

So little place to hide.

Long after she was gone, he lay in his sleeping bag, thinking about the day, and how it felt as though time weighed thousands of pounds. He'd arrived expecting nothing, no answers, and that was about how it had played out. But now, even more questions without answers, more fog and less light.

When a man burns his own house to the ground, is it an act of great sacrifice? Or of desperation? Or is it just the parting wave from somebody who no longer has a choice, or even cares, and is never coming back anyway?

When the bed is freshly made, with a quilt perhaps hiding the box of clean clothes underneath, will she then stock the shelves with coffee, a few cans of food, a book or two, and keep a little firewood cut, believing that some morning she'll find fresh familiar footprints in the yard?

A gust of wind rattled the windows, and he could hear a piece of tin flapping and banging on top of one of the sheds. Then the night turned silent again.

He slipped in a deep sleep, and if he dreamed, the dreams would have been of a man inside a maze of red-rock canyons, going up one canyon after another, running into blind walls of rock, finding no one and nothing, always turning back.

Out of Hiding

LATER THAT NIGHT, she walked out into the trees behind her cabin, wearing a pair of leather gloves and carrying a lantern. In the absence of any piece of the moon, the black shadows inside the heavy growth were as dense as a doomsday fog.

Fifty yards behind the cabin, she came to a stack of old timbers, left over from the construction of the place almost two decades before. She hung the kerosene lantern on the dead stub of a tree limb and bent to her work.

By lifting first one end and then another, she was able to move five of the timbers away from the pile, enough to expose a piece of black plastic about the size of a kitchen table. She folded it over, and, in turn, exposed the rusted top of an old barrel buried in the ground.

She pried the lid loose with a screwdriver, pulled a heavy plastic sack from the barrel, and removed a small box from the sack. Then she dropped the plastic back into the barrel and reversed the process, closing the lid, putting each timber back in almost the exact place from which it had been moved.

The shadows closed in behind her as she moved away, back toward a small point of light that marked her kitchen door.

I still don't know. He lacks the guile, the finish, of a dishonest man. His eyes are the eyes of a man who probably knows better, but can't let go of old images, scrapbook illusions. Does that make him trustable? No, never.

Nostalgia is one of the most unreliable maps, going either forward or back.
Give a man a penny, buy his dreams, or what he thinks he remembers.
I have to be sure.
Tomorrow, we will go to the river. We either cross. Or we do not.

Noche found it hard to sleep with the box lodged under her bed, behind a couple of cobwebbed crates filled with old clothes. It lay there, like a body she should have left hidden, a risk beyond her means.

She had tried every trick she could think of—placing small aspen leaves so that the opening of any door, any window, would move them before they could be seen; dusting over her own tracks; lining up the fifth tooth of her rake with the edge of the shed door—and never had she found any evidence of visitors.

She knew full well that their craft could easily overcome her cleverness. But she trusted her sense of things that could not be seen, handprints left upon the air, the smell of skin, and she had finally stopped sneaking up on her own house.

They had, she believed, never been inside.

Probably, we can soon burn the rest of all he wrote. I so want to. And I so desperately do not.

A Fishy Smell

"THE FISH WERE BLOATED," she said, "almost round, and their eyes bulged out like buttons. They were an ugly pale gray and yellow color, and they'd washed up on the banks, lodged between the rocks, floating in the eddies like rotten corks.

"In the shallows, birds that had been forever coming there to drink—sparrows, chickadees, robins, jays, juncos—were all dead, too. They were scattered around the little backwaters, feathers everywhere, almost stacked on top of each other, covered with flies and those nasty yellow wasps.

"We even saw a dead muskrat float by."

That next morning, Jackson had opened his eyes just at the edge of daylight, and for a moment, had been bewildered, not certain for a heartbeat or three where he had just spent the night.

Then had come the muted clang of the goat bell.

He got up, stepped out into the faint light, and walked over toward the wire pen, feeling a dozen pairs of eyes watching his every move, sensing that if he jumped or jerked, all twelve of them might bolt and cram themselves against the wire on the far side of the pen.

He found a water hydrant just inside the fence. The water was cold, sharp as a snow-fed creek, and washing his head in the stream of it brought on a refreshing pain. Just as he was drying off, the sun broke over the high jagged edge of the east.

Shades of brown became shades of green and orange in the brilliant crystalline morning light, and the valley took on a subtle rolling beauty unlike anything he could recall seeing before. It was easy to forget that this was a land crying out for water.

He was sitting in the sun on a bale of straw, sipping tea, when he heard her jeep and saw her coming through the fence.

Beyond the polite "Hello" and "How did you sleep?" she'd said very little. Instead, she'd hauled out two milk buckets, walked into the pens, and shouted out a name he didn't catch. Then, like animals trained to perform, the female goats lined up in formation, each waiting to be milked in turn.

"Every twelve hours, whether you're ready or not," she said as she loaded the buckets into the back of her jeep.

Then she got in and fired the engine.

"I have to take this into town," she said. "I'll be right back. Then I want to show you something."

She handed him a cloth bag. Inside, a couple of muffins and a pint jar filled with juice.

"This will hold you for now," she said. "I have more for later."

Noche drove for nearly an hour before they came to a small river cut in against the edge of the western foothills. There she turned onto another road that followed the course of the stream upward to where it came bucking and frothing out of a side canyon.

Where are we going? He couldn't ask. Small talk was impossible in the open jeep at the speed they were traveling, so he just sat back, waited and watched.

Her long black hair streamed out behind her as she drove, and her hands, in soft leather working gloves, worked the steering wheel and gearbox with a practiced ease.

As they climbed higher, he could see thick stands of willow and wild rose, thick mats of fern and tall bent grass, little pockets of aspen and blue spruce.

But after they'd been in the side canyon a half hour, things started to change. The riverbanks were bare, and vegetation had pulled well back away from the water. Most of the aspen were dead, lying in jumbled piles along the rough bottom.

They climbed higher still, and the river course turned to nothing but bare rock, with scattered patches of green moss that only emphasized the gray granite of the canyon.

Finally, she pulled down a trail, a couple of ruts, leading down to the water's edge.

She shut the engine down, eased herself slowly out and walked randomly upstream a little way. Jackson wondered if Isaac Po might step out from the shadows behind a boulder, if maybe there was some sort of cave tucked in among the higher cliffs, if he should hear something above the water's little roar.

Then he noticed the nearby rocks: right at the waterline, they were coated and stained an odd color that was partly yellow, partly orange.

"This little creek used to be great fishing," she said, sweeping her hand toward the water. "You could catch something in every hole. Brookies, some rainbows, even an occasional cutthroat."

She paused.

"Now there are none. Not one, for about five miles in either direction from here."

She sat down on a dead log.

"I thought you ought to get some idea of the place, the wound, the insult, that drove our man past the point of no return."

Then she'd told him, in more detail than he wanted to hear, about the dead and bloated fish.

"I don't like to come here," she said, "Not anymore."

They were sitting on the rocky ground, each leaning back against a wheel of the jeep. Noche had brought out a lunch of goat cheese, hard bread, hardboiled eggs, and sausages, plus a cooler of iced tea.

He was starved, content just to let her talk while he stuffed the food away.

"The memories are sad, and they're bitter."

"Then why go to all this trouble? Why take so much of your time to bring me here?"

She finished chewing a bite of bread.

"Much of what you need to know is right here," she answered. "The dead fish, the dead birds, the poison water, the emptiness of this place. Do you hear any bird songs?"

"This doesn't tell me where he's gone."

"No."

"But it's supposed to make me understand."

"Some, anyway."

"I understand this," he said. "But I don't understand the sound of nothing, the sound of the disappearing man."

"Give it some time, Jackson. That's all I can tell you. Nothing here is easy."

There it was: a trace of sorrow in her voice.

When they pulled back onto the canyon road, a sheriff's patrol car sat parked about a quarter mile further on. And when they passed it, the car pulled in behind and followed for a mile before the red light began to blink and spin.

"Mother of Christ," she said.

"What is this about?"

"You tell me."

She pulled the jeep onto the shoulder and waited. The cop sat back in his car, talking on his radio for a minute, then got out and walked up next to the jeep. He was young and thick through the shoulders; he wore no hat, and his hair was cut short.

"Good afternoon," he said, with an expression that reminded Jackson of a door-to-door magazine salesman: pleasant, at ease, as though he was just there to make the world a better place. "May I see your driver's license, please?"

"Why did you stop me?"

"You were driving a little fast for conditions, ma'am. That's all. I just wanted to warn you."

"I was going thirty-five."

"Well, you know how it is."

She dug through a leather bag stuffed between the seats of the jeep and handed her driver's license over. The cop clipped it inside his notebook, then looked over at Jackson.

"And you, sir, can I see some sort of identification, as well."

"Was I driving a little too fast for conditions, too?"

The cop ignored the sarcasm, but the smile had vanished, and Jackson could see a drill sergeant set to his jaw.

"No, sir," he said. "I just need to see some identification, that's all."

Perhaps he owed it to Isaac Po. Perhaps it just came from a lifelong problem with rules. But he was unwilling to produce anything.

"You have no cause," Jackson said. "I'm just a man going for a ride, that's all."

His name was Deputy J. Stovall. It was engraved on a tag over his right shirt pocket. And Deputy Stovall walked around to the passenger side of the jeep.

"No, sir," Deputy Stovall said, and now his eyes had turned to little metal marbles. "You've got that all wrong. I can tell you what to do anytime, anyplace I want. I can tell you to get out of that vehicle and lie face first on the ground, if that's what I feel like. I can handcuff you to the door handle of my car. You see, if you don't cooperate, you're what we call a presumed criminal. And a presumed criminal, well, that changes the rules of the game."

He reached back and unsnapped a pair of handcuffs from his belt.

"Now, why don't you just make it easy on yourself?"

He flipped the handcuffs into the air, and they flashed in the light of the sun, and seemed to turn over and over slowly, in freeze-frame, and Deputy Stovall reached out to catch them by their chain.

And why don't we just kiss your ass?

Jackson reached out and snatched the handcuffs out of the air.

The next couple of seconds would come back to him only as a painful blur. Before he'd even closed his fingers fully around the chain, he was hauled from his seat and slammed into the ground. In one clean and perfect motion, Deputy Stovall twisted his arm behind his back and jammed a knee into his spine. Lying there face down, he could taste and smell dirt and the blood that was leaking onto the ground from somewhere. His shoulder felt like it would either come out of its socket or snap.

"Now, you trouble-making piece of shit, let's see about that ID."

Through the pain, Jackson could feel his billfold being jerked out of his rear pants pocket.

"Miz Apodaca, Mr. Jackson, you both have a nice day."

After a few minutes on his radio, the deputy had walked back with their licenses, and his life-is-good smile suggested nothing about the tone of the few minutes just past.

Then he'd patted the hood of the old jeep like it was a big friendly dog and walked on back to his car.

Jackson looked back as they pulled away, and saw the police car reverse across both lanes, turn around, and head upstream again.

Noche handed him a handful of tissue, and he dabbed at his raw cheek and bleeding nose.

"Congratulations," she said, shifting gears, picking up speed.

"For what?"

"You just made the list."

"What list?"

She didn't answer while she shifted into high and overdrive.

"Do you fly often?" she asked, raising her voice against the wind.

"Not much. Two, three trips a year."

"Next time, you might leave yourself an extra hour or two."

"Why?"

"They'll be waiting to talk to you at the airport security gates."

Noche finished her evening milking and loaded the buckets into the jeep. Someone else was making cheese for her now, she said, and she just had to get the milk into town sometime before nine.

"I don't have time to make the cheese anymore. I just can't keep up."

As earlier that afternoon, he heard a note of quiet remorse in her voice.

But before she left for the night, Jackson was quick to haul out the bottle of brandy. His shoulder was a knot of pain, and the rip on the side of his cheek still burned.

They sat inside the straw bale shed and drank the liquor straight and warm from the coffee cups.

"What was it you wanted to tell me?"

"I don't know. Hell, I do know, but it doesn't seem quite as important now."

And it didn't. Somehow, the events of the day, the things he'd learned, seemed to carry so much more weight than news about unclaimed money.

Where does money even fit into the picture? It's a little too much—like a doctor stopping in the middle of a heart transplant to take a call from his broker.

"Let me clear my head. Let me tell you tomorrow."

She nodded. Most likely, the day had already been heavy enough for her as well.

For a while they sat quietly. A warm fire popped in the barrel stove, and in the fading light, the goats had gone mostly silent.

"I'd like to ask you something," he said. "Something simple."

Her big eyes said, *Go ahead, ask.*

"Why are you staying here? The house is gone. Isaac is gone. What's the point in fighting the fight, whatever it is?"

She didn't answer for a while.

"Well," she said, "you have to understand how I got here to understand why I stay."

"Tell me."

"No," she said. "Perhaps some other time, when we've had an easier day."

Then she was gone, pinpoints of light fading off into the darkness, and

Jackson was left standing alone under a sky of a thousand flickers, under a dome so deep it had no beginning and had no end. A wedge of a moon topped the ridge, just south of the highest peak, and its edges were so sharp they could have been drawn into the cobalt sky with black ink.

A little cabin by a creek, she said. Pine logs, probably, and a rock fireplace. Where she could go home after milking goats, chilled and tired, and draw a hot bath. Strip off her work clothes and heavy boots, and maybe pour herself a glass of red wine. Open the window and listen to the wind and the creek.

He tried not to think about that. Tried not to think about soft skin and, maybe, the smell of wild roses.

No, I cannot afford that sort of foolishness. These are not the old days, not that blend of wine, not that flush of roses.

He looked at the sky for a few minutes more, breathed deeply of the cool night air, and walked back into the shed.

Roots

AGAIN, SHE LAY AWAKE, looking out her windows and seeing nothing.

Why did I stay?

He'd asked a much more complicated question than he could ever know. At times, the answer seemed as clear as the water in the creek: she had so much to gain, so little to lose. Other times, nothing about the passage of the last few years made much sense.

Perhaps she would be able to explain it all to him when the time was right. Or perhaps she would lose the ability to explain it to herself.

She'd grown up in the valley, a little further to the south. Her mother, a white woman, was a nurse who had married a Mexican rancher. Both gone now, after a terrible mid-blizzard car wreck. She'd gone away to college and come back to teach in her hometown. Only a few years later, perhaps old enough to know better, she'd married the son of the valley's biggest, richest potato farmer.

After a few years, he'd turned into a drunk, a woman beater, a man who flew into rages and went around driving his pickup into fence posts. She'd stuck it out, then, because they had a newborn son. But at the end of one frightening night, she'd run for her life. The scar that she saw in the mirror each morning was enough to bring it all back into focus.

The boy was ten years old now and with The Family. They had the money, the political power, to take him away. In Mexican culture, families banded with families. Little armies. Even the judge was an Apodaca. She never had a chance.

She couldn't even see the boy on a regular basis—only when she begged the grandmother or when the child showed an interest, which seemed to wane with the fading of the years.

"But you see," she heard herself saying to the ghosts, the memories, that lived in the corners of the room, "I'm going to get my son back."

And in the darkness, she rolled over and looked out into an empty room.

To leave here, now, what is that? It is the sound of a bell, the bell of the long good-bye, the end of all hope.

The last thing I hear before I die.

Eduardo Abeyta

Outside, in the early morning light.

He'd heated enough water for tea and sipped from a cup as he waited for the sunrise. Light was building behind one particular peak where the jagged horizon would start to burn, to glow like a welding rod, just as the ridgeline dropped down to expose the sun.

Why do we always say the sun comes up, when, in reality, the horizon rolls down?

Then he saw it, the blazing solar ember, and felt it, the air suddenly warmer against his skin. And like the morning before, the valley was brushed in broad and pastel strokes.

Behind him, the sound of a vehicle, and he turned, expecting to see the jeep. But it wasn't the jeep. Instead, it was a nearly new four-wheel drive truck, bright red, freshly washed, carefully waxed.

And the driver wasn't Noche. The door opened, and the woman who got out was as distinctly not Noche as he himself was not Popeye. She was taller, in fact, bigger by every standard of measurement. Her shoulders and hips were wider, her legs and waist thicker, her chest a prominent geography of its own, and her hair was an explosion of wild red curls. She was dressed in bib overalls, a sweatshirt, and thick-soled boots.

"Jackson," she said coming forward, holding out her hand. "I'm Samantha."

Even her voice was bigger than Noche's.

"Good morning."

"Nice to meet you."

He nodded and smiled.

"I came to milk the goats," she said. "Today is Sunday. On some Sundays, Noche gets a break. These bitches don't, though. You oughtta see me jerk those little tits."

She laughed.

"I'm surprised they don't jump the goddamned fence whenever I drive up."

She laughed again.

"Anyway, I do most of the cheese-making now. Now that Noche doesn't have any help."

"I see. Did she say whether she was coming around today?"

"No, not that I recall. But she did say she would meet you for breakfast at Rosa's, if you wanted. She likes to go there on Sundays. She might even be there by now."

"Where is Rosa's?"

"Just go into town, turn left at the post office, and go about a half a block. You'll see it on the right. It's a rundown old building. But, shit, that's not saying anything. They build 'em thataway in San Tomas."

Ha, ha, ha.

Samantha was hauling buckets out of her truck when he headed down the road toward town.

"¿Quiere café, señor?"

"Uh, yeah, sure. Café."

Rosa's was a little place, filled with maybe ten old kitchen tables and about four times that number of mismatched chairs, some held together with wire, some patched with odd pieces of wood. Most of the patrons were weathered men who sat around in a blue haze of smoke cast off from their hand-rolled cigarillos. Almost to a man, they wore old stained Stetsons, and their boots were scuffed and, in some places, worn through.

They talked steadily in Spanish, first one, then another. And after every third or fourth exchange, they all laughed.

Tome Coca-Cola, said one old sign nailed to a wall and another advertised Budweiser, *el rey des cervezas*.

Noche was not there, but by the time he got his coffee, she was walking through the door. She had swapped her work clothes for tighter and more fashionable jeans, a loose sweatshirt, and sandals. Her hair was tied back loosely at the neck. She looked like a woman taking the day off.

She carried a book in her hand.

"How's your shoulder?" she asked as she sat down.

"Pretty damned sore, if you want to know the truth."

"I thought it would be. He cranked your arm pretty hard."

"Ever see that guy before?"

"No."

"I thought so."

"Why?"

"Seemed a little overqualified to me, that's all."

She didn't say anything.

Noche ordered for both of them, at his suggestion, when the woman came back around.

"Dos burritos, por favor, con salsa verde y jugo de naranja."

"Sí, gracias."

"So tell me," she said.

"Tell you what?"

"Whatever it was you had on your mind."

They sat drinking coffee, two people with an empty Sunday resting as easily in their hands as an old flannel napkin.

He still felt a little like a man about to deliver a present that nobody would want or even care about, but in the end, those kinds of judgments were not his to make. He would just deliver the facts and let the string of consequence unwind from there.

"It may or may not be worth knowing," he started, "but Isaac may be a little better off than he realizes."

"In what way?"

"Money."

She looked down at the cup in her hands.

"Money. You mean, like more than ten dollars? More than a milk bucket full of spare change?"

"More than that."

She shook her head.

"You're serious, aren't you?"

"Dead serious."

She shook her head again.

"This might be the cruelest joke ever, you know."

Jackson just looked at her.

"He probably wouldn't be in this mess if he'd had money to put up a real fight."

"Maybe."

"So tell me, Jackson. Make me understand, once and for all, why you keep hanging around."

Thus, sitting there at a scarred old wooden table, drinking strong coffee in San Tomas, Colorado, Jackson told Noche how he'd stumbled across Velma Widell, and how she'd told of selling Isaac Po a mining claim he might not even remember, and how she'd been approached by people who wanted the claim they thought she owned. And how the real owner, as far as he himself could figure out from courthouse records, was still Isaac Po.

"How much is it worth?"

"There's no way of knowing for sure. But if they want it badly enough, if they have to have it, I wouldn't be surprised if he can get more than a hundred thousand for it."

Her big eyes grew even wider.

"Mother of God."

"I don't know for certain that these guys are still going through with their plan. But if they don't, somebody else probably will one of these days. There's not much private ground in that canyon."

She sat quietly for a couple of minutes, rubbing a finger around the enameled cup rim.

Then she laughed, a small laugh, not as though she was genuinely amused.

"Do you see the irony in this, Jackson?"

"No, I can't say that I do."

"You might recall he went to prison over a mining claim."

For a few minutes, she seemed lost in a quiet journey.

"I wonder what he'd say," she said finally.

"I wonder, too."

"He'd never waste an hour out of his day for money."

"No."

"I'd like to see his face."

"I intend to," he said.

"But how?"

"You tell me."

"I can't do that."

"Can't, or won't?"

"Can't."

"But you know more than I do. More than you've told me. Is that true?"

She looked back into the bottom of her coffee cup again.

"Yes, I guess that's probably true."

While Noche went into the back room to pee, he paid the bill and waited for her by the door. They walked outside into a perfect early autumn day.

"What now?" he asked, leaning against the side of the building.

For a moment, she didn't say anything.

"I need a little time to think this through."

"I have time," he answered.

"I hate to waste it for you."

"Whitewater is a waste of my time. This is not."

She walked with him over to the truck.

"I have a couple of things to do today," she said. "Promises I made to other people. But maybe we can talk again, later."

He wanted her to take her time. He wanted her to realize that unless she dug a little deeper, that hundred-thousand-dollar promise was no more than, as she said, a cruel joke.

"I'll be down there with the goats."

"No," she said. "Don't waste the day. I have a better idea. I'll meet you here in an hour. We'll take a little drive to the top of Deadman Pass.

"And?"

"There's an old silver mine up there. The remains, anyway. A few buildings. Isaac went there a lot, mostly by himself. Said it reminded him of the old days around Whitewater."

"I thought he didn't waste his time with old memories."

She smiled.

"You have to look back, now and then, if you want to know if you ever got away."

They spent part of the late morning and early afternoon walking across a dozen or so meadows scattered through the thick timber on the top of the pass. They walked slowly, stopping often in the shadows at the edges, watching for elk, listening to the wind, enjoying the day.

The grasses were deep and yellowed and dry, and the leaves on low-growing bushes had turned to reds and browns. Here and there, shriveled berries and little patches of stagnant water.

The high, sharp peaks above were giving up their last vestiges of color, turning to gray.

Fall came early to the high country.

The old mine, like so many before it, had lost its struggle against weather and time. The dump was overgrown with gooseberries and stinging nettles, and only a big shed with a rusted motor inside stood strong. Pieces of old beds stuck out from under the rotten remains of a collapsed bunkhouse, and the parts of other walls and roofs were scattered among the weeds.

The entrance to the main tunnel was caved in, but others, higher in the cliffs, were still open holes cut into the solid rock.

They found an old bench next to a fire pit made with sharp-cornered rocks and sat down in the sun to rest.

Above, one, then two, hawks circled in the flawless sky.

The only sounds were the squawkings of jays.

He is not here, of course. Foolish to even play that game. But he might have been. Might have stayed here once for a day or two, or a week, in one of these old workings or in an old cabin hidden somewhere in the trees.

Good, fresh water runs in a little creek not far below. There's protection from the wind and rain. A man could live here for a while.

They sat in the doorway of the motor shed, not moving, watching every fluttering leaf, hearing every sigh of the wind. Somewhere above, a rock fell and rolled, then stopped. A pica squeaked a time or two, then crawled underground. Silence.

He held the remains of an old shoe, dried and cracked, small, with an elaborate pattern of hooks and eyelets.

"Once, she was the belle of the ball, and the music played on and on."

She smiled a little bit at that.

"Souls and bones and stories are buried here," she said. "Old voices, whispering. Old eyes, watching from a long way off. Waiting."

Long pause.

"That's why he liked it here. No cemetery."

She touched the old shoe.

"Just grave markers like this."

She dug around in a small pack she'd carried along over one shoulder, and took out first a bottle of water, then a brown envelope.

"I have something I wanted to show you."

"What?"

"Just a little bit of Isaac's writing. A few pages of his later stuff. I thought you'd be interested."

I'd been behind those bars for eighty-two days when I received

an unexpected letter. I received very little mail, so the delivery of anything at all came as a surprise. There was no return address, and the postmark said Calexico, California. These are the letter's exact words:

"Dear Isaac Po:

"A friend of mine recently down from Santa Fe told me of a story she'd read in some newspaper that caters to the fantasies of deluded anarchists and Quixotic windmill tilters such as myself. Said story talked about your encounter with the Phucking Mining and Pillaging Company, and of your subsequent banishment to the Cañon City Institute of Poorly Disguised Fascism. I lift a shot of cheap tequila in your honor.

"As I've often said, lofty intentions without real action have roughly the same value as do tits on boars.

"At any rate, I, too, am concerned about the ease with which bloodsucking corporations have been able to deplete, desecrate, and destroy what little wilderness, wildness, we have left in this country. Meanwhile, our friends in such agencies as the US Forest Circus stumble around, playing pin the tail on each other's honking asses.

"A slap to our faces, gauntlets thrown to the ground.

"Unless our corporate benefactors have voted to suspend the Constitution (a possibility, by Christ), I assume you will be a free man one day. What then? What are your options, once you've been adequately punished for your good deeds?

"I hope that we can correspond, since we apparently share the same level and manner of fear mixed with disgust. However, our exchanges will generally be protracted. Mail is sent to me at the California address below, but, because I've become a paranoid old fool, this is just an intermediate stop. Pigeons and peons carry it the rest of the way.

"Yours sincerely,
Eduardo Abeyta

c/o North Mexico Transport
PO Box 29A
Calexico, CA"

I didn't write back, not at first. I was not interested in confessing my sins to some penal system imposter, some underpaid snoop operating out of a dung-colored federal office on the California border, systematically stealing possible evidence from sad and lonely pen pals. Who was Eduardo Abeyta? I did not know. Was this a real person, or just an alias, a made-up name? I didn't know that either.

However, I read a raw cynicism in what he had to say, and a sense of the ridiculous, that no corrections officer (that's funny— we're just here to correct you, punishment being just a way we kill time) could ever muster. After a week, then, I decided to take a chance.

I was, to be honest, pleased to know that the story was getting around. I still believed in the rightness of the act, just on its own merits. But those sorts of gestures serve a greater purpose yet if they can rise out of the bullshit of everyday life to serve as metaphors. And metaphors are only as good as the stories that carry them around.

So I wrote him back, and I said I'd be happy to stay in touch, to trade comments on this sad experiment we call mankind. But, I wrote, don't ask me questions I can't answer, and don't tell me anything you wouldn't want the warden to know. The prison goons might not understand everything they read, but words like arson and arsenic would certainly get their attention.

He was right. It was a slow process. I didn't hear from him again for about three months.

Jackson skimmed the two typewritten pages a second time, then learned back against an old post and sat quietly for a couple of minutes.

"What do you think this is about?"

"I don't know. I thought maybe you would have an idea."

"Who is Eduardo Abeyta?"

"I can't say. If he had his mail sent to Calexico to confuse the hounds, then he probably wasn't using his real name, either."

They sat quietly for a couple minutes more. A few clouds had started to settle in around the higher peaks, and a cool breeze lifted from the lower valley, as it always did later in the afternoons.

"Is there more?"

"More?"

"More about letters from Abeyta in Isaac's writings."

She didn't answer for a while.

"Yes," she said. "But there shouldn't be."

"The fire?"

"Yes. He said he wanted his prison papers burned."

"But you didn't?"

"No."

"Why?"

"It was the way he phrased it, almost as though he was trying to tell me something else. He said, 'And the prison papers, too,' those were his words, 'but, if you want, you can read them first.' As though, against his better judgment, he was trying to give me some insight into the game."

She paused for a moment, looking off into the sky.

"Or, perhaps, he was trying to leave some faint tracks for you, Jackson."

She stopped again.

"You see, he always knew that you would come. He told me so, after he had seen you. He'd always known that you would come."

In his February letter, Eduardo Abeyta seemed finally to be getting to his point. I think, before, he'd just been working up to it, testing me, to see if I was worth the paper and ink.

One thing I knew for sure: Señor Abeyta was a writer. He hadn't said as much. But he laid ideas down with a clarity and style that betrayed a practiced hand.

The next morning, she'd brought a few more pages with her when she'd come down to tend the goats.

"It takes me quite a while to find this stuff."

"What do you mean?"

"He wrote like a man possessed for several months after he got out, and references to Eduardo Abeyta only crop up now and then. I don't necessarily want to read everything he wrote. I don't think he was ready for that, or, perhaps, am I."

She paused.

"Besides, it's a tangle of sorts. The pages are not numbered. No chronology that I could find. Some of it, he may have already destroyed himself. I don't know whether he was trying to rearrange it according to some plan in his mind, or if he just wanted to scramble it into a mess only he could understand."

"Did he take any of it with him?"

"He may have. But any of these Abeyta pages? How could I know?"

"We'll have to thirst and strangle the sunsabitches to death," *Abeyta wrote. "Without water, they'll be no new slumdivisions* *creeping out into the desert like some sort of venereal disease. No* *new 'wastelands' will be sacrificed to the Jolly Green Giant and* *Elsie the Cow, worked by wetbacks for a desperate five dollars a* *day.*

"Jackrabbits can play the golf courses, and wild pigs can run *up and down the grown-over roads.*

"In short, the desert, never meant for human habitation, will *revert to its natural, beauteous, god-awful and treacherous state,* *where heat and turkey vultures sit at the top of an ever-diminish-* *ing food chain."*

That afternoon, while she was taking care of affairs of her own, Jackson took to the highway again, going nowhere, lulled into reverie by the drone of the tires.

Why does nothing hold still here? Every face, every place, lacks hard edges, seems eventually to vaporize.

By sticking to the pavement, he ended back at the top of Deadman Pass. There, on foot, he followed a creek that wound slowly through the meadows before it dropped off the edge and rattled through a short canyon of steep rocks.

He sat by the water's edge, watching as gusts of wind stripped the last yellow leaves off the aspens and dropped them into the slow-moving serpentine creek.

Even the seasons seem to be running out of time.

He realized he would not be going back to Whitewater. Not soon, anyway, and maybe never.

But now what?

Noche's grip on the present was so tenuous, her vision of the future so clouded with old dreams and new nightmares, that he could not see a place for himself. And even if he could, how, even on the coldest and loneliest nights, could they shake themselves free from the Ghost of Isaac Po? How long until, finally, they looked up from the dinner table one night and the chair at the other end was empty and the Ghost had gone?

They talked that night over bowls of chili at her cabin, over glasses of a strong red wine that Samantha had made, and Jackson told her he was leaving the next morning for Calexico.

At first, she stood and opened her mouth as if to protest, but instead, she walked through the door and out into the quiet darkness, into the whisper of the wind in the pines. After a few minutes, he followed and found her sitting on a bench

"You don't have much to go on," she said as he sat beside her.

"True," he answered, "but time is not on our side. I lie awake at night and feel like another day, another chance, something important is slipping away."

"Yes. I understand."

For several minutes, neither spoke.

"Anyway, maybe there's something to be said for white lines and deserted little towns and sleeping on different ground every night," he said at last.

"Which is?"

"I don't know. Maybe it's because you become somebody else once you lock yourself out of the house."

I live inside a mothball, a Tampax box, a plastic Easter egg.

"Maybe that somebody else is wiser and has better eyes. One day, maybe, sitting outside an old gas station in the desert, drinking coffee in the morning sun, the years start to come back into focus again."

She thought for a moment.

"You're deluding yourself, Jackson. Once you come to the conclusion that your life is in order, that every screwdriver and every broken promise and every shovel and every bad marriage are all in their proper places, nice and tidy, it just means you've forgotten about the huge pile of inconvenient crap, the loose ends, the raging inconsistencies that mark most of your life. You're just hoping that while you're out there on the road, somebody will haul that whole mess to the dump."

She paused for a moment.

"You just want to start over. Maybe we all do. But, eventually, we run out of time. What happens if you look in a mirror and see that your hair has turned from gray to white and your fingers don't bend anymore? What happens if your legs give out and you're five hundred miles from home?"

He smiled at her, strangely affected by the power, the passion, of her words.

"Remember what you said?" he asked. "About not being able to live on what ifs?"

"You'll do me a favor?"

"What's that?"

They were standing outside under the faint light of a waxing moon. Stars spread across the sky, and the night had brought down a little chill from off the peaks.

"Check in by telephone once in a while. Tell me what you've learned."

"How, exactly?"

She handed him a slip of paper.

"This is Samantha's number. Call her and leave a number, or just call back in a couple of hours, after she's had time to find me. Either way."

"Sure. I can do that."

Then came the silence, the shifting of feet, the stall that sets in while two people try to figure out what ties them together and how much of something else holds them apart.

"Well, take care."

"Yes."

She took his hand.

"I wish you knew what you're getting into."

"You expect the worst."

"No, actually," she said, looking him in the eye. "I've learned not to expect anything at all."

"If you find him, tell him—" She stopped. "No, I guess not. He'll have to find some things out for himself."

Then she put her arms around Jackson's neck and kissed him, quickly and with power, and walked away into the shadows. He stood there for a moment, looked up at the scant moon, fished his keys out of his pocket, and moved on.

Water Resources 102

From a news release issued by the National Geographic Society on February 13, 2008:

Changes in climate and strong demand for Colorado River water could drain Lake Mead by 2021, triggering severe shortages across the region, scientists warn.

Researchers at San Diego's Scripps Institution of Oceanography said Tuesday that America's largest artificial reservoir faces increasing threats from human-induced climate change, growing populations, and natural forces, like drought and evaporation.

There is a 50 percent chance Lake Mead will run dry by 2021 and a 10 percent chance it will run out of usable water by 2014 if the region's drought deepens and water use climbs, the researchers said.

"We were stunned at the magnitude of the problem and how fast it was coming at us," said marine physicist Tim Barnett.

"Make no mistake, this water problem is not a scientific abstraction but rather one that will impact each and every one of us that live in the Southwest," he said.

Currently, Lake Mead—located in Nevada and Arizona—is half-full, as is Lake Powell, another manmade reservoir on the Colorado River.

Both lakes help manage Water Resources for more than 25 million people in seven states.

Researchers said that if Lake Mead water levels drop below 1,000 feet, Nevada would lose access to all its river allocation, Arizona would lose much of the water that flows through the Central Arizona Project Canal, and power production would cease before the lake level reached bottom.

PART THREE

Hecho en México

THE RAGGED EDGE OF ANOTHER WORLD.

North Mexico Transport, SSA, was located in a big brick warehouse down near the railroad yards. On one side, a high chain-link fence around some junked cars; on the other, a yard where a gang of men with a cement mixer were making bricks.

The door of North Mexico Transport was padlocked, and no one was around.

Jackson sat there in his pickup most of the day, leaving the parking spot only long enough to eat and find a gas station where he could take a leak. Around him, a sea of trucks and vans moved back and forth, bumper to bumper, horns blaring. Exhaust fumes colored the air blue and burned his lungs. But the building remained deserted.

He checked into a rundown motel for the night, listened to Mexican television through a thin wall, and tossed and turned until the streets quieted down, and he could finally drift into a restless sleep.

The next morning, he drove back to the rail yards again, expecting to find the same thing—a locked door, no sign of life. But the padlock was gone, and a fairly new Ford flatbed truck was parked in front.

Just inside the door, a small office. The air was musty, and the light dim, and dozens of boxes and crates were stacked and scattered around the room.

A middle-aged Mexican man sat at a metal desk reading a Spanish language newspaper. He wore a white short-sleeved shirt, crisply pressed—the business suit of choice in that part of the world.

"*Buenos días.*"

"*Buenos días, señor.*"

He studied Jackson closely.

"American," he said in English. "How may I help you?"

"I'm trying to locate someone. I thought maybe you could give me some information."

The man stood and moved a pile of newspapers off a chair.

"Please, *señor*, have a seat."

He extended his hand.

"I am Rafael Montoya."

Jackson shook his hand, gave his own name, and sat down at one end of the desk. Then he explained that as he understood things, a man by the name of Eduardo Abeyta received mail at the North Mexico address, and he wondered if the man behind the desk knew his whereabouts.

The Mexican blinked his eyes a couple of times, then smiled sadly.

"I like to help you, señor, but I'm afraid I can do nothing for you today."

"You don't know anything about such a man?"

He shook his head and smiled sadly again.

"My friend, you must understand something. This is a border town, you know. Many things come and go through Mexicali, through a place like this. We accept shipments for people, truckloads, mail, ever'thing. We forward things on, both ways. Ask no questions. Just move the goods. *¿Comprende?*"

He nodded. He'd seen the life on the streets. He did understand.

"We start talking about our customers, to the police, maybe you are the police, I donno. Soon, we have no business. Maybe dead, floating in a ditch somewhere. *¿Comprende?*"

Jackson didn't say anything.

"I am just a little company. Run my truck to La Paz, run my truck to San Diego. Pick up. Drop off. That's all. That is all I know."

Jackson got to his feet and headed for the door. Then he had a thought.

"But if I wanted to get a letter to Mr. Abeyta. I could pay you a fee and leave it with you?"

The Mexican thought for a minute.

"Yes, *señor*. I think, for you, maybe I can do that much."

Then he stood and walked Jackson to the door.

That night, he called Samantha from the motel room and left her the Calexico telephone number.

"Anything else?"

"Tell Noche I found North American Transport, but the guy in charge guards his secrets well."

"How long will you be there? What can I tell her?"

How long? Sitting there with a phone in his hand, he suddenly realized how, already, time had begun to form and harden like a wall of handmade bricks. Unless he could make a connection in Calexico, find some tracks to follow, he had nowhere else to turn.

"Tell her three days," he said. "After that, I don't know."

The next morning, he drove to the North Mexico Transport office with a letter addressed to Eduardo Abeyta. The message was short one, stating simply that he was looking for a man named Isaac Po, and if Sr. Abeyta knew of his whereabouts, he might advise Isaac Po to call Colorado.

Rafael Montoya was sitting at his desk, just as before.

"I have the letter," Jackson said and dropped it on Montoya's desk. "How much do I owe you?"

The Mexican shrugged.

"Nothing, *señor*. My client pays to have his mail sent on. No need to pay me again for the same job. Here, I am an honest man."

"I thought perhaps I could offer you a hundred dollars."

"I am sorry, *señor*, but I cannot help you in that way."

"Well, then, maybe you could just answer a reasonable question. The kind anyone might ask."

Montoya looked at him, waiting.

"How long before the letter will be delivered?"

Montoya sat back in his chair, thinking, making sure of his answer.

"I leave for La Paz tomorrow. Many stops along the way. Somewhere along there, I drop off mail for my client. I do not know where he lives. I do not know when he picks it up. I just leave it at a *tienda* along the way. More than that, I cannot say."

"So he could get this tomorrow?"

"I don't think so."

"But he could?"

"*Sí.*"

"*Muchas gracias,*" Jackson said and turned toward the door.

"*Señor.*"

He turned back toward the desk.

"Give me, say, twenty dollar. No more. I will give to the man who owns the *tienda*, and ask him maybe to do what he can do. Maybe he has a way of getting word across. I donno."

Jackson laid two twenty-dollar bills on Montoya's desk, shook the other man's hand, and walked out the door.

He couldn't sit and watch and wait.

More than anything, the little city of Calexico would drive him crazy. The maps said it was part of America, but life, as lived on the streets, said it was just a piece of Mexicali that got caught on the wrong side when Americans fenced the border. Its people were Mexican to the core, in language, habits, and soul. Dark eyes stared at him from narrow doorways, and the sounds of accordion and guitar flooded the alleys. Signs in both English and Spanish warned visitors to leave nothing of value in their cars overnight, and vacant-eyed lettuce pickers climbed slowly and painfully onto old school buses.

Tides of vehicles swept back and forth across the border, starting before first light, tapering off toward midnight, but only for a few hours. Then, again, horns honking, engines coughing, the world moving inside a thick blue haze.

The town had an edge to it, an undercurrent of noisy despair.

More than once, alone in the room, he'd watched the telephone and finally picked it up, listening for dial tones, hanging up, repeating a half hour later. The phone worked, but it never rang.

What am I doing here? In this place? Anywhere?

He'd driven out of town back toward the east, trying to kill time, trying to clear his head. On the way back, he pulled off next to a half-finished concrete building, old, overgrown with bushes, a bank of tumbleweeds stacked against one wall. Inside, where he stood to piss, broken bottles, tin cans, and dried animal dung were scattered across a buckled concrete floor.

Waiting for a phone that never rings, looking over my shoulder, watching strangers watching me. What good is this?

He saw a new wine bottle, empty, and beside it, a pair of panties, blue, left there like a flag that marked a spot, a memory, a celebration. He could see her, call her Maria, legs wrapped around his waist, call him Sancho, her back braced against the dirty block wall, her eyes closed, a whimper on her lips.

The image made him ache.

It's hopeless. I'm ass-deep in a jungle of desperate souls. Why have I come?

A police car went flying by with its siren blaring, lights flashing, and he felt himself shrink back into the cobwebs against the grimy piss-stained wall.

What am I doing here?

When he checked with the motel clerk, the young kid told him that he'd received a telephone call earlier that day. The name Noche and Samantha's Colorado telephone number were written on a small yellow pad.

He returned the call, left a message with Sam, and waited. The afternoon dragged on. Evening crawled by as though his watch had almost stopped. Finally, just as the streets were growing dark and lights were coming on, the telephone rang.

"Jackson," she said, "I talked to Isaac last night."

"What?"

"I told him you had news he needed to know. I didn't attempt to explain it to him. I don't think I understood everything you said."

"And?"

"He says you should be on the seawall in San Bruno three days from now, in the afternoon."

"From when?"

"Today. Now."

"Is that all?"

"He said he'd be there when he could. He never knows for sure. He mentioned a truck and said sometimes it runs on time, sometimes it doesn't. Sometimes it breaks down, sometimes it doesn't. So if he doesn't make it, try again the next afternoon, he said. He'll get there one day or another."

"So he's there now, somewhere around that part of Baja?"

"I mean, well, you decide. What's a truck ride? To where, from where? California? Arizona? Mexico? I think about it, but I don't know. His whole world is an unmarked road."

The tide was out.

Jackson walked slowly along the sea wall, the malećon, the promenade that looked out upon the Sea of Cortez, and watched the break of the distant waves. The surf was nothing more than a faraway roar.

The sound of Mexican music, accordions and guitars, rose and fell on the wind, and with it, the smell of frying lard and fish. The sun was warm, and high in the bleached-out sky frigate birds sailed without a movement of wing.

In the air, the faint taste of salt.

He studied the faces of the old men: anxious, selling hand-painted wooden fish. He watched the faces of the younger men: mocking almost, hawking blankets and silver. He scanned the faces of oddly dressed men from Germany and Chicago and Montreal: uneasy, afraid of little kids selling pieces of gum.

No one was familiar.

No Isaac Po. *El hombre no está aquí.* Not yet anyway.

He had expected to wait. What difference would another day or two make? But where? Wait where? The one-way street that ran along the top of the *malecón* was clogged with cars, some moving, every parking space filled. On the seaward side of the street, only a walkway and a low rock wall. Across the street, toward town, countless open-air *cocinas*, all selling the same shrimp cocktails, fish tacos, and Tecate. In front of nearly every one, a man or woman waved a menu and tried to drag business in off the streets. Between the food sellers, a collection of pharmacies, liquor stores, and tee-shirt shops.

How can I find anyone here? How can anyone find me?

Finally, toward the north end of the seawall, he spotted an empty bench in front of a *cantina*, sat down, and opened a book he'd carried along. *Sorry, Sold Out*, by one Isaac Po, a book he'd read once before, but with a far different set of eyes.

So he waited there through that first afternoon, reading in the sun, watching an olio of Americans, Europeans, and Mexicans working their way along the *malecón*. Some stopped to talk among themselves, others marched by as though destiny had called and the seascape was a backdrop painted poorly, something to be ignored.

Children laughed and threw popcorn to the swooping gulls.

"Lo siento," he said over and over to the street vendors. *"No dinero."* Sorry, no money. He frowned into the book, making it seem important, and the armloads of blankets and hats and silver moved on.

It was mid-afternoon, and the tide was coming in, moving relentlessly toward the dozens of white *pangas*, Mexican fishing boats, pulled up onto the beach, ready to go out with the next high tide. Dark-skinned *pescaderos* mended and sorted nets, cleaned outboard engines, crouched in the sand, smoking and laughing. A radio blasted mournful Mexican ballads from its place on top of an overturned hull.

He bought a couple of fish tacos in one of the cafés, wrapped them in napkins, and walked a hundred yards in both directions while he ate. The faces of men on the benches, of men who passed him by, were the same faces, over and again, telling nothing. For a while, he sat on the flat rocks atop the masonry wall and looked out to sea, watching shrimp trawlers well off toward the horizon.

Meanwhile, the sun moved further toward the west and finally disappeared behind clusters of trees and houses, where fingers of civilization jabbed out into the desert. Shadows began to inch across the seawall, and vendors packed up their cases and carts and disappeared into the tail end of the day.

Still, he sat on the bench and waited.

When darkness swallowed the horizon and lights began to flicker on, he stood and walked away, toward one of the cheap motels along the street leading into the center of town.

Mañana. There will always be another day.

Afternoons.

Jackson thought about afternoons as he sat in Tres Gringos, a little American-style café, the next morning. Noche had said Isaac Po would be there some afternoon, but not morning. So sitting along the seawall in the earlier hours would be useless. Pleasant, perhaps, watching another day take life. But useless.

He ordered eggs smothered in chili sauce, tortillas, beans, and coffee. The young Mexican girl who smiled and took his order with laughter coming out of her almond eyes spoke English as clearly as he did. Her long black hair gleamed in the sunlight, and her body was quick and lithe, and twice she caught him watching her, and twice he turned away.

But there was something in her look, a knowing, an easiness, a balance that reminded him of a half-tamed cat and made him want to spend the rest of the morning at that table, waiting for a chance to talk.

Nonsense. The song of the lonely road.

He left a foolish amount of money on the tray and walked out into the rooster calls and the rapidly warming sun.

He drove south, drawn that way by intuition more than anything else, in search of nothing more than a workable, believable sense of direction.

Ten kilometers outside of town, he ran into soldiers. Seven *federales* dressed in green camouflage lined both sides of the road, and the sign said *Todos Altos*. All stop. Several tents were pitched back near the ruin of a farmhouse, and three more soldiers sat there, leaning against trees, perhaps asleep.

Two of the soldiers, neither of them more than young boys, waved semiautomatic rifles in the general direction of the road, the sign, his truck.

He rolled down his window and came to a stop.

"Buenos días," a slightly older-looking soldier said. He walked with a definite limp and had an angry, sullen look in his eye. Someone, somewhere, would be made to pay.

"Whey djew fron?"

He didn't answer because he didn't understand.

"Whey djew fron?"

The voice was tougher, raspier, now.

Then he got it. Where you from?

"Colorado."

The soldier, probably the *jefe*, the leader, nodded knowingly, but Jackson wondered if the name, despite being Spanish, meant anything to him at all.

Another soldier, a short, round man, opened the passenger door and looked behind the seats. Then he opened the toolbox in the bed of the truck, took out a crescent wrench, and put it into his pants pocket.

Jackson said nothing.

"Whey djew hetting?"

"Just south for a few miles. Just looking around. I'll be coming back soon."

The soldier nodded knowingly again. Likely story.

Then he waved Jackson through.

A few more kilometers south of town, past the last of the towering gringotels and condos, past the trailer parks and tourist zone, the road began to fall apart.

Without warning, his right front wheel dropped into a hole so deep that the tow hook welded to the bottom of the front bumper scraped the asphalt, and the jolt was so heavy that his head hit the roof of the truck. Did anything remain of his tire? It had survived mainly because the edges of the hole had been worn smooth by other bushwhacked drivers like him.

The farther he drove, the worse it got. After a few more kilometers, staying on the asphalt was almost impossible, even when he swerved from lane to lane. Clearly, other drivers had given up and worn the sandy ditches on either side into a much smoother sort of road.

After a half an hour of slow going, he saw what appeared to be the white fender from an old vehicle stuck in the sand above the ditch, with two interconnected circles in bright red paint. There, a rougher side road climbed up and out, and snaked away through the scrub brush and cactus.

Tired of driving, thinking about turning around, he eased onto the rutted road, stopped, got out, and stretched. So far, he'd seen only one other vehicle, an old half-wrecked Volkswagen headed toward San Bruno on the other side of the ruined pavement.

Time to turn around. Time to get the hell out of here.

Then he saw a second old fender alongside the bush track, maybe twenty yards farther toward the east, toward the sea. He walked a ways until he could read the red paint.

It said, simply, *Jackson.*

Barely forty yards beyond the second fender, the track topped a sandy rise and faded, disappearing entirely as it approached the high tide line. Ropes of seaweed bent across the sand. Gulls and curlews worked the water's edge.

A more primitive track cut slightly back toward the south, and he saw a small bleached and battered house trailer, jacked up and sitting on cinder blocks. Next to it, a thatched-roof, open-walled *palapa*, with a table, a couple of chairs, and a little propane stove, partly in shadow, protected from the sun. An old truck, faded blue, scratched and dented, was parked at the far end of the trailer.

He stood there waiting. No one came out of the trailer or from anywhere else.

"Buenos días," he said in a loud voice.

No answer.

He walked past the end of the *palapa*, staying wide of the trailer and noticed that the outdoor room seemed heavily and recently used. Dishes were piled on the table, and the sand was tracked and packed down.

Out toward the bay, toward rocky tide pools interlaced with fingers of sand, a flock of gulls rose as one giant bird, cackling and swinging out over the water.

In the spot where they had been milling around, thrashing, beating each other with their wings, he found the partly rotted carcass of a hammerhead shark, about three feet long, its protruding eye sockets picked clean.

Then, a second flurry of gulls took to the air. Off to the south, walking in the froth at the edge of the surf, a lone *hombre*, a thin stick of a figure, was coming his way.

He was a tall and thin old man, back straight as a plank, with long white hair blowing wildly in the little breeze. He paced slowly through the tide, using a long piece of broken oar as a walking stick, and his loose white shirt and baggy pants billowed around his body.

The thin body seemed almost transparent, and Jackson somehow expected the shape to change, lines to thicken and blur, and a giant egret to rise slowly from the sand and wing its way out to sea.

In that gauzy light, anything seemed possible.

The old man kept his eyes fixed on Jackson as he walked along, but showed no surprise, no concern, no emotion of any kind. Though his hair was wild, he had no beard. The skin on his face looked to be smooth and soft.

"Hello," he said as he approached, and the music, the softness, in his voice left Jackson unsure whether he was hearing the voice of any sort of man or whether it was the voice of an old woman.

"Welcome to Campo Jackson."

The old man, the old person, smiled broadly, and a pair of green eyes flashed as though the name might be meant as a joke.

They talked for a while then about how they shared the same name, about how Elder Jackson had come down from Chicago many years before, about the fishing village just around the headland to the south and how the Indians there called him *El Brujo*, the old wizard.

"They see what they want to see or perhaps what they need to see. They insist that I bless their marriages and their boats, help them bury their dead. What choice do I have? It is useless, if not a little risky, to tamper with these people and their sense of god."

Then *El Brujo* asked Jackson what had brought him out to his little piece of coastline.

"Just driving, looking. Looking, really, for a man I used to know."

"Once, but no more?"

"It's been as long time. I can't say."

"A friend?"

"In my eyes, at least. I cannot speak for him."

The old one reflected on that and said nothing in response.

"His name is Isaac Po."

"Such as the raven who sayeth nevermore?"

"No. P-O. A river in Europe, I think."

"Italy."

"He's a thinner man with long hair and little round glasses. About my age. He has a talent for getting himself lost."

"Do you have high hopes?"

"Of what?"

"Of finding him."

"Some days. Then they fade."

"Good."

"Why?"

"Your disappointment will not be so great."

"What do you mean?"

"Tracks are hard to follow here. Sand, rock, a constant cleansing by the wind and the sea. Crumbling walls. Short memories. Stories you want to believe, but you know you cannot."

El Brujo took a couple more steps as though to walk on by, then stopped.

"Come along. It's a good day for it."

They walked together, silently, partly in and partly out of the thin tide. The late morning sun had grown warm, and shorebirds scattered ahead of them. A solitary pelican perched on the half-rotted bow of an old dory sticking out of the sand.

They came to the remains of the hammerhead shark.

"These waters are full of them," the elder said. "But they don't seem to get very big. This is the biggest one to wash ashore in a while."

Then *El Brujo* did something that surprised Jackson: he made the sign of the cross in the air over the fish carcass. And he could tell from the look in the other's eyes that it was not an idle gesture.

Then he pushed the fish farther out into the surf with his bare foot.

"High tide will carry it out."

He paused.

"But it makes no difference. Tomorrow there will be another one and another one the day after that. It's the rule. We die, we wash up on the beach, and then we're gone. Someday, somewhere, we wash up on yet another beach, as an otter, an ibis, yet another kind of fish."

They were sitting in the shade of the *palapa*, and *El Brujo* had produced a jug of some kind of colorless murky wine, bittersweet to the taste. Even though the sun was not yet perfectly overhead, they drank. It was not a wine of celebration they took, but something more like a ritual—a communion of people alone, but with similar names.

"Disappearing is pure white magic," the old one said then, his eyes fastened on something far out to sea. "No strings, no mirrors. But, one day, it ends. Our hands grow slow, and we are no longer able to slip away through the mystery of our own smoke. Sooner or later, we all get caught in the act."

Then, for a full five minutes, neither of them said a word. The only sounds were the small washing of the surf and scattered cries of distant birds.

"This friend of yours," the old one said finally, "in your searches, have you asked at the Tres Gringos Café in town?"

"I ate there today. But, no, I couldn't do that."

El Brujo thought about that for a minute and seemed to understand.

"Still, they seem to know most everything about Americans that pass this way."

"The girl?"

El Brujo smiled.

"Lucia, yes. She knows many people, many things. She ..." But then his voice dropped away.

"I'll keep an eye out for your friend," *El Brujo* said as they stood and made their farewells. "But I must warn you, Mister Jackson. These are not good times for Americans down here. Remain long enough, and you can feel it in the air. Listen closely enough, and you will hear a kind of whispered warning on the edge of the wind. In time, perhaps, we will all disappear."

When they shook hands in good-bye, *El Brujo's* grip was soft, the fingers without much strength, and Jackson drove back to the north toward San Bruno, feeling a sting, a burning, in the palm of his hand.

He needed it, that little pain, along with a slight throbbing behind his eyes caused by *El Brujo's* sacramental wine. Without them, the whole morning could be chalked up to imagination, dream, the trailing feathers of a giant white bird that lifted off and floated out to sea.

By 1 p.m., Jackson was back on the seawall, sitting on the same bench, watching the same parade of the same tourists. An old Chevy with speakers mounted on the roof passed by a couple of times, bellowing bursts of rapid-fire Spanish interspersed with a few seconds of loud music.

Pelicans sailed by on patrol, skimming the water like low-flying drones.

Again, he studied white-skinned faces, strangers trying to look at ease, strangers who were deceived by their eyes. Don't speak to me or try to sell me anything, the eyes said. I don't trust you. We are not brothers. There is nothing I can do.

Once again, the sun was dropping toward the western horizon. Impatient, tired of sitting, he got to his feet and walked a block to the west, onto another street busy with rug and glassware merchants, with currency changers and beggars, where he remembered seeing a telephone kiosk.

No, Samantha said, there had been no further calls that she knew of. No, Noche hadn't mentioned anything about a change in plans. No, so far as she knew, nothing was any different from what it had been a day, a week, a month before.

He thanked her, hung up the phone, and turned away. Off to the west, the last of the day's light was fading fast.

Another day gone by. Another mañana. What else can I do but watch and circle and wait? How long before I become the odd duck, and the cops patrolling the seawall begin to follow me around?

Unease, doubt, was beginning to hang on his mind, and he wondered if something important had been misunderstood.

Inside the window of a small shop, coarsely woven blankets and rugs were on display. But it was his own face he saw, reflected in the window glass, and it was a tired face, with tourist eyes, wary and unsure. Shadows had settled into the wrinkles at the corners of his mouth, and his hair had been scrambled by the wind.

What in the hell are we doing here, he silently asked the face in the glass.

That's when he noticed another reflection, another face with features he remembered, just behind him. He turned quickly, almost too quickly, and nearly stumbled into the person standing only a couple of feet away.

It was the Mexican girl who had waited on him at breakfast, the one *El Brujo* had mentioned by name.

She stepped back a pace and smiled.

"Hola," she said. And before he could answer, she said, "I am told your name is Jackson."

She led Jackson back past the northern end of the seawall. There, on a deserted section of beach, well back from the water and beyond all but the highest of tides, a dozen or so old hulls, the remains of big trawlers and shrimpers, lay partly on their sides, close together like a family of foundered whales. Some wood, some rusted metal—all with missing parts; none would ever see the water again. As she led him between the hulls, they moved from bright sun to deep shadow, more light, more shadow, until they were out of sight of the street.

There was movement, noises, from the dimness beside an old gray wooden hulk with Tampico painted in white across her stern. He moved closer to the shadow and, there, perched on a massive rusting anchor sat Isaac Po.

Jackson turned to catch his bearings, but the world had closed in, become overlapping panels of rust and decay and dim and shifting light. Nothing back there moved. The Mexican girl was gone.

South by South, the Hard Way

"THIS TOWN IS SAFE ENOUGH," Isaac Po said after they'd shaken hands and said their greetings. "Except for out there along the seawall. The few cops they've got all prowl around here and scare money out of the gringos. Hell, why not? It's honorable in a Mexican sort of way and much easier than peddling wooden fish."

He shrugged.

"You learn it, quick or the hard way. It doesn't take much to get your ass thrown into a Mexican jail. Some patriot slick dressed like a farmer from Omaha slips five hundred pesos to a hungry cop, points to you and me sitting on a bench, and away we go. No charges ever filed. A year later, we're still trying to get out."

He looked mostly the same, but perhaps thinner. His short beard had grown out some, and his hair, gathered in the back as before, seemed longer, shaggier.

His eyes looked very weary and a little sad.

"What is this all about?" Jackson asked.

"You tell me. You wanted to come down here, to find me, and here we are."

"You make it tough."

"Circumstances, that's all."

"You should be glad to see me."

"Explain it to me. Tell me why."

"I'm starved," Isaac Po said. "What would you say to a little dinner?"

Jackson was hardly surprised when he led them right back to the same little café where he'd eaten that morning. He was more surprised to see the Mexican girl back at her job, waiting tables, as though she'd never taken her apron off.

"*Buenas tardes*, Lucia," Isaac Po said, and she looked bashful and pleased. "Again."

"*Si*, again," and she laid menus on the table.

"*Dos cervezas, por favor.*"

As she turned to walk away, Jackson noticed how she put her hand on Isaac Po's shoulder.

"My Spanish doesn't amount to much," Isaac Po was saying. "With her, I just practice, and she can laugh at me and ask me what in the hell I'm trying to say."

"You know her, I see."

"We're friends," he said, and the tone of his voice suggested that Jackson was edging their conversation in the direction of a locked gate.

"Where are you staying?" Isaac Po asked while they were eating.

"Last night I found a little motel not too far from here. Cheap, hot water, clean sheets, not too bad."

"Tonight?"

"The same, I guess. It wasn't full."

"Makes sense."

"You want a room there, too?"

Isaac Po shook his head.

"Lucia's family are friends of friends, part of—," and then he stopped himself. "They would expect me to spend the night there. I usually do."

They ate in silence for a few minutes more.

"How long are you staying here?" Jackson asked.

"Don't know. We need to talk about that."

"What do you mean?"

"It can't be long. I need to turn it around in a day, two at the most."

Jackson waited. His old friend looked tired, in need of rest, more than just a single night's worth. Taking to the road again should be the last thing on his mind. This was the land of *mañana*, not of the forced desert march.

Isaac Po looked up and paused.

"I have an old man to look after. An important friend, and I can't leave him alone for very long."

So it was as simple as that. Obligations, maybe as simple as life and death.

"Eduardo Abeyta?"

Isaac Po stopped in mid-bite.

"How do you know that?"

"I got some information from Noche. How do you think I got as far as Calexico?"

Isaac Po just nodded his head. Details. Maybe he hadn't bothered trying to put them all together. Or maybe he knew exactly where the pattern led.

"Did he ever get my letter?"

"What letter?"

"I wrote and asked him if he knew where you might be."

"No. I mean, I don't know about it if he did."

Jackson sat back and sipped on his beer, watching the other put away his food.

"Some days, things are okay. Other days, well, I have to keep a close eye on him. He's a good man, but he's old, grouchy, and I don't know how much longer he's going to last."

He dropped his napkin onto his empty plate.

"So I have to get back."

They stood outside in the darkness, just beyond the light streaming out of the café's windows.

There, Isaac Po apologized and asked if they might wait until morning to try to untangle the snarl of questions and explanations and stories.

He had another job still to do.

"Señor Torres brews a powerful mescal," he said, as though Jackson would understand how important that might be. "He and his crew cut agave in the hills around here, a lot of it. They distill it in old barrels built into a rock oven, cool it through a copper pipe in a wood trough filled with cold water. Quite a rig. You ought to see it."

Señor Torres would be Lucia's father, Jackson guessed but didn't ask.

"I need a shot or two of that right now, while I give him a medical report on the condition of his old friend."

He rubbed his eyes.

"Then I need some sleep."

"I can see that."

"Here, at seven, for breakfast. Then we'll talk."

They shook hands, and Isaac Po clamped his left hand around Jackson's forearm for ten long seconds. Then he turned and walked slowly off into the San Bruno night.

"You said you have to get back," Jackson said, and the other man stopped. "But back to where?"

"*Mañana*," Isaac Po said and walked on.

"Okay, Jackson, let's get to the point. Why are you here?"

The café had been crowded at breakfast, and on every side of the table, the air had been thick with English. So the two of them had talked only about things that could be overheard and mean nothing: careful questions about Noche, about Whitewater, about goats and weather and the Main Vein Saloon. The answers were, likewise, doled out in careful and unemotional words.

Only later, when they'd walked to the far south end of the seawall and sat among the big rocks there, could they talk about more urgent matters.

"You expect a five-word answer?"

"There are cheaper places to drink bad tequila and eat stale fish tacos."

"Probably."

"Cleaner beaches."

"No doubt."

"Well?"

So Jackson told his story then, about Whitewater in the spring. He took his time, picked just the right lines with which to draw a picture of Main Street just before midnight, of a man sitting and watching the traffic, caught in an ebbing flood of old memories. He told Isaac Po about the girl who came out of the darkened doorway across the street, and about Velma Widell, the crippled and drunken old woman who sat in her wheelchair and watched the streets at night.

"She told me how she watches until first light until the mysteries have all gone home. Inside her own world, looking out."

"Then she hasn't changed."

"So you remember?"

"Some."

"Skin and bones, wrapped around a pretty spooky soul."

Then Jackson told him the important part, about the man who'd come to call, the man who wanted to pay good money for his placer claim—the hillside and sandbar that had produced less than one single ounce of gold.

Isaac Po sat quietly for a while, studying the surf, the crash and froth of the incoming tide. White wings swooped by, closely, hoping for pieces of tortilla, scraps of anything like meat.

Each of them seemed to be waiting for the other to certify this as good news or bad news or no news at all. Two shrimp trawlers moved from behind the rocky headwall of the marina, rusted, with sea-scarred hulls, and pushed steadily out into the choppy bay.

Isaac Po stood and brushed off his pants.

"C'mon," he said. "Let's walk."

They walked to the west, away from the waterfront, across streets filled with noisy traffic, into the neighborhoods of simple and shapeless houses, then turned north. Little children played in the streets, and round women stood in shadowed doorways and watched the two gringos pass by. Dogs slept in the dust and barely opened their eyes when the two strangers stepped around them and walked on.

Isaac Po, for his part, didn't seem to be seeing any of this, just seemed to be walking for the rhythm of it, paced by some metronome in his mind.

They passed a school, quiet, with the children all inside. Then a church, quiet in just the same way, with the spirits behind closed doors. More houses.

The farther they walked, the more flocks of cackling chickens seemed to own parts of the streets.

After they'd been on the move for almost an hour, Jackson began to understand that Isaac Po had no destination in mind. They were just walking. Part of that, he supposed, was merely a cog in the other's thinking process. Part of it, maybe, was a plan to stay on the poorer side of town, away from the street corners with big ears and sharp eyes.

Finally, they stopped in front of a little *mercado*, and Isaac Po went inside and brought out two bottles of Coca-Cola, and they drank while they sat on a bench in the sun.

Around the corner, an invisible rooster crowed over and over again.

"What is it worth?"

"They didn't put a price on it. Not as far as I know."

"What do you think?"

"It depends on how critical that piece is."

"And?"

"My guess is that it's fairly important to them."

"So what does that mean?"

"Hundred thousand, maybe a little more. Most of those old claims are pretty damned small, as I remember."

Isaac Po didn't answer, didn't show any reaction at all, just sat there, taking in the morning air.

"But that's just my guess. Keep that in mind. It could be less, maybe far less."

The sun was higher in the sky, and the day had begun to warm.

"Do you still own it?"

"I don't know."

"What do you mean?"

"I haven't sold it. I haven't given it away."

"Well then."

"But I haven't paid the taxes on it for a while."

"How many years?"

"I don't know. I would have to look it up."

"That probably doesn't matter. Even if someone else has paid the back taxes, you can always redeem. You might have to fork over a few hundred dollars, but the title still belongs to you."

He nodded, as though he knew all that. And possibly, Jackson thought, he in fact did.

"Is this going to help you?"

"In what way?"

"How in the hell would I know?"

Isaac Po took the bottles inside, and they began, generally, to retrace their steps—different streets, around different corners, but randomly working their way back toward the south and east.

"How hard would it be to get it done?"

They sat on a concrete bench at the edge of a rundown basketball court. The rims were rusted and bent. Old newspapers and candy wrappers and pieces of torn cloth were blown halfway up a chain-link fence.

"Simple. We cross the border, fill out a deed, you sign it, and we get it notarized. You sign a power of attorney, we notarize that. I go back, do the deal, sign the papers in your behalf, fill in the buyer's name on the deed."

He nodded.

"In fact, once I have the power of attorney, you don't have to sign anything else. I can sign the deed. I can just pick up the check."

"And cash it."

"I suppose."

"Same-day service."

"What do you mean?"

"I don't know. I don't know how these things work."

Pause.

"Take the money and run, I guess is what I mean."

"Is that what you want me to do?"

"I don't know yet."

"Why?"

Isaac Po didn't answer for a couple of minutes.

"Think about it," he said. "If there's one thing those government bastards know how to do, it's follow the money."

They stood and walked on.

"If I wait for the truck to come back through, I'll be here two more days," Isaac Po said once they'd approached the center of town. "At least. I never know."

The thought seemed to agitate him a little.

"If you drive me, we can leave now."

"To where?"

"South."

"How far?"

"All day."

He paused.

"And then some."

Jackson waited while his old friend doled out information in little, barely usable, chunks.

"Let me put it another way," Isaac Po said. "Today, tomorrow, two days after that, I'm headed south. I have no choice. If you don't come along, you can't help me. Maybe, then, you brought me information I can't even use."

Jackson had not considered that.

"We could go north right now," Jackson said. "We could cross the border, get the paperwork done, then you could go back to wherever you came from."

"Then what?"

"I bring the money to you."

"If you're going to do that, you might as well go with me now."

He paused.

"At least you'll know where you're going."

He paused again.

"And what you're getting into."

A beat-up dump truck with no muffler crawled past them on the street, and for a couple of minutes, neither could talk or be heard.

"Besides, I think the old man ought to have a vote here. If things go to hell, he's the one with the most to lose."

Destination, somewhere south.

Isaac Po stocked up on a little food, some tequila and rum, and water for the trip, then had Jackson change five hundred American dollars into pesos.

"American money is not always good farther south. And people remember gringos waving hundred dollar bills around. Pesos are safer, quieter. Most importantly, they show a little respect."

At the last stop, a Pemex station, they filled the truck and two five-gallon cans with gasoline.

"We can't make it on one tank. And you won't get back on one tank, either."

Then they pulled out into the tourist traffic, another license plate in the sea of license plates from everywhere, and headed south.

The soldiers were still there, and Jackson could feel Isaac Po tense a little as they pulled to a stop.

Same questions, same nods, same bitter look from the soldier in charge, and they were waved through again.

"Those guys are everywhere now, on every road. They make me nervous."

"Yeah."

"They stand there for days on end, months on end, same thing over and over again."

"What are they looking for?"

"Drugs. Guns."

"Not terrorists?"

"That, too."

Pause.

"Those kids stand there, in the wind, in the rain, maybe with no days off. Their pay doesn't amount to shit. Nothing. And so you know what they want to do more than anything else in the world?"

Jackson couldn't guess.

"Shoot those fucking guns."

He'd not been surprised when Isaac Po had pointed them south along the very same road he'd driven before. So his instincts had been correct, earlier, and his foray in that direction had not been a total waste. He knew, at least, about the holes in the road.

Jackson saw the shadows and lines that marked the edges of the craters, and he knew when to hit the brakes, to swerve, to move to the wrong side of the road.

"This road is the shits."

"I've been down this way before," Jackson answered, "a few miles at least."

Isaac Po looked over with a question in his eyes, but he didn't say anything.

Then Jackson turned the truck down into the sandy ditch and drove on.

When they passed the old fender buried in the sand, the one with the two interconnected red circles, Jackson asked Isaac Po if he knew anything about the *campo* tucked away back there at the end of the rutted little road.

He shook his head.

"He says the fishermen call him *El Brujo*, the wizard. Might be a man, might be a woman, might just be a dream."

"This stretch of coast is thick with those kind. Lot of people don't have a place in the US anymore. Mostly by choice, I guess. But even in the interior, every bleak little campo you come to, seems like there's some wild-eyed *gringo* holed up there. Chickens and little kids scatter, and out comes this unshaven old fart in his undershirt, scratching his balls, ready to offer you his daughter or something strong to drink."

Pause.

"Then you find out he's a philosophy professor from Princeton. A physicist from Berkeley. A bond trader from Chicago."

Another pause.

"But that just tells you who he was. It doesn't tell you who he is. Or what he did. Or what he might be trying to hide.

"He could be anybody," he said. "Or nobody. Once you're here, it doesn't make a helluva lot of difference. He could be an escaped Nazi, he could be Ambrose Bierce. Who's to say?"

"You probably think I don't know who Ambrose Bierce is."

"True."

"They made a movie about him a year or so ago."

Isaac Po shook his head and frowned a little, as though that news was made no sense.

"With Gregory Peck. I always liked Gregory Peck. Maybe that's why I read about it. I don't know. I can't remember."

No answer, and they drove on, bracing themselves every time Jackson slowed for a hole or a loose piece of asphalt.

"What did the movie say ever happened to him?" Isaac Po finally asked fifteen minutes later. "Ambrose Bierce. How did he die?"

"I don't know. I only read about it. I don't spend much time at the movies."

"He was old," Isaac Po said. "In his seventies, sick of writing, pissed off at the world. So he came down here to fight with Pancho Villa, to get killed, to find his own way into the darkness, into the desert, or so he said."

"But nobody knows?"

"No. If the old bastard wanted to disappear, I guess he got that. If he wanted to get killed, he probably got that, too. Hell, maybe these desert coyotes are still dragging old Ambrose around. It's dry here. A good bone lasts a long time in Mexico."

Jackson pulled onto the pavement again to avoid a washout in the sandy ditch.

"Anyway," Isaac Po said, "if that old man back there is Ambrose Bierce, he's got to be about a hundred and fifty years old."

"He knows your friend Lucia," Jackson said. "He mentioned her name."

He looked over at Jackson and shrugged.

"Maybe he knows her better than I do."

"If that's true, I don't want to hear about it."

Early in the afternoon, they passed along the edge of a little fishing village, squatting bare and gray on a cliff overlooking a small bay. As they drove by the first of the scattered shacks, Jackson asked if this was it, the place where they were bound.

The other man just laughed.

"I wish to hell, amigo," he said. "We've still got a lot of miles, a lot of dirt to eat and rocks to scrape before we get back on our own two feet."

All vestiges of pavement were gone. The road had turned to hard-packed sand and sharp rock.

They drove on.

"At the motel where you stayed, did you use your credit card?"

"No."

"When you used the telephone?"

"No."

"When you filled up with gas before?"

"Yes. But that was in California."

"Good."

"Why?"

"Then maybe they don't know where you are."

As the afternoon faded toward evening, the road got steadily and obviously worse. For mile after dirty mile, the washboards, corrugated ridges cut by spinning tires, jerked the truck and threw them around like little rocks shaken inside a paper bag. Rattles came from everywhere, and at times, it seemed the truck would fall apart into a pile of fenders and windows and knobs that had all pulled loose at the same time.

Now and again, they slowed to five miles per hour, just to keep the truck on the road.

As darkness fell, they climbed into barren mountains. The roadbed turned to boulders, and they eased their way down into rocky washes, then spun and churned up the other sides. They rode for miles along the tops of spiny ridges, then down into the dry washes again. More than once, Jackson heard his back bumper catch and scrape on rocks behind as they started yet another climb.

The world was reduced to only what they could see inside the tunnel of light ahead: jumbled rock and cactus, scrubby brush and scrawny tree trunks, pieces of old metal and rusted and stripped car bodies.

They didn't meet another vehicle or see any lights behind them.

The only animal they saw was a desert jackrabbit that sat frozen in the headlights for a moment, then ran down the dim tunnel a ways and veered off into the scrub.

Jackson's eyes burned, and his shoulder and arms were aching from fighting the steering wheel for what had seemed like more than one long night.

He got out and stretched while Isaac Po emptied one of the five-gallon cans into the gas tank.

"How far have we come?"

"Not nearly as far as you think."

"Not far enough."

"We'll get there. An hour more maybe."

"Is this the only way in?"

"No. There's another road that comes in further south. It's rough, too, but not like this. But it would have taken us at least five hours longer to go that way. Up to Ensenada, then back to the south again."

"I forgot to check the air in my spare tire."

"Relax. We'll make it. Two or three trucks make this same trip every day."

"Yeah. Two or three leave town, and one makes it through. The rest have to be used for spare parts."

"Funny."

"Yeah. Ha, ha. I'm a funny man."

Sometime near midnight, they dropped out of the mountains, and as they rounded a bend, he could see, in the light of a slivered moon, the waters of the Sea of Cortez, spreading off across the eastern horizon.

It seemed that weeks of dry and painful time had passed since the last glimpse of water.

"We're here," Isaac Po said. "Bahía Obregón."

Five minutes more and they were riding across the tide flats, and the smooth sand felt like velvet slipping away under the tires of the truck. Nothing Jackson had ever driven upon felt so perfect and sublime.

Then a row of houses appeared between the road and the sea. In the headlights and in the dim light of the moon, he could see cubes of buildings, hard to separate, hard to tell which was attached to what. Boats, some old, some new, were strewn around as were piles of boards, barrels, and pieces of nameless, undefined machinery.

"Turn in here."

It was a lane between small buildings, deep in the shadows, just wide enough for the truck.

"We'll unload in the morning."

When they stepped out of the truck, Jackson could hardly straighten. His back had grown too stiff, too tired, from the long and jarring ride, and his shoulders felt like they had been nailed into the frame of the truck.

He followed Isaac Po onto a boardwalk alongside a house and could see the sea again, much closer, and could hear the crashing of a small surf. The thin moon left a jagged pale yellow line across the mostly calm water, and he had no way of knowing if the tide was in, out, or somewhere in between.

Down the beach, only two other lights, both some distance off.

"You can sleep in here."

He opened a door, and then Jackson saw what had seemed to be a house was really a small trailer enclosed on three sides by wood. He was in a room with a bed, a small table, one chair, and not much more. The only light came from a bulb hardly bigger than his thumb.

Then the light went out, as though power to the trailer had been cut off for the night.

He took off his shoes and lay on the bed in his clothes, relieved, at last, to be able to stretch out, loose, like a bag full of bones. The temperature was cool, and he pulled a blanket from the foot of the bed.

The last thing he heard was the sound of footsteps going up a set of stairs and the muffled sound of voices, of two or more people talking.

Then the darkness took him in, and he was asleep.

Another World, Far Removed

HE AWOKE TO SCREECHES AND SHRIEKS, the mixed and ragged sounds of shorebirds fighting over something that had washed ashore with the changing of the tide. Light streaming into the trailer was intense, and when he first opened his eyes, he could see nothing but glare and ghost images, as though he'd been staring into the sun.

Outside, he could hear the slap and rattle of the incoming surf.

His watch said 7:55 a.m.

Perhaps the long trip through the nighttime hours had done it, the bumping and swerving and jarring, driving through a corridor of light with nothing on both sides but broken rock, sterile and yellow dirt, and plants that looked as though they had been half-dead for a hundred years. So he awoke in a scratched-up and grimy mood, and at the dawning of an unknown day, he expected nothing but more of the same.

Water, the gulf, wouldn't necessarily change anything, he knew. More than one formless rock pile had sprung out of the sea, covered with nothing more alive than iguanas, bird shit, and crusted shells.

But when he walked outside and took his first real look at Bahía Obregón, he could only blink and stare. He'd come awake in a world of soft edges, muted colors, and spectacular light.

To the south, or what he believed to be the south, the bay looped away in a series of coves until, almost due east, a rocky headland jutted out into the horizon. Beyond that, a high peninsular mountain guarded the right side of the entrance to the bay.

To the north, the beach and its houses—maybe thirty, maybe sixty, maybe more—ended against a sheer gray cliff that was part of another peninsula. Beyond, a rocky island, with a lighthouse at its tip. Further in the distance, more steep granite closed off the left side of the entrance to the bay. Thus, the gateway to the open sea was just a hole between rocks, a small stretch of watery horizon straight off to the east.

Below the little patio where he stood, the beach fell away in a sand that was light brown and fine and smooth, all the way into the oncoming surf, into water that was at times emerald, at times ultramarine.

His bare feet felt the coolness and softness of the sand, and the heavy, moist air washed its way into the folds of his parched and brittle skin.

On dry lips, the faint taste of salt.

Another world, beyond his grasp.

A delicious sense of ignorance.

"I'm glad to see you didn't die in your sleep."

Jackson heard the voice coming from above and behind, turned, and saw Isaac Po sitting on a high deck at the top of a flight of steps, directly above where he had been sleeping.

"Otherwise, I would have had to cut you up and feed you to the fish."

Jackson could not find his voice.

"I have coffee here," Isaac Po said. "Come on up."

He turned and stretched into the morning sun.

"Where's the pisser?"

"After dark, you'd be about standing in it. In the daylight, we use the one inside. Go through that door on the left. You'll see it."

The south end of the trailer butted against a two-story white box, which added another room over the top of the trailer, like an inverted L. Next to that upper room, the small deck where Isaac Po sat.

He opened a door into the wooden structure and went inside.

"What's the layout here?"

They were sitting side by side on canvas chairs, looking out over the bay, holding coffee cups. Isaac Po was dressed in baggy shorts and a thin shirt, and looked more rested than he had in San Bruno.

A small table with a coffee urn sat off to one side.

"The trailer has been gutted and made into two bedrooms. Next to it, they built a kitchen and bathroom. Running water, but don't drink it. Up here, another bedroom and an office."

Curtains were closed across the front of the room next to them.

"The old man?"

He nodded.

"How's he doing?"

"Better in fact. He got up when we came in last night, and he was up and around for a while this morning. The sun rises just a little past six."

They drank coffee, black, and watched as pelicans, a dozen of them, swooped back and forth across the near reaches of water. Out past the peninsula to the north, in the lee of the island, a white sailboat was anchored, barely moving on the calm water there.

"Who's that?" Jackson pointed toward the boat.

"I have no idea. People come, people go. Some nights maybe a quarter of these houses show lights, other nights they're mostly dark. Some nights, there seems to be no one here at all."

He gestured back over his shoulder, inland.

"There's a landing strip back there," he said. "More people get in and out of here that way."

"Easier on the kidneys."

"Tires. Bones. Attitudes."

A door clicked closed below, and Jackson was surprised to see a middle-aged Mexican woman, slender with slightly graying hair and kindly eyes, coming up the steps. She carried another urn of coffee.

"This is Marcella," Isaac Po said, and added "*gracias*" as she put the coffee down and took away the empty urn.

She nodded and smiled and walked away.

"She's the boss. She watches after the old man, cooks, cleans, finds parts, and people we could never locate on our own."

"She lives here?"

He shook his head.

"The other road out, to the south, forks in places, and old trails cut back into the mountains. She and Paco, her husband, have a rancho up there. He brings her in his old truck every day at first light, then comes and takes her home about dark. No two finer people on the face of this earth."

Then they sat quietly for a while. From behind, out on the road, Jackson heard the sound of a motor, fading off inland, maybe toward the north. Further down the beach, toward the south, a dog barked for a few minutes, then fell silent.

"I didn't expect this."

"No?"

"When we left San Bruno, I thought we'd end up in some thatched-roof hut somewhere down this way. In the jungle. Dark. Rain dripping from the palm leaves. Cholera. Dead monkeys. Beetles the size of your fist. Iguanas bigger than warthogs. I don't know."

"I expected the same thing. But the old man said if he had wanted to wallow around in misery and die in the arms of a shit goddess, he would have stayed in Arizona."

"What does that mean?"

"Desert poetry, I guess. I just let him think I understand."

Isaac Po said he had work to do with the old man and suggested that Jackson get more rest or walk around on his own.

"Down at the far end," he said, pointing toward the north, "there's a six-room hotel, and a little restaurant with a bar. I can have Marcella cook you up some tortillas and eggs. But maybe you just want to have a look around."

He paused.

"Maybe that would be better, for the time being, anyway."

He stood and gathered the cups.

"Stick to the road or to the beach. Look all you want. But don't get too close to the houses."

He looked off down the beach.

"Most of the windows are shuttered anyway."

There is no electrical system in Bahía Obregón.

It was a thought that came upon Jackson as he walked back along the beach after breakfast, wandering, with the slow eyes of a man who had been stripped of his compass and map.

He'd felt hungry even before Isaac Po had mentioned food, so he'd walked out onto the road and made straight for the little hotel—noticing the houses, noticing the cubes and the rust and the clutter, but not stopping to look closely or to try to figure anything out.

The waitress, a teenaged girl, had spoken no English, but between pointing to menu items and having her write numbers down on a pad of paper, he'd managed to get the order made. The meal of eggs, chorizo, and tortillas was the best he'd had in a while, and he'd eaten like the underfed man he'd indeed become.

Afterward, he'd walked back along the beach.

Most of the houses were painted white, but a couple were green, one was turquoise, and one was red. Several others were either painted brown or left to weather to a saltwater gray.

At least half, probably more, had been caterpillars before they'd been butterflies. They showed a clear morphosis from bleached and battered trailer to something planted in the ground and meant to stay. Some were totally enclosed, some had decks built over the top, some had a mere shed or two tacked on. A few, in particular a couple made of stone, were houses in the real sense.

Every structure, someplace, somehow, featured glass that looked to the east out over the sea. And nearly every structure showed one or more solar panels on a roof, or a porch, or fastened to a homemade rack. Under little roofs and inside partly open sheds, he could see generators, some old and some new, flanked by barrels and cans that must have held gasoline.

People hoard power here. More precious, maybe, than water or solitude. That's why, last night, the light went out.

"If you need something to read, there are plenty of books in the bedroom where I sleep."

Isaac Po had come downstairs in search of something and found Jackson sitting in the sun, staring at the birds, watching the rhythm of the incoming waves.

"Maybe later. What I really need is more sleep."

"I hear that."

So he went back to his bed, and though the air inside the trailer was close and still, his tired mind took little notice of it, and he fell easily back into a deep and dreamless coma.

When he woke again, the sun was far lower in the western quadrant of the sky, and the tide was lapping higher on the beach.

His watch said 3:10.

For a while, just the stillness of the bay.

Behind him, the rattle and ring of pans and dishes, and he guessed that Marcella was beginning preparations for the old man's evening meal and perhaps theirs as well.

The white sailboat. Although the craft was far from shore, he could see two people moving around on deck, and they seemed to be at work.

Who are you? If I knew the answer to that question, then perhaps I would know something about this place, something about the winds, fair and ill, that bring people into this bay.

To the north, hundreds of pelicans sat on a tide flat, side by side, nearly all facing out to sea, toward the boat.

Then the two people disappeared below decks, and though he watched and hoped they would launch their dingy and come ashore, they did not reappear.

One by one, the pelicans took to the air and sailed out over the waves.

No one else was around, no sounds came from above, no other people moved along the beach.

He had a strange feeling of being left behind, as though they might have evacuated the bay while he was asleep and decided not to wake him, to leave his body in its bed.

He decided to read.

In Isaac Po's end of the trailer, a small bed was shoved against one wall, and opposite it, a desk had been made from concrete blocks and an old door. It held a manual typewriter and a clutter of papers and books. Next to the old Smith Corona, as though someone had arranged a still life of simpler days, a kerosene lantern.

Several boxes of books lined the third wall, and he began to pull them out, one by one, and put them back again. Some of the titles in the first box were familiar—works by Hemingway and Cather and Steinbeck and such—but many were not. He found nothing that matched his mood, whatever that mood was turning out to be. Confusion? Ignorance? Anticipation? He wondered who had written *Stranger in a Strange Land*.

In the second box, however, he found books that were not what he was looking for, but what he needed. They had nothing to do with Spanish soldiers or dead Catholic priests, nothing to do with migrant farmers or the charting of the coast. But they kept him reading, kept him pulled along by a thick and powerful string for the next two hours.

The books spoke of sandstone and tamarisk, of uranium miners and Mormons, of bleached skeletons and the panic of thirst. Old trailer houses. Sunsets. Snakes that lived under the floor. And somewhere out in a nameless desert, in a bleak side canyon off a dry creek that showed on no map, at the end of a trail that disappeared through a crack in a wall, Jackson began to assemble clues and footprints.

And those led to the real hide and the real bones of the man who liked to call himself Eduardo Abeyta.

"Who is the old man?"

The two of them were sitting on the patio, each with a rum and soda in hand, watching the light begin to lift off the far peninsulas. Just as morning came early at this latitude and longitude, so did evening.

"What are you asking?"

"When I was looking for something to read today, I came across a box of books."

"I told you there were plenty of books."

"Not just any box."

"Meaning?"

"It appeared to be filled with every book that Quentin Behr has ever written."

Isaac Po was silent for a minute.

"I'd forgotten about that box of books."

"So?"

"So then you know a part of the story you probably didn't know before. Doesn't matter. I would have explained it to you anyway, sooner than later, or at least tried to."

"I don't get it."

"Get what?"

"He died in the late '80s."

"Yes. As a matter of fact, he did."

They sat and drank and talked until the sun was gone, and after that, they lit the kerosene lantern and talked more. Marcella and Paco had gone back to their place in the mountains, leaving the old man to himself and the two of them alone with the sea and the bottle of rum.

Now and then, a cool rush of breeze blew in off the water, but just as quickly, the evening stilled and the forces of the night seemed to sit in perfect balance. As darkness closed in, their bodies were swallowed by shadow, leaving only two faces, two masks in the lantern light, moving and shifting very little at all.

"Early on in his writing career, Quentin Behr met a young couple, both doctors who tended the rural poor, mostly in Mexico. Their names were Rita and Howard Ellison, and they remained friends for life. The three of them saw the world the same way: big government and big business walking hand in hand would lead us down a pathway to hell. That's oversimplified, but you get the drift."

And for a while, the Ellisons were also part of a group that believed in something akin to utopia, he said. Along with friends from Santa Fe, where they lived, and Taos and Aspen and San Francisco, they found Obregón Bay. It was just a little fishing village back then, no real contact with the outside world, and they'd all hauled their beaten-up old trailers in and built the camp.

"The Ellisons built this place," he said. "It still belongs to them. Or to her. Howard died a few years ago. And they flew in here whenever they could. Rita Ellison learned to fly in order to haul medicine and emergency care into little villages like this."

Most of their friends moved on, he said, sold their interest in Obregón, but the Ellisons stayed. Being doctors to the poor, this would be the closest they would ever get to a villa by the sea.

"Then, in 1989, Quentin got fed up with life. Because of his writing, his speeches, his finger-wagging, the feds were trying every trick they knew to paint him as the one man responsible for all the spiked trees, burned castles, dead cows, closed roads in that part of the world. The squeeze was on. And it worked. Editors were afraid to use him. Every time he spoke, trouble broke out. Even after all he'd done, he was still living on a pretty paltry income. And he was sick, physically sick, and sick at heart for the poor world he'd made for his wife—the last of many, the love of his life."

The kerosene lantern had started to smoke, and he stopped to trim the wick.

"But he did have one thing left. He had an insurance policy. Not huge, but enough. So he decided to die."

The Ellisons agreed to go along with his plan. So they, Quentin's wife, and a couple of other close friends gathered in the Arizona desert one morning and pronounced him dead. They mourned for an hour or two, made a few phone calls, then took a simple plywood coffin that Quentin had made and filled it with just enough sacks of sand and nailed it shut. Howard Ellison signed the death certificate, and they left for the canyon country to bury Quentin Behr in a place known only to the five of them.

"Quentin had written more than once about the high honor of an unmarked grave, about being left alone when he died."

After dark that day, the group of mourners stopped somewhere in the ponderosa country north of Flagstaff, dumped the sand out of the bags, broke up the plywood and made a fire. Then they passed bottles of good bourbon around and celebrated Quentin Behr's untimely, but not unexpected, death. After all, he'd had kidney problems for years.

"That same night, Rita Ellison flew Quentin down here, and with few exceptions, he's been here ever since."

He paused, watching as a small moon rose over the island to the north.

"So now you know," he said. "One of the best-kept secrets in the brotherhood of malcontents, the posse of missing men. Quentin Behr at rest. "

Then he went quiet. Jackson could have asked more questions, even offered a comment or two. But the story, the stage, even the silences, all belonged to Isaac Po.

"It's odd," he said after several minutes had passed. "More times than one, I've sat here and thought about that night—the night they flew down here together. It rolls over and sticks with me like a scene from a poor man's tragedy."

He let the words hang in the air like smoke before he went on.

"I met Rita only once, when she flew a batch of medicine down for the old man. A wonderful lady. And when the two of them were together, it was like everyone, anyone, else in the room had just turned to dust and blown away. Maybe I just don't know how two old friends act when one of them is sick. But there was more than just hand-holding at work. Like an old sweet song, an old secret. I don't know. Private pictures no one else could see."

He paused.

"Anyway, so I think about them, about that night they flew down from Tucson. Sitting side by side here, maybe, sipping their whiskeys, watching the moon, thinking about what might have been."

He said nothing more for a while, then stood.

"Marcella fixed dinner before she left," he said. "All we have to do is heat it up."

The next morning, when Jackson climbed the stairs to share a pot of coffee with Isaac Po, a serious and sad look clouded the eyes of his old friend.

Without saying anything, he poured a cup of coffee and sat down.

"Quentin wakes at first light," Isaac Po said, as though he might have more of the story to tell. "Up here, with all this glass, he sees the first bands of morning sun off to the east. Though he doesn't always stay with us for long, he's always poking around, ready to eat, when Marcella puts breakfast together. Always."

He turned to look Jackson's way.

"Until today. This morning, we had to wake him. We had to get him on his feet and convince him to eat. He was grouchy. He's always grouchy now, I guess. But he didn't want much to do with us."

He shook his head.

The voice and eyes of Isaac Po were heavy with the weight of surviving, of being the one left with the chore of a heavy, dragging load. Jackson had seen a little of it that night in San Bruno, when dirty and tired from his trip, he'd talked about turning around and coming right back south.

"We give him what he wants. But time could be running out much faster than any of us had counted on."

He said no more, and they sat quietly. That's when Jackson noticed the sailboat was gone.

The kitchen held a small table, and the two of them had eaten breakfast there, while Marcella worked outside on an old wringer washing machine.

"We save every drop of water here," Isaac Po had explained. "The rinse water from the dishes becomes the wash water for the clothes.

Then it gets filtered and is used to water the cactus and the palms."

Now they were sitting upstairs again in the sun. A shrimp trawler had pulled into the bay and seemed to be coming right at them.

"Every few days, that shrimper comes in here and drops anchor. They fart around on deck for an hour or two, then they're gone. I guess they sleep the rest of the day. Just about dark, the boat heads out again."

For five or ten minutes, they just sat there, watching the gulls swarm around the trawler, squawking, diving as though they might be getting fed. From a distance, the thrashing, the shifting colors on deck were just part of a disorderly dance.

Then he began to talk again.

"After I'd been in prison for about six months, I got a letter from a man named Eduardo Abeyta."

"Noche told me about that." His statement wasn't exactly true. She'd showed him the writings. But he didn't want to make a mistake, telling him more than he needed to know.

"He suggested we might be kindred spirits. That we should stay in touch. You know this?"

"Pieces, that's all."

"So we did that. We exchanged long slow letters over the next two years or so."

Jackson was amazed at how close the trawler came to shore before it swung around. Then the anchor chain began to unwind with a rattle, lowering the hook.

"Did you know who you were dealing with?"

"No. I had no idea."

"But it didn't matter?"

"I took it for what it was. A voice I needed to hear."

Until that moment, his inside life had never come into focus for Jackson, never really registered as the days of a man in jail.

"Then, in the third or fourth letter, I can't remember which, he did a very clever thing. In the middle of a paragraph about living in the desert, he quoted Shakespeare. He wrote, 'To be, or not to be, that is the question. Or is it QB, or not QB? I can barely remember the pathetic old bastard anymore.' At first I didn't get it. I was pissed that I was being trifled with, and I couldn't move past it. Then the answer came to me, two nights later, when I had given up on sleep."

"And you believed it? Believed it was really him?"

"At first, I wasn't so sure. He was supposed to be dead. But I reread everything he'd written me, studied the style, and I knew it had to be true."

Just as he had said, the fishermen were scrambling around on deck, working with their long green nets, hosing down the deck.

"When I wrote him back a week or so later, I said that when I'd lived in the valley, I'd also turned to Shakespeare to help me through those long cold desert nights, through those three winters of my discontent. Do you remember?"

"Remember what?"

"The title of Quentin's best-known book. *Three Summers of My Discontent*."

Jackson remembered. Remembered the spring snowstorm that had pinned them inside the old mill shack, and his friend's suggestion that desert stories could take the edge off alpine ice.

"The prison goons, they never got it. If they read at all, they probably had to wade through all of *Richard the Third* and a little Steinbeck before they gave up in disgust."

He laughed.

"It was difficult. Hard to write about the anger we both felt about all that had gone on, knowing that prison apes were opening all incoming and outgoing mail. But we kept at it. And at times like that we even got a decent laugh from our inside joke."

The shrimp trawler had gone to sleep. Gulls still swooped around in big waves, but nothing was moving, nothing worth eating was floating in the slicks around the boat.

"So it went," he said. "So it went for many months."

Jackson tried to imagine the routine, the edginess, of waiting for loaded mail, but he could not.

"Then, after I got out, after I'd been home about a month, I got a letter. It was more direct, to the point. He was assuming something I never could, that as a free man, I would again get mail that had not been tampered with. Maybe he was right. Maybe not. I still worry about that and I still don't know. Anyway, he said his health had taken a serious turn for the worse. He was having trouble writing. He was having trouble putting together his last big chance. Or, as he put it, an old fool's last mumbling prayer. He said he needed both a writer and a fighter and asked me to come see him."

He shrugged his shoulders.

"How could I turn him down?"

He had met Paco in Calexico, stowed his truck in Señor Montoya's shipping warehouse, and come south.

"So you wanted to know how I got here? That's it. That's all there is."

The soft hand of the late morning sun.

Isaac Po had holed up in his side of the trailer, back at work on the old fool's last prayer. Jackson could hear him banging away on the tired typewriter, and the clatter of the keys only added to his sense of coming awake in another world, back in time, as though he might have fallen and hit his head.

"I don't think Quentin is going to be doing any work today," he'd said and gone off to his task.

So Jackson sat alone, out in the sun, watching the silent, motionless trawler.

So this is all supposed to make some kind of sense? A man you only know from twenty-year-old books asks you to walk away from a life you've worked so long and hard to build, and you do it? I can't see through Isaac Po's eyes, and I never could. But I know what he has forsaken, left behind, abandoned. And for what, really? For what?

A couple of questions find answers now. Yes. But the story is far from fully told. Isaac Po did not come all this way, is not sweating all this blood, simply to watch an old man die.

Tired of thinking about it, he walked back inside and began to sort aimlessly through a stack of paperback books taken from the next room.

Chekhov's short stories would be good for another time, another place. He tried Pablo Neruda, but poetry demanded more focus than he could muster.

The third book was *The Treasure of the Sierra Madre* by a writer named B. Traven. He was familiar with the title, had seen the old black-and-white Bogart movie perhaps twice. But the author's name meant nothing.

Still, the story took place in Mexico.

Quentin Behr had written his name inside the front cover. Also there, a piece of paper folded inside: a brief biography of B. Traven.

In the 1920s and '30s, the paper said, a man writing under the name of B. Traven published twelve works of fiction. His manuscripts were all written in German and mailed from Mexico. His only address was a post office box.

Most of the many scholars who have tried to solve the mystery of the identity of this man believe he was born in Chicago in 1890 under the name Traven Torsvan, had worked in Germany as an anarchist named Ret Marut, and lived in Mexico under two names: Berick Traven Torsvan and Hal Croves. However, other scholars have concluded that he was born in Germany at about the same time and had an entirely different name.

In either case, a man calling himself Hal Croves appeared on the movie set of The Treasure of the Sierra Madre, saying he was there to represent the interests of the author B. Traven. He was hired on the set as a technical advisor. Most experts agree that the man who passed himself off as Hal Croves was the author.

After reportedly living in the jungles of Chiapas for many years, a man named Traven Torsvan Croves died in Mexico City, in relative obscurity, in 1969. Neither the agent/screenwriter Hal Croves nor the author B. Traven were ever heard from again.

Somehow it seemed that being a writer and disappearing into Mexico was, for some, the perfect final note. Ambrose Bierce. B. Traven. Quentin Behr. Or maybe Jackson was the only one who had noticed. Besides,

Q. Behr had not, so far as the world knew, disappeared. So far as the world knew, he was simply long-time dead. But perhaps that was the most sublime form of disappearance: leaving an empty coffin without being missed.

And what about all the writers who had disappeared in Paris, had drowned in bottles of Irish whiskey, or had walked into Asian whorehouses, never to be seen again?

Is the mystery, the silence, of slipping unnoticed into an unmarked grave an important part of this, and something only a writer can understand?

He didn't realize he'd fallen asleep until he felt a hand on his shoulder, shaking him.

"Wake up," Isaac Po said. "Quentin wants to talk to you."

Now approaching the age of eighty and sick for more than twenty years, Quentin Behr had become a shell of a man. As he sat up in bed, his thin arms stuck out from the sleeves of his nightshirt like willow sticks caught in a flooded culvert. His hands were long and gnarled, flesh gone, bones held together by rawhide.

His shoulders were narrowed and his neck was long and thin. Much of his face was hidden behind a wild snow-white beard, which betrayed the hollows in his cheeks in the way that shadows in grasses betrayed ditches and dips. His eyes were sunken, tired from the effort it took to bring them to bear. His hair was the same dazzling white, the same uncontrolled chaos.

"Quentin, this is Jackson. Jackson, Quentin Behr."

No effort was made to shake hands.

"I understand you've risked the wrath of the pecker-headed patriots to come all the way down here and bring us a little good news. I appreciate you for that."

His voice was stronger than Jackson expected.

"It was just a long trip, nothing more."

"A long trip for us all, my friend. A trip of many years, bad whiskey, good women, and bloodied feet. We haven't abandoned all hope, we luckless bastards, but only because we're too ignorant to know when to quit and go quietly into the godless, waterless, meat-eating desert."

They waited for him to go on.

"At any rate, welcome to Obregón. Now get the hell out. The best thing you can do for all of us would be to load your ass right back in that truck and drive on north, the way you came in."

The old man leaned forward off his pillows, staring hard at Jackson.

"The longer you stay here, the more you will learn. And the more you learn, the more they'll get out of you when they wrap electric wires around your balls."

He coughed and wiped his mouth with the back of his hand.

"Anyway," he continued, "I thought I should at least check you out before Lucifer checks me in."

Silence.

"That was a joke, goddammit. Laugh."

They smiled, the two of them, but they could not laugh.

"Check-out time? Sixty-five, seventy? Here's your pill. Leave your shirt and shoes on that chair over there. Try not to shit your pants."

"All of us, maggots on a bloated sheep. A scourge, a disease, a plague swarming over this poor fucking globe like lice on a border-town whore."

His eyes had turned bright, as though all the power in his body was focused there.

"Another set of bones bleaching in the sun? Yours? Mine? Who gives a shit?"

He lay back against his propped-up pillows, eyes closed, and for several minutes he didn't say a word. They sat in two chairs at the foot of the bed, waiting.

"Pseudo-Europeans, an inferior race of piss-blooded pacifists," he said suddenly, opening his eyes. "Easy meat for Ayn Rand's soulless fucking psycho-industrialist troglodytes. Too late for hanging. Too late for words. We need guns."

As he'd talked, Quentin Behr had straightened and come forward off his pillow again. Now, exhausted from the effort, he sank back down.

They all sat quietly for a few minutes more. Then the old man's heavy breathing began to quiet down, and for a couple of minutes, he closed his eyes again. One more time, he came awake.

He lifted his hand, as though waving good-bye.

"Find a good woman, Johnson, one that can put up with your bullshit. Build her a strong house back among the rocks. Learn to raise vegetables and shoot a deer now and then. Try not to pick fights you can't win."

He caught his breath.

"Go home."

He sat back and turned his head away, and they closed his door quietly and walked out into a day that had grown darker. Black clouds were rolling in from the north and had just overtaken the sun.

"Christ," Jackson said.

"Of a sort, anyway."

Then there are Dylan Thomas's famous words about raging against the dying of the light. Quentin Behr can feel the dimming, the fading, and he knows the sun and the moon and the light behind his eyes will leave him all at once. Birth in the east, death in the west.

Isaac Po had gone back into the trailer to do more work, and Jackson was walking alone along the beach.

Although the sky looked to be alive with weather, a mass of boiling gray and black clouds dancing across a dim sun, little wind stirred the waters of the Sea of Cortez. The surface was flat and pewter, barely reflecting a lone pelican, late to his nest, gliding silently by.

"He's an angry man," Jackson had said as they came down the stairs.

"There's more to it than that."

"Such as?"

"He's frantic in a helpless sort of way."

"Why?"

"It has to do with unfinished business."

Then they were standing in front of the trailer door.

"We'll talk about it later," Isaac Po said and disappeared inside.

Jackson went for his walk on the beach.

Who isn't angry when the end comes around? Does any man ever go gently into that good night, knowing he's done all he can do?

The shoreline was lifeless as though the gulls and pelicans and frigate birds had never existed at all.

To fake one's own death is to die. To suddenly not exist in the minds of ex-lovers and old friends, to be talked about only in the past tense, is a form of death. Slipping away, hiding out, walking away from faces never to be seen again, skin never to be touched again, is a good enough definition of the end.

The only sound was the darkened water lapping onto the unmarked sand.

So Quentin Behr has died once and is about to do it again, and he still isn't satisfied.

What hope for the rest of us?

Ahead of him, an old woman walked out the door of a house, stood for a few minutes looking out at sea, then lifted her head to look at the gathering clouds.

She turned and disappeared inside. If she'd seen him, she made no sign.

Early afternoon.

He tried to read the first chapter of The Treasure of the Sierra Madre, but after only a couple of pages, he drifted into sleep again. Thirty minutes later, a gust of wind blew the unlatched door open, slamming it against the wall with a bang.

Still groggy and a little confused, Jackson staggered out into the open air and saw how the weather had changed. The sky was still layered with thick gray clouds, but the sea was not so calm. Now and then, sheets of wind slid across the surface of the water, erasing the reflections, leaving behind creases and foam and swells.

There came a sound, a rustling, from behind him and above, and when he turned, there sat Quentin Behr in one of the canvas chairs, with a blanket across his lap. His white hair was blowing in the wind and his loose clothing filled and spilled in the moving air.

Slowly, like a child running his hand through water, the old man beckoned to him and pointed to the other chair, and Jackson climbed the stairs.

"Damned fine day, Johnson," he said as Jackson sat down. "Or do you feel otherwise?"

"No, sir."

"We need a little weather like this now and then. Little rain, little wind. Cleans the air. Sweeps the beach. Discourages real estate investment and unnecessary optimism."

For a couple of minutes, neither said more. They simply watched the tilting of the sea and looked off toward the east, where the line between water and sky had disappeared behind a gray fog.

Then a single pelican sailed by, just inches above the waves, wings barely moving, sliding along on the wind. At the north end of the beach, the bird turned and glided back the other way.

"Notice that old pelican never even bothers to look our way," the old man said. "Know why?"

Quentin Behr was in command of his voice. It was reasonably strong, not loud, but easily enough heard.

"He's fishing."

"Maybe. Maybe not."

More was coming.

"He knows we don't count for shit. Tomorrow, next month, fifty years, whatever it takes, we'll be long gone. He's seen Mayans and Mexicans, priests and goat herders, whores and horse traders. All come, all go. We've got about as much chance as a turd in the oncoming rain.

"Couple more generations ought to about do it. By then, we'll have things so fucked up we'll all have to emigrate to the moon. And after we screw that up ... " His voice trailed off into a gust of wind.

The old man kept his eyes fixed on the water, as though watching for the pelican to slide by again.

"Homo erectus stupidus, Johnson," he said. "The American dinosaur, soon to be gone, soon to be nothing more than piles of bones waiting for some one-eyed archeologist from outer space."

He looked toward the sky, then back at Jackson.

"Spotted owl, my tired ass. How about the gray-bearded nut scratcher? How about saving guys like you and me?"

He wiped his mouth with the back of his hand.

"Across the gulf there, on the mainland, a couple of thousand years ago a tribe of monkey worshippers carved out a little kingdom that worked. Part of their so-called success was built on shit known as jungle lime. Everything they built was covered with a smooth coating of lime plaster. Temples, pyramids, little huts—everything."

A puff of wind shook its way through his hair.

"More importantly, the tribe grew more food than they could eat in a jungle where the soil was poor as hell."

A door slammed below them, probably from the wind.

"How did they do that? They lived on the edge of a million-year-old bog that had, since the first frogs drug their asses onto shore, been rotting jungle leaves and logs, making perfect soil. They carried that rich shit back to their towns in baskets and made hundreds of raised garden beds."

He stopped and looked over, as though he just realized that he was not alone.

"Then something went wrong, Johnson. What do you suppose that might have been?"

He paused, waiting for an answer he knew he would not get. The old man's voice was beginning to weaken, and the hand that lay on the arm of his chair had begun to tremble.

"Pride. They got so damned proud of their lime walls, they lost their heads. In order to make enough of that shit to plaster a new temple, they had to burn hundreds or thousands of trees, hell maybe more. After three or four generations, the firewood and wood they needed for posts and beams were gone. But they kept right on making that famous plaster, proud as hell, using those trees until they were gone.

"Worse, without those trees to hold the soil, the clay and caliche from the jungle floor started to erode into the bog until it killed the peat. No trees, no soil, no food. No future. Starved, they drug their asses off into the jungle and were never heard from again."

He got to his feet, and for a moment, in a gust of wind, he wavered. Jackson tensed, ready to catch him if he started to fall.

"You know what mankind learned from that," the old man asked.

Then he paused.

"Apparently, not one goddamned thing."

He turned and took three steps toward his bedroom, then stopped and turned around.

"See? That old pelican, that grizzled old bastard, he knows. He sure as hell knows."

Then he turned and limped away.

Water Resources 103

IN AUGUST OF 1975, rainfall so heavy that it was called a one-in-two-thousand-year event, fell in the river basins blocked by China's Bangiao Dam. Even had the rainfall been half that amount, the dam probably would have failed because so much silt had built up behind the 387-foot-high dam that its sluice gates, through which excess water was designed to flow, were blocked.

In an attempt to get the dam open during the torrential rain, the Chinese government was in the process of authorizing military planes to bomb the dam open, but the action came too late. A dam upstream from Bangiao failed, and thirty minutes later the Bangiao collapsed, sending enough water raging downstream to breach another 60 dams. The total of 62 dam failures sent 1.5 billion tons of water, an inland tidal wave, into the lower valleys.

Consequently, the failure of that dam and several more downstream is estimated to have drowned 26,000 people, and another 145,000 are estimated to have died from disease and famine.

About 5,900,000 buildings collapsed and approximately 11 million residents were adversely affected. A number of other dams had to be destroyed by military bombs.

Twenty years later, the Chinese government commenced construction of the giant Three Gorges Dam project, which, by 2007, had cost $25 billion US. For a time, it looked as though the project might never be completed, since more than 90 landslides had started an unanticipated siltation process, which had governmental officials revisiting the Bangaio incident. Officials talked openly of calling the world's largest dam "a disastrous failure" and halting further construction.

However, work continued, and in November 2009, the final dam height of 175 meters, approximately 525 feet, was reached.

Meanwhile, 13 cities, 140 towns and 1,350 villages had been inundated, creating what some have called "a festering bog of effluent, silt, industrial pollutants and rubbish."

PART FOUR

The Old Fool's Last Mumbling Prayer

By the time Jackson and Isaac Po sat down for rum and sodas, rain had started to fall out of the darkening sky, so they moved their chairs just inside the doorway of Isaac Po's room. The wind had had laid completely down, and the sea was mostly calm again. Only a few birds could be seen bobbing in the water, and the trawler had hoisted anchor and headed out to sea.

"He won't eat tonight," Isaac Po said.

"He seemed stronger to me."

"When?"

Jackson told him about their conversation, sitting on the edge of the incoming weather, and about the story of the jungle lime.

"He's got that story imprinted on his brain. He's told it to me at least three times, and I think he could tell it if he were in a coma. But there's not much left tonight. Marcella is sitting in the kitchen crossing herself and wringing her hands."

"Is he finished?"

"He's not that far gone."

"No, I meant with this last project, whatever it is."

He took his time before he answered.

"That depends on how you look at it, I guess."

"What does that mean?"

"I don't drive his chariot," he said, plainly not answering Jackson's question. "I have no say. If I did, I would keep him here for more years than he would care to live."

The rain was gentle, but steady. The sand had turned shiny, and several different choruses were being sung by the water as it dripped from roofs and railings.

"Half of these houses will have water on the floor by now," he said. "They don't put much money into their roofs. It rains so seldom that nobody gives a shit."

He took a sip from his drink.

"During the last storm, I was down at the hotel. The old lady down there was just standing around in water up to her ankles, saying *'muchas aguas'* over and over again and laughing, like she'd never had so damned much fun."

He smiled.

"I like that in a woman."

The bottle of rum swung back and forth a couple of times, slowing with each arc, while they talked about the old man and his writings. How his books had forced people to stop looking at the desert as a place to leave old junked cars and dead horses, as a place to bomb and dump and discard. He'd found color and life and peace in those red-rock canyons, and he made damned sure the rest of the country understood. Somebody had to defend the vast and the empty, and he was mad enough, in every sense, to take on the job.

Still, he felt as though he hadn't done enough.

"That's what started all of this," Isaac Po said. "He wanted to give it one last shot, say whatever he had been unable to say in all of his other work."

"What is it about?"

"That is never an easy question to answer, not with one word or five sentences or a page full of paragraphs."

He walked over to his makeshift desk and returned with two sheets of paper. Then he began to read.

"Roger Forsythe stopped his car in the middle of the block and got out. It could have been any block in any of the hundreds of neighborhoods ringing The City.

"It was empty.

"Row after row of houses, block after block, had been abandoned. Windows were broken out of most, and doors stood wide open or had been torn off their hinges and laid in the yard. Pieces of furniture, mostly damaged, were scattered around, along with old tires, fuel cans, and mattresses.

"Tumbleweeds filled the narrow streets and blew back and forth with old newspapers and pieces of ragged blue plastic as the seasonal winds moved from north to south and back again.

"A thick silence lay over the bleak and wounded scene.

"Forsythe heard the sound of a door opening and closing, and looked up to see a woman standing on the front step of one of the houses. She might have been forty, or she might have been seventy. Her graying hair was pulled back and tied, and she was dressed in a plain and tattered dress. Her eyes darted back and forth from Forsythe to his car and up and down the street. She looked like a deer caught in the headlights, about to spring and run.

"'Get out of here,' she yelled in a high, scratchy voice. 'We don't want any.'

"He took a couple of steps toward her, and she shrank back against her closed door.

"'This is my house,' she yelled. "'All these are my houses. You got no right to be on my street. I'll tell you one thing, mister. I've got a gun.'

"She reached behind her and opened the door, and as she did, six or seven underfed cats slipped outside. They gave Forsythe one glance, then darted under the house.

"The woman went inside and slammed the door.

"No street, no district, no enclave had been spared. He'd driven around the entire perimeter of the city, and every street looked the same: desertion and squalor, garbage and starving dogs, with a few old recluses and outcasts still hanging on.

"Most of the others had walked away, driven away, taking with them whatever they could carry or haul.

"The day had finally come. The water had run out."

Back in the 1960s, the character named Roger Forsythe, a young hydraulic engineer, was employed by the federal government. He was the man responsible for monitoring all major water projects in the West, from Washington down to the Mexican border and west through Colorado and New Mexico. Each quarter he reported to officials in the capital, recounting the number of dams under construction, the number of kilowatts that had been generated, the number of acres irrigated and the gallons of water delivered for personal use.

After Forsythe had been on the job for a year, the Bureau of Water had sent him to India and Pakistan, Iraq and China, to observe how some of the older masters of water diversion had built and run their systems. What he learned there was indeed significant, leaving him in a state of shock, a state of desperation that lasted for several weeks. After looking at dams, talking to farmers and engineers, and spending endless, exhausting days walking miles of canals, Forsythe had concluded that the water projects of the American West were doomed.

Salt was the first culprit. After nature had spent a million or so years covering over the salts of ancient seabeds with layers of healthy topsoil, irrigators had come along and soaked the grounds of the arid regions. The water reached the salts, dissolved them, and brought them to the surface—where they killed all living plants.

Forsythe had walked more than a thousand acres in the Northwest Provinces of India and had seen the land covered in fine layers of white alkali, abandoned, able to grow nothing but a few noxious weeds, and he began to understand: the legacy of the irrigators was to water, grow, ruin and move on.

Meanwhile, the peasants, who had once been able to eke out a living on that same land, were left with nothing but barren, lethal salt flats. Meanwhile, for the same reasons Mesopotamia, the birthplace of civilization, had become little more than a salty desert in southern Iraq.

Salt took its toll on the grand water projects in another way as well. River water trapped behind the giant dams carried large amounts of natural salts—and those salts were left behind when vast quantities of river water, trapped behind concrete and sitting still, had evaporated. Later, when that water was released for use downstream, it was often too salty for irrigation or consumption.

"Believe it," he said.

"Believe what?"

"The Colorado River alone loses five hundred million gallons a year to evaporation, mostly out of the man-made lakes. It was all in Quentin's notes, early stuff, that I can trust."

Silt was the other culprit. Silt had built up behind dams at a rate far, far faster than anticipated, threatening to fill all dams and eventually leave them clogged and useless. Forsythe saw one dam on China's Yellow River, which carries over a billion tons of silt each year, unable to hold water after only two years of operation. Meanwhile, silt was clogging canals and pipelines, ruining power generators and leaving millions of acres with no water at all.

Forsythe saw what a grand disaster the entire idea of trapping wild rivers had become. But as bad as things might have become in China and India, he saw a far worse threat looming on the horizon: the death of the American West.

Power would dim, and water taps would run dry. Salt-laden farmland would be left to bake in the sun. Migrant workers would be left with no work and no food. Dams would break and floods would scour the canyons clean.

So Roger Forsythe returned to America after a year of thought and study, determined to change the course of human events.

"Not likely," Jackson said.

"No, not likely. But, shitty as things get, we're still allowed our heroic dreams."

The rain had stopped, and the rolling clouds showed flashes and pieces of a half-full moon. They'd moved their chairs out into the cooler evening air.

They sat quietly, drinking, listening to water that still dripped and to the hiss of the kerosene lamp. Isaac Po had lit the lantern and hung it on a hook screwed into a beam, and the light only served to darken the shadows that wrapped around them like black wool. His glasses turned to small circles of flashing light.

"Is this it? Our brave new world?"

"Let me put it this way. In my next life, I want to come back as a turkey vulture. They might be the only ones getting fed."

As would be expected, Forsythe had no luck. Industrial agriculture, major landowners, politicians and bureaucrats were all in lockstep against him. Newspapers, radio, television, all unofficially controlled by the government, ignored his pleas. Stop building new water projects, he warned, and begin the task of taking existing ones apart.

We can avoid disaster, he said, if we begin to wean ourselves from water that will one day cease to flow. We can import more vegetables and grow less. We can give people free land on the Great Plains and start tearing down desert cities that should never have been built. We can gradually increase the flow of water down the old natural river channels.

But no one would listen.

The harder he took to the streets, the more he worked at new methods to get his message across, the more the government began to threaten him. Had it not been for a maverick of another kind, a whiskey-drinking lawyer who lived in a cabin in the Nevada foothills, he likely would have been hauled off to prison as a threat to health and welfare.

T. O. Sawyer, who took on very few cases, and lived on the very little he made, believed everything Forsythe had to say, and felt just as strongly about the coming apocalypse.

Forsythe found another ally.. Leandro Perez had grown up in a little farming community in northern Sonora, married an American woman, and worked for years as a teacher in the Los Angeles barrios. After his wife had died of cancer, he'd returned to his home town, only to find it withered and dying—the big water projects had cut off seepage into the aquifers, and the wells and springs had begun to dry up.

Leandro Perez feared for the future of all of the people of northern Mexico. He'd seen their government turn its back on them and seen them become slaves to the tomato and broccoli growers of the north. Now, he could see them starving, workers without a country, as the water trickled and stopped.

Together, they worked the streets and floated leaflets and spoke from park benches. They wrote letters and made long impassioned telephone calls.

But no one would listen.

Finally they were forced into an act of desperation. Their most powerful enemy was the senior senator from Wyoming, Curtis Thornton, a man who had in one way or another been behind every major water project proposed or built during his forty years in the Senate. For his tenacity, he'd earned the nickname Water Dog. For that same support of water interests, he'd become a very rich man.

Roger Forsythe and Leandro Perez kidnapped Water Dog from his Teton ranch one spring afternoon as the old man was riding his horse out to the ranch gate to check his mail. Then they hid him out in the deep serpentine red-rock canyons of southeast Utah. A week later, they sent a copy of a document they'd been working on, called The Free River Manifesto, to the Los Angeles Times. If the paper would publish the manifesto in its entirety, they would set Water Dog free.

Time dragged on. Promises were made, then pulled back, while army patrols and local cops went around looking inside old buildings and under rocks.

Finally, time and thirst and the army proved to be too much for the two desperate souls. They were trapped in a canyon, and torn apart by gunfire coming from all directions, despite the fact they had no weapons. Water Dog and Leandro Perez were killed, and Roger Forsythe was badly wounded and near death.

Charged with kidnapping, sedition, treason, and manslaughter in the death of Curtis Thornton, Forsythe was sent to prison without right of appeal or chance of parole.

Through the years, Roger Forsythe and T. O. Sawyer wrote volumes of letters back and forth, mostly philosophical exchanges about the ignorance of man and the resulting wounds inflicted upon the planet. But through those letters, also, Forsythe learned that, one by one, the disasters he had predicted were coming to pass.

"The cities were in ruin, the valleys caked in alkali, and poor Mexicans had armed themselves and taken over the state of Sonora. They were shooting *federales* and *gringos* alike, something they should have started doing about eighty years sooner.

"Dams overflowing, filled with silt, had begun to weather and crumble. The rivers had resumed their steady, timeless march toward the sea."

But times and governments changed, and after twenty-three years, Roger Forsythe was set free. T. O. Sawyer, sick at heart and hounded by the government, had immigrated to Leandro Perez's homeland in Sonora.

Forsythe made his way to the tiny Sonoran village, only to find T. O. Sawyer near death. Day after day, he sat by the older man's bedside and they talked, and their conversations became a summary of what it means to fight and lose, but still fight, and have no regrets at the end.

And Sawyer told him how, in little trickles at first, now a little more each year, tiny springs had begun to run, and water could be drawn from the bottom of deep wells.

In the evenings, as he sat alone watching the sun fade from the little valley, Forsythe could see small swathes of greenery spread toward the horizon: patches of beans and peppers and tomatoes, corn, squash. And he knew that he would stay, even after T. O. Sawyer had gone. Because here, and only here, had he found the seeds of hope.

Isaac Po, the story finished, poured himself a strong, straight shot of rum and handed the bottle to Jackson, who took it and stood leaning against a post, looking out to sea.

The night was still. The incoming tide, with no wind behind it, hit the beach with a sound that was more soft roar than crash. Off in the distance, we could barely hear the faint growl of a generator running.

"What do you call it?"

"Call it?"

"A title."

"Adios, Water Dog."

For ten minutes, then, neither of them said anything.

"The story, it's the best thing he's ever done," Isaac Po said finally. "And I could give you a hundred reasons why. Passion. Wisdom. Realizing it's heroes we really need, not real people with warts on their asses and rotten teeth and poison in their minds. Heroes, bigger than we are, hauling loads that would break the rest of us down.

"But there's something else, too. Despite what he says and what he's been through, he holds on to some kind of crazy hope. He says we're doomed, but, behind his back, he's got his fingers crossed."

"Something just doesn't make sense to me," Jackson said, after watching his old friend sink back into a sort of reverie. "As shitty as things have become in our so-called civilization, the last I knew it was not illegal to write a book. Why would anybody, two people, have to hole up down here in order to put this story down?"

He nodded his head, as though he'd been anticipating the question.

"Well, it's illegal for Quentin to be anywhere, isn't it? He's dead. He can't afford to have the insurance company going after his wife and kid. And he damned sure doesn't want to die a second time in the pen, convicted of fraud."

"Is that all there is to it?"

"We know they want me. I don't know what that really means, and I damned sure don't want to find out."

He looked out into the night for a moment, then went on.

"Quentin thinks we're being watched. I can't say. He's paranoid, no doubt, but it's starting to rub off on me."

Having told the whole story, Isaac Po seemed lost in it. Jackson made a comment or two, and the other man didn't respond. He asked a couple of questions, and Issac Po's answers were short and vague.

Finally, Jackson said goodnight and moved toward the door.

"Just remember, Jackson," said a voice from out of the darkness behind him. "People have killed each other over water. It will happen again, only this time it won't be two old West Texas sharecroppers swinging round-pointed shovels at each other's heads."

The hour was late, and the rum pooled heavy in his gut, but Jackson lay awake, staring off into the darkness of the little room.

Something did not feel right. Although twenty years had passed, and the Isaac Po he once knew had aged into a different soul, his intensity had not diminished. He'd seen that in San Bruno, when he turned around on little rest and rode the nasty road back to Obregón as though every moment was precious. He'd seen that here, when Isaac Po bowed his neck and walked off to do his work.

But something in his eyes, his choice of words, his long silences, made Jackson think Isaac Po regretted the way things had turned out.

Still, his intolerance of small ideas, of fiddlesticks of the soul, had not changed. Jackson felt certain of it.

So he could live on that for a while, could wait and see. Or he could go back to Whitewater and choke to death on a bite of overpriced meat.

Jackson did not come awake until late in the morning. The sun was well up in the sky, low tide had come and gone, and the air and water were filled with a mayhem unlike anything Jackson had ever seen. Birds, hundreds of them, were crashing into the surface of the bay, thrashing it to a froth, and at the same time filling the air with a racket of loud screeches and high-pitched caws. Terns and boobies dived from high in the sky, while pelicans and gulls plowed in from lower down. Cormorants swam and dove, and herons and egrets pecked at the water from nearer the shore. Small herring-like fished boiled on the surface and wriggled in beaks and disappeared down gullets at a rate too brisk to follow.

Then, suddenly, it was over. Two- or three-dozen birds cruised just offshore for ten minutes, then floated or flew softly away. The surface of the water had gone totally flat again.

Jackson stood in his doorway, both amused and stunned, wondering how the frantic birds had avoided wounding each other and breaking their own necks.

But, obviously, they'd been practicing that same drill for decades, centuries, forever.

After the scene had quieted, Jackson could hear voices coming from Quentin Behr's room, more than one, but no one came out. He didn't feel right about troubling Marcella for breakfast at that hour, but hunger gnawed, so he walked down the beach to the little restaurant.

Twenty minutes later, Isaac Po walked in and sat across from him.

"Here," he said, handing over an envelope.

It was addressed to Quentin Behr, and it was in Jackson's handwriting.

"The letter you asked me about," he said.

"Where did you get it?"

"Señor Torres just brought the mail down from San Bruno. I guess it's been awhile since he picked it up."

"What do you mean?"

"Every now and then, he drives to Calexico and fetches Quentin's mail. Then, eventually, either he or Lucia brings it on down here."

"What? What about Señor Montoya's story about how he brought it down the highway in his truck on the way to La Paz and dropped it off at some *cantina* along the way?"

He smiled.

"Ah, that was just some bullshit story Quentin invented to cover everybody's tracks. Torres owns Montoya, one way or another."

He didn't say anything more for awhile, just sat there and watched Jackson clean his plate.

Then he shook his head.

"Like I said, Torres is here—and he bothers the hell out of me. I don't trust him. I don't like having him come around this place. Quentin trusts him seriously, so maybe I'm wrong. It's just a feeling, one that I can't shake."

He toyed with a spoon that was lying on the table.

"You see, he and Paco are brothers. And I'd trust Paco with my life. But not this hombre. I told you he makes mescal. Well, he makes a lot of it, barrels full, and bootlegs it on both sides of the border. Besides Montoya, how many people do you suppose he has to pay off just to move his goods? Everything boils down to money with him. Wave a dollar and his eyes light up. He runs all sorts of little enterprises out of his wallet, and I don't know how many of them are legit. Damned few, I'd wager."

"Sorry I missed him."

"Don't be. Maybe he doesn't know who you are. And that might be important later on."

"I don't get it."

"This one, Ruben is his name, and Paco grew up on a farm just west of the delta where the Colorado used to flow into the gulf. Then the Americanos dammed the river and their water was gone. They had to abandon the farm that had been in the family for at least a hundred years. Back then, they were bitter, both of them. That's another thing that bothers me. Paco has learned to live with it, and lets life play its way out. Brother Ruben, though, still carries a grudge like an old rusted knife. And some day, some way, he'll slip it between somebody's ribs. Some *gringo*. It's a feeling, dread, that's all."

The young waitress was walking toward the table with a menu.

"*No, gracias*," Isaac Po said, waving her away.

"But you sleep at his house." He couldn't say anything about Lucia, couldn't ask.

"You do what you have to do to get along, to make things work, that's all. It all has to do with manners, an odd kind of code."

He ran his fingers back and forth across the grainy wooden table.

"Anyway, I don't know how they got together. Maybe Quentin heard their story. Maybe they heard his. I don't know. I just know they've been dealing with each other for quite a few years. Money changes hands, and I don't want to know about that."

He shrugged, turned to the windows that looked out over the water, and said nothing.

"How is the old man this morning?"

He shook his head.

"Not worth a damn. Yesterday he asked me to rewrite a couple of pages, and I did that. Today I read it back to him, and I thought it did what he wanted. But he looked at me like he didn't understand a damned thing we had been talking about."

He shook his head again.

"I guess it's the pain. Great, increasing pain. He still won't eat. That can't go on."

"Do you ever think about getting him to a doctor, or at least getting Rita what's-her-name to fly in here and give him some help."

He shook his head another time.

"No, that was part of our deal. When he got that far around the bend, all bets were off. No tubes, no priests, no painkillers. Besides, he wouldn't be the first. Some of the wisest old people in the world have said enough is enough, I have nothing left to give, and gone off and starved themselves to death. Interfere? No, I can't get in the way of a decision like that."

They talked that night, but neither had much to say. The late hour of the evening before, plus the residue of the rum and the lingering drag of the trip south, seemed to be adding up to a great weight on their collective bones.

Isaac Po, for his part, stayed mostly inside his own mind, staring out over the dark water as though he were waiting for some light to appear far out at sea.

But before Jackson retreated for the evening, he wondered if B. Traven had any significance in the way of things.

"I read him a long time ago," Isaac Po said. "And the name has come up a couple of times here, in one or another of Quentin's rants. I don't know that he thinks much of the writing, but he damned sure appreciates a good anarchist when he stumbles across one. Why do you ask?"

He told him about the piece of paper he'd found describing the mysterious life of the man.

"It feels like a writer's inside joke," Jackson said.

"What do you mean?"

"Lost in Mexico, pissed off, fading to black, gone. Books, the only grave markers. How many lost writers' souls are roaming around out here in the dark?"

"A man could do worse. Funeral music fades away pretty damned fast, but these fables, mysteries, whatever, seem to age better than wine. But no, there's no script. Quentin is Quentin, not a copy of anybody, accidental or otherwise. If, in his prime, you'd have asked him whose ashes he was born out of, he would have named some flute-playing philosopher you'd never heard of, then told you in great detail why the miserable bastard was both a prophet and a fool."

"And now? Now what would he say?"

"He'd give you an answer you could never understand and, sadly, neither could I."

After that, they'd both gone to bed, and Jackson had fallen into the hard dreamless sleep of the exhausted. He heard nothing and felt nothing, and only moved when the evening chill caused him to pull a blanket tighter around his chin.

Then, from out in that foggy world that floats way, way beyond dreams, he could hear somebody calling his name.

"Jackson. Jackson, wake up."

What was it? Who was it? He fought the confusion until he came awake and then wasn't certain whether he'd heard anything at all.

Then it came again.

"Jackson, are you awake?"

It was Isaac Po's voice, and it was coming from just outside the door.

"Well, hell, I guess I am now."

"I need to talk to you for a minute."

He pulled on his pants, went out the door and into the adjoining room.

Isaac Po was sitting on his bed, lacing a pair of rough worn boots. He wore the same clothes, as though he hadn't yet gone to bed, and when he looked at Jackson, his eyes were wide and they gleamed, a look bordering on shock.

"What—?" Jackson cut himself short when he saw Quentin Behr sitting in the shadows of the far corner of the room. He was dressed in faded pants and an old shirt, a pair of sandals, and a stained old Stetson hat.

He was holding a gun, a pistol, and the bore looked as big as a man's thumb.

He was not aiming at Isaac Po or at Jackson, but he held the pistol firmly in his hand, and let it play slowly back and forth around the room in a manner that suggested, if not intent, then definite possibilities.

The old man nodded his head, but said nothing.

Jackson stood there in the doorway, unsure what they expected of him.

"I need the keys to your truck," Isaac Po said. "That's all."

The old man nodded his head again.

"That's all," he repeated. "This is between the two of us, nothing for you to be involved in. Just give me the keys and go back to bed."

"I don't have them. They're under the floor mat."

"Good. That's all I need then. Go back to bed."

The barrel of the pistol seemed to be swinging his way, so Jackson backed out the door and stumbled back toward his room.

Then he heard the closing of the latch, the footsteps of two men walking away, the slamming of metal doors, and the sound of the engine turning over. After that, all sound faded away.

He looked at his watch: 10:45 p.m. He'd been asleep little more than an hour, yet it felt as if midnight had come and gone, as though he'd been tricked by some reset clock. He lay there in fearful silence, dressed in his pants, listening. Nothing, except for an agitated heart thumping in his chest.

What could they be up to? He thought of dramas unfolding, from armed robbery to self-defense. He thought of Quentin Behr turning the gun on Isaac Po. But why? In his imagination, he could see soldiers moving along the beach, moving slowly from house to house. But they wouldn't have left him there to be hauled off in the night.

He thought about Señor Reuben Torres and wondered if he played a part, and that thought led him to Isaac Po's fears and all manner of nightmares of betrayal.

He tossed and turned for two or three hours, got up, looked out, then went back to bed. Finally, after two more hours had passed, he fell asleep again, more exhausted than before, and heard nothing the rest of the night.

When his eyes opened again, the sun was well above the peninsula to the east and the room was flooded with that same glaring light. For a moment, he struggled to recall why this morning should be any different from any of the days before. Then the events of the middle of the night came back, and he dressed as quickly as he could, ran a brush through his hair, and walked outside.

All appeared calm, little different from the day before, except that the gulls could only pace and squawk and sort through the detritus of yesterday's feeding frenzy.

He walked around the end of the trailer and saw his truck parked where it had been, alongside a pile of old oil drums.

When he walked back around to the steps leading to the deck, Isaac Po was sitting in his usual chair. He was dressed in the clothes he had worn the day before, and his eyes looked as though he'd had very little sleep, if any at all.

"Let's take a little time for coffee" was all he said, and the flat tone of his voice, the set of his jaw, told Jackson that silence was the only tolerable response, and his questions would have to wait.

Isaac Po gave directions and Jackson drove. After just a couple of miles to the south, they turned toward the water and worked their way through the sand, along a network of unmarked and overgrown trails. Mostly they followed a set of tracks that might have been recently made.

The road ended on a sandy point overlooking a spit of round black rocks exposed by the low tide. There, an old weathered brown cabin sat back among the dunes. Once the roof had been covered with tin, but it was now just bare boards, splintered and half rotted away.

He shut the engine down, and they sat quietly for a minute or two.

"He had me bring him out here one morning early on," Isaac Po said. "Mostly, he just walked around saying nothing. But he did say he used to camp here, just to be able to see the world from a different direction, to be alone for a few nights at a time. He'd camp next to this old shack and would go inside if the wind or rain got to be too much."

They got out and walked up to the shack, and Jackson could see a shabbiness that distance had kept out of focus. The door hung at an angle, supported only by its top hinge, and sizeable gaps had opened between the boards that covered the walls. He looked through a vacant window frame and saw empty rusted cans and wine bottles scattered around on a bare dirt floor. Small wooden shelves on one wall had been taken over by piles of dried turds and nests of string and grass and paper.

They rounded the corner, and on the east side, facing the water, they came upon Quentin Behr sitting in the morning sun. His hat was resting across his legs, and his head was slumped off toward his left shoulder.

A single bullet had entered and exited just in front of both ears, and trickles of dried blood ran down both cheeks. The pistol lay next to him in the sand.

A hundred feet inland from the cabin, they dug a deep hole in the sand. Digging was easy, and in less than an hour, the shoveling was done.

Then, using sheets Isaac Po had brought along and ropes from the truck's toolbox, they lowered the body down. Isaac Po turned away as Jackson threw the first shovel full of sand onto the tangle of white cotton.

When the grave was filled, they left it unmarked, as Quentin Behr had wished. In a matter of days, the coastal winds would obliterate his passing, their passing, all evidence of the drama and pain that had ended that morning in the silent dunes of the Sea of Cortez.

Then Jackson left Isaac Po there alone and walked back to the truck. After about twenty minutes, he came along.

"It's hard to know just what to say," Isaac Po said as he climbed into the cab. "Thanks is about all there is. Thanks for living, thanks for writing, thanks for not giving up."

Pause.

"I hope the going home was worth the getting lost."

That afternoon, they agreed to head north on the second morning following—through Ensenada, over the mountains, and across the border at Tecate. Isaac Po had heard from other travelers that Border Patrol routines were soft there, and cars were not backed up for miles, as they were in Mexicali.

"Less time in line, less time for some bored cop with a clipboard to come by and write your license plate number down."

After they'd taken care of business in El Centro, Jackson would drop him off in Calexico. There, he could pull his own truck out of Señor Montoya's warehouse and drive back to Obregón.

"I might want to find a way to get my hands on some Mexican license plates, title, registration, but Montoya probably has plenty of that kind of thing around. Or knows where and how to get it. Anything, for a price."

They fixed themselves a scant and early dinner. Isaac Po had sent Marcella and Paco home for a week, allowing them time to grieve for their master who had "died during the night."

Afterward, he wanted to walk. Tensions and raw nerves, Jackson guessed, still would not let him rest. Sitting back, toasting the sinking of another sun, was not enough.

The night was a soft and quiet one, befitting the end of a solemn day, as though Quentin Behr's first evening in the embrace of the earth should be peaceful and sublime. They walked slowly north, past the little hotel, and saw no one. Once facing the rocky headland further north, they turned and walked back. The lighthouse glowed orange in the last rays of the day.

They stopped from time to time, looking out to sea, and tried to talk about the life, the passions, of Quentin Behr, but the words all seemed hollow and weak, and neither of them could bring anything new to the last hours of the old man's last day. His life had been heroic, and they said as much in three or four different ways and left it at that.

The little restaurant seemed to be closed, so they sat there, on concrete steps that led down to the sea, and listened and watched as the evening took shape.

"What about the book?" Jackson asked after a while. "What happens now?"

Isaac Po didn't answer, not for several minutes, and when he did, the tone of his voice was even more solemn than it had been earlier in the day.

"I haven't misled you, Jackson, but I have let you mislead yourself. Is that the same thing? You think you know what is going on, but you do not. You think you understand what this is all about, but you don't. You see, my friend, there is no book. There has never been a book. An illusion, a charade, but more complicated than that."

Jackson wasn't certain he had heard the words correctly. It was as though Isaac Po was telling him that Obregón and everything that he was a part of had all been built with mirrors and cardboard and fog.

"What are you talking about? You told me there was a book."

He shook his head.

"No, I told you there was a story. I told you there was a plan. But never did I tell you there was a book."

"You read part of it to me."

"We see what we want to see. I'm sorry, Jackson. Let me try to explain."

The story outline, the full story line that Isaac Po had told him that night, had been written down by Quentin Behr maybe twelve years before.

Sometime following, he had written the first four chapters, part of which Isaac Po had also read aloud that night.

"Beyond that, I have very little. Bits and pieces that he has written over the years, much of it disconnected, garbled dialogue, the work of a failing mind. He hasn't written a coherent sentence in a very long time."

Then he stood and brushed off his pants.

"Come on," he said. "I have something to show you."

They walked back to their quarters, side by side, but without saying a word. What was there to say? The questions rolling in Jackson's mind were so broad, so confused, he couldn't make language out of them.

Isaac Po walked into his room and returned carrying a large brown envelope, overfilled and tied shut.

"I have this."

Jackson held out his hand absently, to take it and open it, but Isaac Po did not hand it over.

"No need to look," he said. "In here are carbon copies of all the letters he wrote to me in prison as well as the original of every letter I wrote back to him."

Letters from Eduardo Abeyta. How clearly Jackson could see himself, then, reading through Isaac Po's writing, sitting on the porch at the old silver mine. Reading about the very letters inside that envelope.

"When Rita Ellison told him about my problem in Colorado, he realized the parallel with the story that had for so long been festering inside his mind. So he started writing letters. He saw this as the basis, the body, of the work we would do together. This was how we would finish the book."

Jackson didn't understand and told his friend that.

"You have to remember that most of his letter writing was done years ago. And even then he might have had help."

"Rita Ellison?"

"I don't know. But well before I got out, the letters had stopped."

Darkness was setting in. Shadows were deep inside the little patio, but Isaac Po made no effort to find a light. So they sat there, waiting each other out.

"What, all these months, have you been working on?" Jackson asked.

"Collecting his thoughts, his expressions, his words, as fast as I could. But, each day, I could see his memory, his ability to frame his thoughts, going to pieces. Some days he would be extremely lucid, like the day he talked to you. Then for three or four days following, he might say nothing at all. Just stare out through the window and mumble to himself. Gradually, I came to grips with it."

"So this typing, this rewriting, this time together—you've just been humoring a dying old man?"

Isaac Po shook his head in the dimming light.

"No, not totally. Some of the work is real. Strangely, he could re-member statistics about water. Evaporation. Flow rates. Salt content. But, to a certain extent, what you say is true."

"Did he understand?"

"No. In his mind, there really was a book. All we had to do was as-semble all the scattered pieces. Our old letters, he thought, were just a book waiting to be organized. But he didn't understand how much of it he had never written down."

He took the envelope back inside, and Jackson sat silently. When Isaac Po returned, he also sat quietly, but Jackson couldn't tell what he was staring at and couldn't see the look in his eyes.

"Are you going to finish it, make it into a book?"

"I don't know. Sometimes I think I have to. I told you how strongly I feel about the story. But what would be the use? Without his name on the cover in big bold type, it would be just another book, maybe never published, maybe never read."

"You can't fake it?"

"What do you think?"

He understood.

"I might just do it for myself. Just to know, somehow, that the whole story got told, if only by me, to me."

Bits of blackened paper, with words about Tibetan death chants and sandhill cranes. Jackson remembered.

"The message would still be the same."

"Would it? How much of the message is colored by the soul, even the reputation, of the messenger?"

"Why didn't you tell me about this from the beginning?"

"I didn't want to disappoint you. Didn't want you to feel like you'd made this long trip for nothing."

"I came to tell you about your mining claim. That's all. And I've done that."

"Is that the only reason you're here?"

"It's the reason I came. Why I'm still here, I don't know. I sure as hell don't."

The silence of nothing left to say.

The whistle of a nighttime wind.

The pounding of the waves.

Like a slow pulse, the flashing of the lighthouse light.

Isaac Po got to his feet and—without another word—went into his room and closed his door for the night.

Twenty Years, and for What?

Isaac Po spent most of the following day sorting through Quentin Behr's books, clothes, and other belongings. Jackson didn't ask what he was looking for or how he might be intending to dispose of the property, preferring instead to leave him in peace.

In the morning hours, Jackson walked the beach to the south, mindlessly setting one foot in front of the other, often not seeing the birds ahead of him or even really hearing anything beyond the questions that continued to rattle him.

After a couple of hours of walking, he suddenly realized that he was coming upon the rocky point that fronted both the old shack and Quentin Behr's final resting place. He walked closer, but almost timidly, as though he might find something he didn't want to see.

Then he heard the sound of a vehicle and watched in some surprise as his own truck came into view.

Isaac Po got out, picked up a few pieces of old wood from around the shack, and started a fire. Feeling like an intruder, Jackson stepped further back into the dunes and watched Isaac Po unload boxes of loose papers, file folders, old newspapers, and magazines. And as Jackson turned and eased away, Isaac Po was silently, slowing feeding his load into the hot, almost smokeless, fire.

"I used your truck to haul some clothes to the mission down the road a-ways."

"Good."

"And I hauled old papers and crap that meant nothing, pertained to nothing, out to the shack and burned them."

"I saw you."

"Yes. I saw you, too."

Although no clouds, no rain, threatened the evening, a stiff wind was blowing in off the sea. Waves were breaking hard against the shore, thundering and crashing far more than on any night since they'd come down from San Bruno.

Isaac Po had produced a bottle of Señor Torres's mescal, left behind as part of that earlier day's mail call.

"People kill for this shit in the border towns, Jackson. It may be diesel, but it's high enough octane to run a barge."

Jackson could tell Isaac Po had already been sampling it. His eyes were wide open and intense, and words were rolling off his lips more freely than at any time since he'd read aloud from the nonexistent book.

Rather than sit in the protection of the buildings and walls, Isaac Po wandered out, bottle in hand, to stand on the edge of the surf in the full force of the wind. His gray hair was blown behind him like a cloud of trailing smoke.

Then he retreated far enough to be heard and sat down in the sand.

"Until nighttime two days ago, it was all still possible. Had the old man hung on for another couple of years, maybe we could have pulled it off. Probably not, I don't know. But, still there was always a chance. Now that chance is probably gone, and that means everything has changed. Nothing we knew or were can ever be the same.

"Even for you, Jackson. Having been pulled into this story, you're now a different man. You can go back to Whitewater, or the valley, and you can try to pick up where you left off, or even where I left off, but you never can. Not completely, not precisely, because a part of you has already been born here, and part of you has died."

He took a drink from the bottle and handed it to Jackson, who simply stared at the unmarked bottle for a few moments and handed it back.

He felt something coming on, something more than the wind that was beginning to grate on his nerves.

"We start all over again, now. Sometimes that doesn't amount to much. New hat, new name, the first frost comes earlier or later than it ever did before. Other times, other lifetimes we've got live with pain."

He stared Jackson straight in the eye with a hardness that forced him to look away.

"That's why I asked you, did you come to tell me about the mining claim or for something else? Maybe you don't even know. But I know, and I want to tell you about it, and I never want to talk about it again."

"There was rain," he said, speaking as much to the sea as to Jackson. "But you wouldn't remember it. You were so drunk, river water could have risen above your knees, and you wouldn't have known. But you'll remember the night. Not the details, the madness, the sights and sounds. Not like I do."

Isaac Po had gone to the city to get his eyes checked. That same day, Jackson had a meeting with his biggest newspaper advertiser, working to nail down what, for him, was a major deal—a two-year contract, with half the money paid up front.

Meanwhile, Corinne had been gone for a month—first sitting by her mother's side as she slipped painfully away, then seeing to the funeral and to the doling out of the little money her mother had left. She was flying back into the city that afternoon.

Isaac Po, since he would be down there anyway, had volunteered to drive her home.

"When we got back into town, we went into the Main Vein, waiting for you to show. We had a couple of drinks, but you were not to be seen. We checked a couple of other taverns, and finally we found you."

He sat like a monk, ankles crossed, hands on his legs, still staring out to sea.

"You were sitting at a table with Lydia Sullivan on your lap, with your hand up the back of her sweater. You remember Lydia. We used to call her Big Titia. And you were way over on the dark side of the moon.

When Corinne tried to talk you into going home, you flew into a rage. 'Stop trying to run my fucking life,' you yelled. Then she started screaming at you.

"I had to get one of the two of you out of there before you made a real mess. And since Corinne's bags were still in my car, I convinced her to just let me drive her home. She was bawling like a baby. And I was pissed, really pissed, that you'd gotten me into a situation like that."

Jackson reached for the bottle, and Isaac Po handed it over. Now Jackson knew what was coming, what had been churning under the surface since the snowy night they'd stumbled across each other on the highway.

He remembered the story, at least scrambled pieces of it. It had been one of those brutal nights a sane man could barely remember and a troubled man could never forget. Important details escaped, while ugly details come back like chronic pain. But it was one among many. One card in a fat deck of bad ideas, well-shuffled and poorly played.

He drank and passed the bottle back.

Isaac Po had driven her home, and she'd begged him to stay until Jackson got there. She just didn't know what to expect, and the anger and sadness she'd felt over the way she'd been treated wasn't something she could bear alone. So they'd had a few more drinks. And they'd waited. And they'd waited more hours still.

"You never came home."

An ugly detail. He remembered it.

Somewhere in the course of that waiting, they'd begun to hold onto each other, maybe out of innocence, maybe not. And the holding had become stroking and the stroking had taken on a course of its own, without distinction between right or wrong, a mixture of passion and tears.

"That wasn't sex we were having, Jackson. It was revenge, blind anger, defeat. Once too often, you'd gone too far over the line."

Isaac Po stopped, then, as though he didn't want to go on. He held the bottle, but didn't drink from it, and instead just stared out at the breaking waves.

For more than three weeks after that, Corinne and Jackson had not spoken. Jackson didn't know what had happened that night at home, didn't even think about it, but he did remember most of what he'd done, and a saddened and sorry skeleton of himself had settled in for long nights on the living room couch.

"Then one evening, a couple of months later," Isaac Po said, "I'd been reading, and I was about to go to bed when I heard a knock on the door. It was Corinne, and as soon as I let her in, she started crying, sobbing as though the world had come to an end. I had no idea in hell what was going on. Then, when I got her calmed down, she told me: she was pregnant. And, because she'd been away, because she hadn't allowed you near her for a month after she got back, the cause of that pregnancy was pretty clear."

He reached for the bottle, took it back, and took a sip.

"At first I thought it was nothing. Another pregnant woman. Hell, the mountains were full of them. Zero population growth. A woman gets pregnant, a man leaves town."

He stopped for a moment, looked at the bottle in his hand, and dropped it into the sand.

"But then it sunk in, and I realized that I'd made one big mistake, and I would be paying for it for a long time to come. The baby could not be born. You could not be my friend. I could not stay in Whitewater. All of that came clear to me.

"So I made a rough plan. An aunt of mine was a nurse in Colorado Springs, and she agreed to take care of Corinne's problem. So, about a month later, we pulled out in the middle of the night, she and I. The next morning, I left her there in the hands of my aunt, signed a blank check, and drove on. Where to, I didn't know. Where to, it didn't matter.

"Maybe I would see her someday again. Maybe I would see you again. But on that day, moving on, giving time a chance to work, was the only answer that seemed to make any sense at all."

He finally looked over toward Jackson.

"Still, now, I think it was the only thing I could have done."

Inside Jackson's mind:

Corinne could have had a child, and we could have named it and raised it and walked down the sidewalks of Whitewater holding it by the hand. And everyone would have known. Somehow, from a look, a whisper, a glance across a crowded room. Everyone would have known.

Isaac Po had spared me the agony.

But even if there had been no child, that one rainy night had changed everything. He had it right. For five years, ten years, twenty years, we could never have been friends.

He'd spared me that agony as well.

Isaac Po said nothing more then, just sat brooding, studying a darkened world that had slipped well beyond sight.

Jackson stood and brushed the sand from his pants.

"I've got to go pack my shit if we're going to get out of here at first light."

He walked off a few steps, and Isaac Po stayed behind, adrift in that nighttime sea.

Then Jackson walked back.

"Maybe it mattered then, Isaac," he said. "And maybe it mattered when she came back and left again. But it sure as hell doesn't matter now."

Isaac Po looked up.

"It's the past, Isaac. What is the term you use? The bastard child of yesterday? Well, the bastard child is dead. Buried. Mourned for twenty years. Now we can get off our knees and try to figure out what the hell we're going to do next."

The next morning, by daybreak, they'd packed a few belongings into the truck and were ready to head inland. However, before they left, Isaac Po called Jackson out onto the small patio overlooking the sea.

"I need to show you something," he said. "Just in case."

"In case of what?"

He didn't answer. Instead, he walked over to a chiminea, a small Mexican stove that sat in a corner next to his doorway. He lifted the short clay chimney off and sat it on the floor, then picked up the three-legged stove and moved it out of his way, leaving only a large, irregular slab of sandstone that had served as the stove's base. He grabbed one corner of the rock and slid the piece off to the side, revealing a wooden box buried in a hole in the sand.

"I think of this as our fallback box," he said.

"What do you mean?"

"If I need to get something to you and can't, for whatever reason, I'll try to leave it here. And if you have something for me, and I'm gone, leave it here. Maybe it won't work, I don't know, but I don't know what else to do."

"What are you afraid of?"

"I can't even answer that. But when nothing turns out to be what it should be, the way it was promised, then maybe we need a box. Maybe it ought to be big enough to crawl into, with food and water for a lifetime. But for now, this is the best we can do."

Driving north, they passed through three soldier barricades, but who were they? Just two more guys in long lines, gringos who'd been in Cabo fishing. That was a story they'd made up as they drove along, how they'd gone for yellowtail, how their luck had been poor, how the weather was to blame.

"Las lluvias." The rains.

But the story never came into play. Where you going? Where you been? The questions were always the same.

When they came down out of the mountains into Tecate, the day was mostly gone and shadows filled the rolling valley. Jackson made two wrong turns and drove in a circle before he spotted a dozen or so cars in line at the Border Patrol gate.

"You both American citizens?"

They both said yes and held out their passports.

The patrolman glanced at the documents, returned them, and waved them on through.

"Cameras," Isaac Po said.

"Where?"

"Somewhere. You can count on it."

But they were back in America, and all Jackson could think about was a clean motel room, a hot shower, and fried chicken out of a box.

"Amazing what a little cheap water can do," Isaac Po said.

They were eastbound on the interstate, headed toward El Centro. On both sides of the road, lush crops of head lettuce, leaf lettuce, perhaps spinach and broccoli, ran north and south, brown and green furrows that converged and stretched for miles in both directions.

All of it, every green plant, owed its life to the All-American Canal—the project that had finally destroyed the farm of Paco and Reuben Torres's family.

"As long as you can get Lupe and Juan and Pilar to sneak across the border and handpick all this fucking lettuce for a couple of bucks an hour."

Jackson remembered the peon buses he'd seen in Calexico, the hard-eyed pickers, but didn't say anything.

"Welcome to the Imperial Valley," Isaac Po said. "Coming soon: the site of world's largest salt flat, the world's longest chain of empty ditches. Next water, one hundred miles. Do not slow down. Do not give rides to starving Mexican boys with guns."

The phone rang twice.

"McMurry and Ross."

"Is LaDonna in?"

"May I tell her who's calling."

"Jackson."

Dead air.

"Jackson, where in the hell are you?"

Her voice was just shrill enough and loud enough to tell him that she probably hadn't already stacked his crap beside the road and gone to court to have him declared dead. That was good. The last thing he needed was indifference or worse—lock-jawed anger, which would make everything more difficult to pull off.

"I got pretty damned worried when you didn't come back from your little camping trip."

"It's okay. I'm in California."

"For Christ's sake, what are you doing there? Why didn't you let me know?"

"Look, I'll be in Whitewater in a few days. I'll explain things to you then. But I don't have time right now. Listen, I need a little help from you. Do you know a man named Barry Halverson?"

He was looking at the business card he'd gotten from Velma Widell, kept safely stashed in his wallet.

"Yes, I know Barry. I've done a couple of small deals with him."

Small deals? He couldn't help but smile at her choice of words.

"Is he for real?"

"Well, he and his partners built and operate four or five hotels. Is that for real?"

"Call him and tell him that I'm coming to town to represent a man named Isaac Po, an old, old friend of mine. He owns a mining claim this Halverson guy is rumored to be interested in."

A short pause.

"I've heard about that mining claim," she said. "They decided they would have to bypass it since they couldn't find the owner. They said they would have to come in from another direction, build a longer road."

"Do you think he's still interested?"

"They haven't moved a shovelful of dirt yet. So I would say yes."

"Any idea what he'd pay for it?"

"Since when did you decide to get into the slimy real estate business, Jackson?"

"Come on now."

"I think he said the extra road work was going to cost him around a hundred and thirty thousand. If he goes back to his old design, he'll have to go through the cost of redrawing and refiling his plans with the county. More public hearings. So, subtracting that out, maybe one ten, one fifteen."

"We're not greedy, LaDonna. Tell him we want ninety cash. And when I say cash, I mean hundred dollar bills. He pays for the back taxes, title insurance, whatever else. And whatever commission you think you ought to have."

For heartbeat or two, she didn't answer.

"Do you understand what happens when you deal in cash, Jackson?"

"What do you mean?"

"The bank that handles that kind of cash has to file a report with the government, specifying who withdrew the money, who deposited it, why. The PDA will contact Barry Halverson. He'll have to turn over details of the transaction. Then they'll want to have a little talk with you and your friend."

"Dammit."

"But I think the banks have ten days or two weeks, something like that, to file the report."

"We'll have to make that work."

"What in God's name are you up to, Jackson? Drugs?"

"Sure, LaDonna, you know me. The cocaine king of Whitewater. Sorry, nothing so exciting. Isaac has a chance to steal a piece of property in Cabo, but the seller demands hard American cash. That's all."

LaDonna would understand this kind of talk.

"Another thing. I'm calling from a copy shop, and I need a power of attorney form. I tried a couple of office supply stores here, but they don't carry them anymore."

He gave her the fax number.

"They can notarize it here."

"Just a second."

He could hear her telling her secretary to send the form.

"One more thing, LaDonna."

"Yes."

"Say nothing to anyone. Tell the same thing to Halverson."

"Jackson, what's really going on?"

"I said I would explain it."

"A sheriff's deputy was here about a week ago, asking about you. He said it was nothing important. He'd just been asked to check on your whereabouts, that's all."

"I'm just a name on a very long list, LaDonna. Maybe the government has decided that small town newspaper publishers pose a real threat to Americans everywhere."

"This still smells fishy to me."

"The clerk is waving a fax copy and pointing my way. I guess it came though all right. I'll see you by the end of the week."

Click.

Jackson left Isaac Po in front of Señor Montoya's shipping company warehouse in Calexico.

They shook hands.

"When are you going back across the border?"

"As soon as I can get my truck in gear."

"Maybe you ought to just kick back for a day or two. Check into another motel. Eat some potato chips and drink some cold beer. I've got plenty of money."

He peeled off three hundred-dollar bills and handed them over.

"Thanks, bud. I can use this to buy some food. Maybe a couple bottles of rum. But I won't stay. This place gives me the jitters."

"Where will you cross?"

"Right here. Into Mexicali, as soon as I can. Border Patrol, they're thick as piss ants in this part of the country."

"Okay."

He started to get out, then sat there with the door partly open.

"Jackson?"

"What?"

"Tell her—"

He waited.

"Just tell her not to give up on me. Not totally, anyway. Not yet."

They shook hands again, as though they'd forgotten.

As he walked away, Jackson waited to make sure the office door was unlocked. After he disappeared inside, Jackson put the truck in gear, then put it back into neutral and sat there with the engine running. Perhaps it was Calexico one more time, with its streets that felt bruised and edgy. Perhaps it was just his own sense of being watched. Something made him want to wait and see.

If Isaac Po didn't trust Ruben Torres, and Torres and Señor Montoya did business together, and they both operated in that murky world that leaked unmarked boxes and sacks back and forth across the border, what did that mean? How could he be confident that he was on safe ground? How could he be so certain his truck was even there?

Then the door opened, and Isaac Po and Señor Montoya walked out, talking to each other like old friends, gesturing at nothing, before disappearing through a gate in the chain link fence next door.

Jackson put the truck in gear and headed north.

Water Resources 104

DUG IN 1938 as little more than a big ditch through the desert, the All-American Canal became the backbone of the largest irrigation project in the world, carrying as much as 26,000 cubic feet of water per second.

The water, taken from the Colorado River, was used primarily for the irrigation of 500,000 acres in the Imperial Valley, which lies roughly between Yuma, Arizona, and El Centro, California. In 2008, farmers and ranchers grossed $1.37 billion from canal-watered fields.

But the canal leaked. Particularly where it ran though the Algodones Sand Dunes, the big ditch was estimated to be losing 66,000 acre feet (nearly 21 billion gallons) of water per year.

Mexican farmers were grateful for the seepage—the only source of groundwater on which their farms relied. Happy, too, were the 100-plus species of birds in the Andrade Mesa wetlands, also kept alive by the All-American leakage.

The City and County of San Diego, however, had other plans for that water. Consequently, the State of California appropriated $170 million and San Diego taxpayers ponied up another $130 million, all which has been used to line twenty-three miles of the ditch with concrete and to buy the rights to the 66,000 "rescued" acre feet.

The math, however, raises questions. The agreement whereby San Diego gets the water for domestic use runs for 110 years. The total tab, $300 million divided by 110 says that the debt will be paid back at $2,730,000 per year, not taking interest into account. Divide that figure by 66,000 acre-feet per year, and you arrive at a cost per acre foot of $41, presumably to be borne by San Diego households.

So far so good, but therein lies this simple problem: the farmers in the Imperial Valley pay $13 per acre foot, a cheap price indeed, given the aforementioned $1.37 billion in revenues collected in 2008.

Fast-forward another 20, 40, 60 years and San Diego needs more water to serve its never-ending growth. Who will end up with the Colorado River bounty then—the lettuce grower who pays $13 or the thirsty citizen who pays $41?

Once they see their livelihoods disappearing down the concrete ditch, perhaps the Imperial farmers will decide to do their irrigating with dynamite. And, thus, the Mexican farmers might someday get their water back.

PART FIVE

Marching toward Oblivion

DRIVING ON ALONE, Jackson found himself struggling against doubt, against a nag of worry, about this return to Whitewater. First would come the squaring off with LaDonna, unavoidable, with all the empty answers and phony details he would have to muster.

Would the game be so different from what it was before? Deception was deception, lies were lies.

Even before, they had rarely told each other the truth. But no, it was not the same. The old *where-did-you-go, nowhere, what-did-you-do, nothing* patter rang a little empty when endless weeks, parts of whole seasons, had gone by.

Second, he was slipping back into symbolic old clothes, the soft old shirt and wrinkled pants that had been the past thirty years of his life.

Once back in Whitewater, will I look at myself and see a fool? Will I wake up and decide the old man on the beach, Elder Jackson, was just myself, dreaming about myself? Will I pour myself an expensive brandy, turn on a jazz station and climb into the hot tub, and decide life in Whitewater is not so useless, so twisted, after all?

The doubts nagged him as he drove.

What if Isaac Po and everything he's trying to do, seen in that tiffany light, look foolish, unreal, unreasonable, unnecessary? What if, in these later years, Quentin Behr has been nothing more than a bitter old recluse, and his madness has rubbed off on Isaac Po? What if, then, it has rubbed off on me?

Every mile he drove took him farther from Obregón and blurred his picture of the place and dimmed his reasons for being on the road again. Then, with a sudden burst of green paint and red and blue lights, he was pulled over by the Border Patrol.

"American citizen?" the officer asked as he stood next to Jackson's open truck window. He was young and tall, and hid his eyes behind a pair of dark glasses. His voice carried a Texas drawl.

Jackson handed over his passport.

"Been down in Mexico, sir?"

He couldn't recall that anyone at any stop had stamped or marked the passport. Still, he couldn't be sure.

"Yes."

"The nature of your business?"

"Fishing a little, around the Cape."

"Catch anything?"

"Not much. I hired a cheap guide."

"Well, we get what we pay for. Am I right about that?"

"Yes, I guess that's true."

"And what we do pay for, we fully declare at the border, like good Americans. Y'all wouldn't have paid for anything you're hiding from the authorities, now would you, sir?"

"No, officer. Nothing at all."

He could feel the patrolman studying his eyes.

"Well then, you have a nice day now, and drive careful."

He stepped back and turned to walk away. Then he stopped.

"Sir, you do believe in God, don't you?"

"What does—"

"Well, sir, there's nothing on your car to indicate it. That's all. Just thought I'd ask."

Then he walked back toward his car, still flashing its red and blue lights.

This time, as he pulled away, Jackson was certain the man behind the dark glasses was writing something down.

Headed east, toward Phoenix, then north, and he found himself in a sea of subdivision houses. In every direction, like endless fields of Dutch tulips, houses in shades of red and purple and white and yellow were planted side by side, roofs all the same, fences the same, streetscapes the same.

"This is my house. All these are my houses," the old lady in the book screeches.

Roger Forsythe gets out of his car to walk an abandoned street, filled with tumbleweeds, lined with abandoned furniture and blowing dirt. Empty Bucket Avenue. Thirsty Trees Estates. Hermits hiding out in the discount warehouses. Bull snakes sunning themselves on diving boards.

He could never have seen it before. But he could see it now. When the water ran out, faucets would go dry there first.

He went through Albuquerque in the late waves of rush-hour traffic. For thirty minutes before he made the center of the city, just as the sun was going down, he began to see how traffic moving in the opposite direction, out of the core, crawled for a while, then came to a total stop. Still life on asphalt.

And so, on the day the earth ended, millions of metal dinosaurs would be frozen in place, each with a perfectly good driver intact. And someday they would be excavated, whole, hands on their steering wheels and radio knobs, from underneath the dunes of the sifting, drifting sands.

Headed north, he found himself caught in a different current of that same migratory flow. He was one of them. On each side, tight-jawed drivers hit the brakes, hit the gas, flashed, changed lanes, changed back, honked, came to a stop, scowled.

Where are you going? Why are you here? How many miles do you drive to be able to live outside the madness of a city that will gobble you up in a few years anyway? Look around you. Just a year ago, six months ago, wasn't this just cactus and yucca and washed-out arroyos?

Sitting, waiting, he rolled down the window. The stench of burned gasoline, hot rubber, overheated brakes, new asphalt was too much. It clogged his nose and burned his eyes. He rolled the window up and studied the weary faces to the left and to the right.

As darkness fell, the traffic thinned and he was rolling again.

No lawn watering, the radio said. No car washing. No planting of new grass. The drought, in its fourth or fifth year showed no signs of ending. City water supplies were running low. Reservoirs were filled to less than fifty percent of historical average. Fire danger was severe.

Politicians were talking about building more dams to trap and store spring run-off. Water that could be used to keep lawns green, to suckle more subdivisions. Stop it, bank it, guard it before it escapes to the sea.

More dams. More dams.

It's all they know.

The mantra of the thirsty blind.

More dams.

And as they lay dying, they dreamed of gin and tonics, ice sculptures and Niagara Falls.

It's Not Betrayal

HE LEFT THE REAL ESTATE OFFICE CLOSING ROOM with a briefcase full of money, climbed into the truck, and drove to an empty condominium parking lot on the edge of town. There, he divided the cash into two stacks—twenty-two thousand five hundred dollars in one, sixty-seven thousand five hundred in the other—and put each stack into its own small canvas bag. The fuller one, he stuffed under the driver's seat; the smaller, he held in his lap.

As he drove past a trash container, he tossed the briefcase in.

Next, he drove down Main Street and parked around a corner on a side street. He stuck the smaller canvas bag inside a paper sack, got out, and locked the door. Then he began walking, holding the paper sack under his arm.

He felt like he was watching a cheap video of himself—grainy, soundless—the sort of images that surveillance cameras collect by the millions every day.

The thought did not make him happy.

The old wooden door creaked open as before, and he began to climb the dark wooden stairs. Chunks of plaster and scraps of wood littered the steps, and Jackson wondered who would let that happen. Then, gradually, he began to recognize the sounds of construction: hammering and sawing, swearing, tools hitting the floor. And when he got to the top, he could see all the commotion was coming from the room with the window that looked out over the street.

A crew was hanging drywall, and a carpenter was nailing new trim around the window. All furnishings were gone.

A younger man, someone Jackson had never seen before, was running a tape measure along the perimeter of the floor, and writing numbers down on a clipboard.

"Excuse me."

The man looked up, and Jackson could see no flash of recognition in his eyes.

"What can I do for you?"

"Can you tell me where I can find the old woman who lived here? Velma Widell?"

The younger man shook his head.

"I don't know. I'm not from around here."

He hesitated a moment, then stood and yelled over toward the carpenter by the window.

"Hey, Roy. The old woman who lived here? Where is she?"

"Dead."

"This guy's lookin' for her."

He nodded his head toward Jackson, and the carpenter leaned his level against the wall and walked over.

"Dead?"

"Stories going around," the carpenter said. "The official version is that somebody came in here off the street in the middle of the night and stabbed her to death, maybe robbery."

The cops had been asking about him, LaDonna had said.

"Another story, though, says her granddaughter has disappeared, gone since that same night. And the feds have been in here snooping around. So we hear. So who knows?"

Jackson didn't say anything.

"Odd, though. In a mink-and-poodle town like this horseshit place, why rob the poorest old lady we got?"

Just at dusk, he hit snow.

Although it was the season for it, and a few pockets lingered in the north shadows around town, he was surprised at how easily he'd forgotten about the coming of winter, the onset of this gray-and-white season in the high mountains.

He was climbing a low pass a couple of hours out of Whitewater, headed northwest, and the light snow had not yet begun to stick to the pavement. He turned the headlights on and set the wipers for an occasional sweep.

He'd told LaDonna he would be at the house for dinner, but that had never been his intention. Instead, he'd meant to be at least a hundred or so miles away by the time she'd finished the first bottle of chardonnay by herself, by the time she'd turned on the front light and begun to stare out into the dark, by the time she'd figured it out and begun to curse his mother and his cruelty and his lousy goddamned tricks. And he felt sorry about that, truly sorry.

He watched the rearview mirror for flickering lights, flashing lights, any traffic sneaking along, or coming at a high rate of speed. But there was no movement behind and not much traffic coming the other way.

He pulled over into a place where snowplows turned around and waited. In ten minutes, not one vehicle passed, from either direction.

Even in the cooling air, his palms were wet and sticky.

The deal had been struck somewhere between San Quentin and Ensenada.

Neither of them had said anything for fifteen or twenty minutes. Jackson was concentrating on traffic that had gotten heavier and seemed to consist mainly of truck drivers who liked to pass on curves at full speed.

Isaac Po was looking out the window, first at bright green fields of some sort of edible cactus, then at mile after mile of beautifully tended wine grapes.

"Odd," Isaac Po said. "We have money, coming, but nothing to print."

"That's up to you."

"Who would read it? What's the point?"

"How badly do you want it? How deeply do you care about the last years of Quentin Behr?"

For a long time, he said nothing.

"How much of this money would it take?"

"I don't know for sure."

"Half?"

"Not that much for printing. But there will be other costs. Maybe we'll have to kidnap somebody."

Isaac Po looked over at Jackson.

"Don't think I haven't thought about that."

He turned his eyes back to the vines, the rolling hills, the cows grazing on the shoulder of the road. Miles rolled on.

"So, that old lady, Velma whatever. You know, that mining claim really belonged to her. I always felt like I was just loaning her money on it. Po's Pawnshop. She's paid me back."

No answer.

"So it's only fair, Jackson. You should give her a quarter."

Jackson agreed. It was a gesture few would make. But without the old lady, there would have been no money, maybe no chance, maybe nothing but a couple of wasted dreams.

Strange, he thought then, how we keep running into our old selves. The door creaks open, and there's a scene from twenty years ago, replayed, details that come crawling out of some dark and cobwebbed room. Would all of this have happened, would we be driving through northern Baja, if, one night, the three of us had not hidden out under the floor of Velma Widell's old shack, stiff on drugs and alcohol, waiting to be ambushed by the first light of day?

"A second quarter should go to Noche."

Jackson agreed with that, too. He could think of no one who could put it to better use, whether in an effort to win back her son or to rebuild the farmhouse.

"And the rest?"

"Just hold on to it until you hear from me."

Jackson didn't know what that meant, and in later days, later weeks, he'd regret not pressing him about his heroic dreams.

Late the next morning, he drove into San Tomas. Although the high peaks on both sides of the valley were white with snow, the flat ground across the bottom of the valley was brown, sere, lifeless, waiting for winter. The sun was shining brightly, but the few people he saw wore heavy coats, and clouds of breath trailed behind them as they walked.

Without stopping in town, he drove out to Vaca Road, and up to the green gate.

The old ranch was deserted, still as an oil painting. He was struck with a feeling that all his memories of the place were nothing but dreams. Or perhaps he'd slipped too far back in time.

Then he understood why: the goat pens were empty. No movement, no sound. He walked the packed earth, thinking perhaps the animals were confined in one of the outbuildings, protected against the cold. But no fresh tracks were cut into the earth, no fresh manure softened the ground. They were gone.

Another change: the charred remains of the house had been scooped and hauled away. Only a smooth black stain remained along the sand, and a few small thistles and clumps of grass had grown up before the frost had set in.

The straw bale shed was unlocked, so he lifted the latch and let himself in. Nothing there had changed. The table stood empty. The shelves stood empty. The bed was still unmade.

It was as though no time had passed, no winds had blown, no human hands had been at work.

He walked over to the old table and ran his hand over it. His fingers left a track through heavy dust. He knew the barrel stove would be cold, but he felt it anyway, and knew that it hadn't seen a fire in a long while.

He stood for a while at the window, watching the shadows play across the high peaks to the east as clouds crossed the sun. In the late light of day, the peaks would turn stark white, then gold, then fade to gray. After that, the temperature would fall quickly.

He carried his sleeping bag and a pillow and some extra bedding inside and spread them out on the bed. Then he lay down, watching the light play along the far wall, and for two hours he slept.

Later in the afternoon.

He walked to the woodshed, and carried back a couple of armloads of split aspen and small pieces of pine. Then he built a little fire and sat next to it on a straight-backed chair.

God, how everything had changed.

The scuffed and weather-beaten farm is not just the place where Isaac Po once lived and worked. Now, it is the place he has given up, sacrificed, so he could be on call as Quentin Behr struggled to find a few last words.

For Isaac Po, the valley and its sunrises and changing seasons were gone.

The songs of goat bells and meadowlarks were over.

Warm morning sun will rise and sweep across this bare and quiet table, but Isaac Po, his work, his papers, will not be here. And they will not be back.

All that was left behind would be lost.

Jackson carried two boxes in. One, filled with winter clothes, went under the bed. The other held his favorite books, and he took those out, one at a time, and placed each volume very carefully on the shelves.

The room needed music, maybe the Navajo flute, maybe the rounded and simple notes of a gut-stringed guitar, but that would come later. Later, music would come back into this room.

He wished for a photograph to hang upon the wall, of a bay, with an island to the north, and a shrimp trawler drifting on its chain, surrounded by a flock of white and hopeful birds.

The sun was gone and the valley had turned a colder shade of blue, not quite in darkness.

Two vehicles were parked in front of Noche's cabin: her old jeep and a pickup not much newer. White smoke curled up and out from her old stovepipe, and chickadees chirped and darted around in the thick evergreens.

He stopped short and paused, thinking perhaps she had a guest, perhaps he ought to turn around. But what difference should that make? He was there as a messenger and a friend, and if she was busy, he could return another day.

He knocked. The door opened. And she stepped back and stared, as though she didn't recognize him. He had not shaved since the morning he'd left the valley, his hair was longer, too, and the sun of Obregón had darkened his skin.

"Oh," she said then and stepped up quickly to wrap her arms around him. He could smell wood smoke in the dark and shining hair pressed against his neck and could feel the warmth of her body through her old flannel shirt.

"It's good to see you," he said, and when she stepped back, he could see how her eyes were shiny with small tears.

"I sometimes dreamed of a giant black hole in the earth," she said, "where, one by one, all the people who were important to me had fallen in and were gone. I began to wonder if anyone would ever be coming back."

"Yes. Like Alice. Down into a different world and back out again."

He gave her his best smile.

"I've seen the Mad Hatter, and he's wearing a sombrero now, but he's full of riddles just the same."

"So you found him," she said. "Some days I knew you would. Other days I knew you would not."

She bit her lip, then looked up at him, into his eyes.

"What can you tell me?"

"He says not to give up on him. Not yet."

On the long drive north, he'd asked himself more than once just how much of the story he would be able to tell Noche. Isaac Po, obviously, had believed the less she knew, the better for all concerned. He understood that, and it made a reasonable amount of sense. But, still, that seemed like old thinking, like asking another person to take a beating and never explaining why.

In the end, he didn't know what he would say or do. He would let it come to him, like the player he used to be, and he'd show everything, or a little, or nothing at all.

"I moved my gear into Isaac's old shed," he said. "Tonight, tomorrow, we have time to talk."

She had a warm fire going, and through the glass in the door, flames jumped and flickered, almost without any sound at all. They sat in chairs and drank Samantha's strong wine and talked.

"But I didn't see any goats. The goats are gone."

For a minute she said nothing.

Then he noticed how she seemed to be trying to fight back tears again, how she tucked her chin into her chest and looked away.

"The goats are dead," she said, her voice weak and cracking. "All dead."

"First a fire. Now this. What in the hell is going on?"

About a week before, she'd gone down to the farm early in the morning to milk and feed. When she'd gotten there, the pen was empty.

"Someone had opened the gate," she said. "Unhooked the chain and propped the gate open."

She'd followed their tracks, and about a quarter mile away, on the edge of a ravine, she'd found where they'd been caught and brought down by a pack of wild dogs. Some were partly eaten, and every one was dead.

"They knew," she said. "Whoever let them out knew. They drove the goats over into that ravine. I could see their tracks."

The ravine ran for miles from the north edge of the property into the foothills. The dogs and coyotes used it like an underground tunnel.

"Somebody knew the dogs were out there. In the summer, they stay up high. This time of the year they come down low again."

Outside, a little wind had gathered, and he could hear it rustling through the pines. The fire popped faintly inside the stove.

"Why would someone do that?"

"It's all part of it," she said. "Part of the insanity. If they think you've got something they want, they poison the air around you, choke you until you can no longer breathe."

"Isaac's writings?"

She nodded.

"Or his whereabouts. His intentions. I don't know. I have no enemies here. Only them."

"Without the goats, how are you staying alive?"

"I took a job waiting tables. At that café where you and I had breakfast that day."

"Is that okay?"

"It's okay. I work the lunch hour mostly, and breakfast sometimes. I don't make a lot, but I get by."

She sipped her wine.

"It's a helluva lot less work than milking and feeding the goats. So maybe it was a good thing. I don't know. Maybe it was just meant to be."

Pause.

"I just can't stand the thought of those poor goats, though, being dragged down by wild dogs. Somebody should pay for that."

Noche had cooked a big pot of chili just the day before, she said, and they should share that for dinner. They ate quietly and made small talk, as though his Obregón story should come after the meal, like a good port.

Afterward, they washed the dishes and put them away, piled more wood on the fire, and sat for a while and watched the hot silent flames. There, in the little cabin, they were a lighted boat in the middle of a vast dark sea.

"What can you tell me about Isaac?"

The question, in one form or another, had to come.

What can I tell her? That he is probably never coming back? That I still hold that power of attorney, and if the deed to the little goat ranch is stuck away in a box someplace, we should dig it up, and if it is in Isaac Po's name alone, I should deed the property over to Noche? That Señor Torres had a pretty young daughter with powers all her own?

No, he couldn't tell her any of that. Not that night, anyway. But he could tell her about Bahía Obregón, and he did his best to describe it without making it sound as though Isaac Po had deserted her for some version of tropical paradise.

"But why, Jackson? Why is he there?"

"I have to tell it to you as it comes to me, in pieces. I can't make a whole story out of it, not yet."

She said nothing.

"He went there to help a desperate old man take to the battlefield one last time."

"This Eduardo Abeyta?"

"Yes. It was a brave plan, but flawed. Whether it works out remains to be seen."

She shook her head.

"It seems so small, so unnecessary," she said. "Isaac Po, suspect American, disappears in the night and runs all the way to Mexico just to do what? Write a book?"

"It's not as simple as it sounds."

"I don't understand."

"I know that. But it will come."

"So tell me."

"It's all part of a long story. Too long for tonight. Tomorrow, in the sunshine, where we have a little more room, more time, to unfold it all."

For a couple of minutes, neither said anything.

"Tomorrow," she said.

He nodded.

"But you're going to stay here tonight."

"No. My gear is all down below. I'll stay there tonight."

She shook her head.

"No, Jackson. That's not fair. Not any more."

Fair to whom? And fair in what way? As though fairness has ever really played much of a role.

"How many nights have I spent alone? Six hundred, eight hundred? Does it matter? Half of all passing time is nighttime, and, in big pieces, my life is slipping away, one night at a time. I read, I sew, I hear the elk tromping around back there in the trees. I lock the door. I never ever locked the door before."

What can I say?

"I'll make a bed for you on the couch."

And it isn't as though I want to walk away, to go alone back out into the night, to sit at the ranch of worsening luck and wait and watch the moon.

"Please?"

He could hear her breathing, but could not tell if she was asleep.

Her bed was in a tiny room off the main room, and with the door open, he could see it from his own bed on the couch. Rather than close the door and block the heat from the stove, she had turned off the lights and undressed in darkness.

Now, he could hear her breathing.

What is she thinking? Is Isaac Po on her mind, or did she understood everything I haven't yet said? Has she seen, from the regret that I probably haven't hidden, that nothing had changed and that there is no Isaac Po in her life, tonight, tomorrow, maybe ever again?

The air felt packed in and tight, and he had a sense that she could read the electricity of his thoughts, the way sound could be heard under water. Thinking about her, the parts of her curled up in her bed, made the air tighter still, and she could read that, too. His eyes were wide open, staring at the ceiling, seeing unholy ghosts, and he knew she knew.

The next morning, after breakfast, they drove down to the lower place, and Noche showed him the bones and scattered hides that were the remains of her goats.

"My first instinct was to try to bury them," she said. "But that would have been an empty gesture, atonement for sins of my brothers. They were gone, they were goats no more. So why not let the coyotes and vultures make the most of what was left?"

He asked her where the pack of dogs had come from, and why it was allowed to roam.

"Nobody knows for sure. The pack has grown over the years from huskies and dobermans and mongrels that have gotten loose. They're smart, smart as wolves, and just as good at hunting in the night. Every once in a while, somebody gets a shot at a couple, and they hide out for a while, and one night they come around again."

She kicked at a couple of bones.

"There are a lot of stories," she said. "But none of them are true."

Inside the shed, he collected the sleeping bag and a box filled with food and a bottle of good brandy he'd bought on the way from Whitewater.

She saw the books on the shelves, and just looked at them for a couple of minutes, and didn't say anything.

"He warned us about death."

While she was away at work that afternoon, he read through some of Isaac Po's papers.

Noche had taken him outside her cabin to that place back in the trees where old logs were piled. She moved a couple of logs and told him what lay beneath.

"All that's left of his work is buried there. No reason you shouldn't read whatever you want," she'd said. "You probably know it all by now, anyway."

And, for the most part, he did.

The piece he found after some sifting would have been written after Isaac Po had been set free, after he'd been asked by Quentin Behr to come down into Mexico.

> *"In his books, he told us tough truths about cowboys, two-man logging saws, and oil gushing into the air. About cows and fallen trees and mine dumps and irrigation ditches. They are not heroic. They are not progress. Like locusts and relentless dry winds, they are simply part of an unfathomable death.*
>
> *"Now he wants my help. And so I'll go. Where? I don't know. Am I coming back? It's a nice thought, something to plan for. But*

the choice is not mine and it never has been."

She has read this, he said to himself. On some night, some summer night when she'd had nothing else to do, she'd reached into the box and found that page somewhere near the top. It was hard to believe otherwise. It was hard to believe she did not know how the story would finally end.

She has just been waiting for the news.

Later that afternoon, after she returned from work at the café, they talked. For a while they sat together in the sun, then took their chairs inside when the tall pines blocked the heat and threw cold shadows off to the east. They talked while they drank more of Samantha's wine, they talked while they ate Noche's chili, and they talked while they sipped Jackson's brandy.

He told her almost all he knew.

She had little to say. For the most part, she sat silently and listened to the story, to his version of the way things had unfolded. Now and then, she asked a question, forcing him back to something he'd failed to explain, or causing him to admit that he just didn't know.

He left out two pieces. He did not talk about Lucia. If Noche knew Isaac Po as well as she must, she would know how people, women, were drawn to him, even on the border, even among herds of goats, even in places where it never rained.

He did not tell her that Quentin Behr was dead. He didn't want to revisit that scene, and he didn't want her to ask the obvious question: why, then, didn't he come home?

"So give me hope," she said, as his memory emptied, his last words hanging in the air.

A clock above the kitchen stove said the hour was nearly 10:30.

"I can only tell you what I know."

She studied the drops of brandy in the bottom of her glass.

"It's a war that never ends, Jackson. Do you know that?"

He had no answer.

"Johnnie never comes marching home again, hurrah, hurrah.

233

Remember that old song? The men will cheer and the boys will shout, and the ladies, they will all turn out? It's good to believe that, even if Johnnie has to march home on a crutch. Endings, even unhappy ones, are better than no endings at all."

Then she stood and kissed him on the top of the head, went into her bedroom, and this time she closed the door.

He lay there, on top of the sleeping bag, underneath two of her blankets. More wood filled the stove, and he lay there and watched it burn.

No sleep, not yet. Too much freight had been unloaded, spilled as from an overturned wagon, to allow for an easy sleep. Just talking about the passion of Quentin Behr had put a knife-edge on the night, and the story of Isaac Po lurking like a beach dog in the shadows of old fishing boats had brought tears to Noche's eyes.

Who could sleep after that?

Was she angry or sad or just thinking? Was she crying or simply sorting things out for herself?

She had to hear it. Maybe, at some point, she deserved to hear the parts left out. But after time had done its job, those details might amount to nothing, faint scratches, never there at all.

They could be gently forgotten.

Just before midnight, he heard her bedroom door open.

She walked out into the main room, and he could see she was dressed in a long plain nightgown, and could see her black hair gleam in the firelight.

Then she sat down on the edge of the couch next to his shoulder and began to stroke his hair. For a while she said nothing, just letting her fingers tangle and untangle themselves.

"We're all caught in the same river now," she said. "All looking for quieter, safer water. We don't know what it is, not really. All we know is that there's a difference between right and wrong, a difference between caring and not caring."

Her hand stroked his cheek, then lay tenderly, softly, against the side of his neck, as though she'd found a pain there that could be eased.

"Finally, it comes," she said. "The day when nothing around us makes much sense. But we have to stay alive. To live. What good will it do if we shrivel up and die like mummies from a darker time, waiting for a crack in the sky, waiting for spring? What good does it do? How many more days and nights do we let slip away?"

She moved her hand over his chest, absently, almost as though she did not know. But she was arousing him, causing muscles to tense and breath to shorten. And he knew, as he always knew, that she knew.

"It's good that you and Isaac and all the others can see a way to save us from ourselves. I want that, too. But I want more than that, at least for right now. I want my womanhood back."

She took his hand and cupped her breast with it. It was fuller, heavier than he had imagined. Dressed in flannel and baggy shirts, the true outline of her body had never been clear to him. But he could feel her nipple hard under his fingertips and feel the heat of her skin.

Then she pulled away and stood.

"But I can't have this, can I?" she asked. "I can't ask a friend to betray a friend. I can't betray a lover."

She was breathing deeply, and her eyes shone with tears.

"But this isn't betrayal, Jackson. I don't know what it is, but it isn't that."

Then, with a soft sob, she stepped toward the couch and threw herself on top of him. She buried her face against his neck, and he could feel her kissing him and crying at the same time. He stroked her hair and held her tight against him, and moved his hand down to the mound of her butt and held her tightly against his moving, pushing, groin. And he could feel her trying to take him in, surround him, through their clothes.

The moment was made, and it took only tugging and pushing at cloth, shifting weight, kicking off blankets, stroking and guiding, before she was astride, moving up and down in a rhythm of her own.

He looked at her, barely lit from the flame in the stove, and her gown was bunched around her waist and head was back and her eyes were closed and wet and shiny lines ran down her face.

He tried to hold back, to go on and on.

But he could not.

When he awoke, at least an hour past midnight, she was gone. She had lain with him for a while, but now she was back in her own bed.

He could hear her breathing, deeply, as in sleep.

And he wondered whom, in the deepest and most secret parts of her soul, she had made love to that night.

Over the course of the next four weeks, Jackson allowed his life to take on an entirely new shape—more subdued, more contemplative than it had probably ever been. In many ways, as Isaac Po had warned, he had become a different man.

Most days, he stirred from his bed in the straw bale building around first light, sometimes confused for a heartbeat or two, then built a fire in the barrel stove, and made tea. Then, as the sun fought its way over the peaks to the east, he sat at the old table, making notes, in longhand, on legal pads, of everything he could remember about each day that had passed since he'd run across Isaac Po at the truck stop in the blinding snow.

He had no particular objective in mind. Yet he felt driven to recollect and preserve the events, to write down the gist, if not the actual words, of every conversation, to record as best he could his own thoughts and feelings. Some days, some nights, came back to him clear as the sharp edges of a mountain moon. Others, mainly the Whitewater days, were not so finely drawn. Still, he worked on.

Perhaps I am doing it for Noche. Or maybe I am just testing my own sanity. But the job seems as important to me as anything I have ever done.

As the mornings wore on and the air began to warm, he moved outside for other work just as vital to the challenge of staying alive. He found a good axe and an old bow saw in one of the sheds, and every day for ten days, he drove up an old road leading into a canyon and cut fallen spruce, fir, and aspen into chunks. These he hauled down to the goat sheds and piled on the south side, open to even the lowest of winter suns. Splitting could come later, perhaps after snow covered the hardening ground, and the rhythm of the swinging ax would be as sweet as the beating of his own heart.

I'll still be here when winter comes. Still waiting. Still here.

But despite the fullness of his days and nights, he couldn't shake a sense of uselessness.

With every dawning morning, every passing sunset, the feeling grew in him that he had lost his way. He was waiting for something, but what? A box would suddenly appear on his doorstep some night? Or would the telephone ring? Would he be expected to again find a familiar face among the shadows of old fishing boat hulls?

Why have I heard nothing? Will I ever hear anything? Has something gone wrong?

Those questions and more woke him in the middle of long nights, when moon shadows played across the empty land.

They did not become lovers. Not in the sense that a dam had burst and they were being swept downstream by some long-repressed tide. They touched tenderly, but not so intimately. They didn't talk about it, but it seemed they were both still haunted by the sense that they might be doing wrongly by someone, even if only themselves.

However, on the evening he told her he felt like he had to return to Obregón, they did spend the entire night in his bed, and they did please each other with a tenderness that lasted far into the late hours.

Somewhere in that long night, while they lay resting, he told her that Quentin Behr was dead. And he told her that Isaac Po was left alone, fighting with the question of whether he would make it work or let the old man's dream die.

She stared at the ceiling and, as he'd hoped, had no questions left to ask.

"The pendulum swings," she said two mornings later. "First toward you, then away. Sometimes it comes back to you, and sometimes it never does. Only a fool would expect otherwise."

He had just come to her cabin to tell her good-bye and to talk to her about the money, the proceeds from the sale of Isaac Po's land.

She stood outside the door and watched him put his gear and a box of food and clothes in the truck.

Then he handed her one of the canvas sacks. He'd redivided the money, so that each sack now held half.

"Isaac and I agreed that half of the money should be set aside, part for the old lady in Whitewater, part for you. It's too late for her, but it's not too late for you."

"I can't do that."

"Don't get confused. This is nothing more than a small part of what you've been due for a long, long time."

She just stood there, looking at him, making no effort to take the bag.

"Use this to hire yourself some legal help," he said. "Find a lawyer who can get your son back. Or, if you don't like that idea, hire a half-dozen cowboys to kick in some doors and do whatever has to be done. Then, if you feel like it, you can turn your back on this place, and start over someplace else. Anyway, use the money on your future, on your kid."

"I can't do that," she said again.

"You have no choice. Think about the house. Your goats. Your world is shrinking. Your world is trying to tell you something."

She wiped tears from her eyes with the backs of her hands.

"No."

"If you won't leave, start rebuilding the farmhouse. Buy another dozen goats. I'll come back. I'll help you."

Of the remaining forty-five thousand, he asked her to put twenty-five in the barrel with Isaac Po's last collection of papers. The rest, twenty thousand, he was going to carry to him in Obregón.

"I don't know what he needs right now," he said. "But money sometimes performs miracles. But I don't want to travel with it all. Something doesn't feel right to me."

He put an arm around her shoulders, and together they walked back to the cabin.

As they reached the door, she slipped her hand into his back pocket.

Once More, the Road

FOR REASONS HE COULDN'T TOTALLY EXPLAIN, the idea of driving on interstate highways made him uneasy. Perhaps it was the Border Patrol, the question of whether he believed in God. But he was much too far north for that. Still, keeping to the lesser routes felt better, and he worked his way along those smaller roads through the Four Corners.

By nightfall, he was halfway across the Navajo reservation in northern Arizona. He thought about a motel, but decided against that, too. Instead, he pulled off on a dirt road, drove three miles into the desert and parked for the night.

Enough scattered wood allowed for a decent fire, and he opened pork and beans and let them cook in their can in the coals. Then he heated water and made tea and sat beside the fire and drank the hot brew and brandy out of an enameled cup.

The coyotes knew he was there. He could hear their yipping, barking, howling off in the darkness, and the noise seemed to come from every direction.

What am I to them? Hunched over my little fire here, a silhouette visible to a hundred eyes, movement seen from a mile away, the smell of sweat. A threat? A meal? Just smoke and the sound of broken wood?

Stay off this desert floor, I hear them say. We live and die here, but you have nothing good enough to take. We'll be here long after you are gone.

And as he watched the fire burn down and felt the chill of the night in his bones, he remembered something Isaac Po had said years ago: Old

Quentin would like for the coyotes to eat us all.

He left at first light and drove hard all that day, and by nightfall, he'd made it as far as Calexico. But although he'd intended to check into the same motel as before, he couldn't find it. He felt certain he had the right place and recognized the turns, the street, the block. But, oddly, the lot had been scraped and now just held stacks of old wooden pallets and racks of rusting sewer pipe.

He found another cheap motel on a busier street and checked in for the night. He was tired and dirty, in want of hot water, and he knew the following day would be long and wearing. Sensibly, another night on the ground was out of the question. Desperate Mexicans and the Border Patrol alike worked both sides of the river at night, and either could see his fire and take everything he had and make him disappear.

At first, he thought it was a dream.

He woke to the sound of a radio, the squawk and chatter of a two-way conversation that sifted into the room as though it had no windows, no walls.

He sat up in bed and pulled back the curtain.

A police cruiser was stopped in the parking lot, with its spotlight playing along the license plates of the vehicles parked there. The light stopped, briefly, on his green-and-white Colorado plate, then moved on.

He could hear a radio exchange, but the words meant nothing.

Then, after a couple of minutes, the police car pulled out into the street and was gone.

Two hours passed and Jackson was still awake.

I've done the best I can.

Sometime after 2 a.m., sleep.

A stiff and cold wind was blowing out of the north, and the sky had turned a pewter gray. Jackson couldn't tell if the sun had risen or not. He looked up and down the street, and nobody else seemed to be moving at that dim and edgy hour, nobody watching as he took the canvas bag containing the money and buried it under the wrenches and a socket set, under a set of jumper cables, in the bottom of his toolbox.

By leaving early, he hit the border in light traffic, and the Mexican guard waved him through without a second look. Likewise, with an early start, he was able to avoid much of the chaos of Mexicali's opening act, getting around the glorietas with ease and heading south toward San Bruno on Highway 5.

Traffic thickened a little on the outskirts of the city, mostly incoming cars, then thinned again as he drove farther and farther into the desert. Still, no sign of the sun.

He stopped in San Bruno only long enough to fill the gas tank and spare cans, and to buy breakfast from a young boy working the Pemex station crowd with a plastic bucket full of tamales, kept warm and fresh underneath a thick and heavy towel.

Then south, past the marina and hotels, and out into the land of cactus and scrub, the rocky ridges and yellow sand.

He remembered the curve well. It swept to the left, toward the water, and cut across a low brushy ridge. Then the road dropped back into the flats and straightened out, ran for twenty or thirty yards, and became the place of Todos Altos, all vehicles stop, the only military checkpoint on this roadway running south.

The thought of another face-off with this group of soldiers left an ache in his gut. He hadn't forgotten the surly eyes of the soldier who walked with a limp or the hard stare of the other as he put a wrench in his pocket and stood there, inviting him to make a fight out of it.

But the soldiers were gone.

The tents had been pulled, and the old farmhouse was home to nothing more than a couple of black vultures sitting, sunning themselves, on the top of a crumbling adobe wall.

They watched him drive by, following him with only their beady eyes.

The old fender with the red intertwining circles was still there, though harder to see inside a dune of windblown sand. But he had no time to stop.

Maybe the old man, too, is gone. Maybe he was a memory. Maybe he was a coyote. Maybe he was a dream.

He thought about that as he drove on, dodging potholes, driving for a while down in the ditch, then back on the road again.

Another disappearing man. Is he still part of the local folklore in some town in middle America, the man who faded from sight, the man who took money or a young boy or his own priceless poetry and was never heard from again?

Do they still talk about him and wonder where, and why?

Driving alone, straining his eyes and fighting the steering wheel, he felt like the miles were creeping by at half the pace of the earlier trip. He fought himself to stay awake and every hour or so, stopped and got out and walked back and forth, stomping his feet in the lights of the truck, watching the dust boil and drift.

How could anybody feel more abandoned, more alone?

Isaac Po was waiting for him, and he had to push himself forward, out of that endlessness, beyond the twisted stumps and broken rock. But he could not fend off the need for rest. Twice, with eyes half closed, he pulled off into the cactus and fell into an instant sleep.

As a result, the trip was a long one, and the sun was just easing up out of the eastern sea when he dropped down off the plateau and started across the soft sands of the bay.

Isaac Po's truck would be there, and Jackson tried to remember it from that night in the heavy snow, from that night so long ago. Blue, white, green? But suddenly he realized, with a growing sense of dread, that it didn't matter. It didn't matter at all. The parking space next to the junk in the yard was empty. Not just empty, but blown half full of sand and stems of dead brush, with no tracks, not even the barest of traces.

He pulled into the space and stepped out into the sand, stretching his legs, listening to the quiet rattle of the surf. Then he walked around to the seaward side of the house and saw the same drifted sand, the same look of abandonment.

The door was not locked and he let himself in. Books, plates, shoes: as far as he could tell, nothing had been crated and hauled off, nothing looked much different from the way they'd left it the morning of their departure for the north. The old typewriter was still there, although his stacks of paper, his files, were gone.

He walked out onto the patio and stared for several minutes at the sea, the quiet and beautiful Bahía Obregón. A couple of hundred yards to the south, a dozen pelicans bobbed in the rippling water, and far out on the horizon, he could just make out the dim shape of a shrimp trawler. Other than the rattle of surf, the whisper of the wind, there was no sound.

He walked over to the corner by the door and removed the clay chimney from the Mexican stove. Then he dragged the body of the stove into the middle of the floor and moved the rocks.

There was no manuscript.

Instead, the buried box held only a single sheet of paper, and on it was written only two words.

El Brujo.

For several hours, Jackson sat and stared out to sea, waiting for answers that would never come. As bitter as it tasted, the only thing left for him to do was to turn around and retrace his steps, all the way back across the border, all the way back to another life.

Unacceptable. But what other choices do I have? Still, to turn and walk away feels like a kind of unspeakable treason, a failure on my part to live up to a promise I've never really understood.

He walked down to the little restaurant at the end of the beach, and tried the door. Locked. He looked in through a window and saw an old lady sitting alone at a table, reading a magazine. He tapped on the window, but if she heard, she never looked his way.

The little table in the kitchen was still covered by a stained piece of oilcloth, and he used it to wrap ten thousand dollars—one hundred one-hundred-dollar bills—and dropped the bundle into the bottom of the box.

"There's more," he wanted to tell Isaac Po. "I can get it to you. Just let me know how."

He found a pen and turned the single sheet of paper over and wrote those few words. Then he sat there for a minute or two. But short of trying to atone for twenty years of silence, how could there be anything more to say?

He closed the box and put it back in its hiding place, buried the canvas bag in the bottom of his toolbox again, and began the long ride back to the north.

Late in the day, as the sky had turned to slate and wind was raking the truck with sand, he rounded a corner, expecting more of the same rocks and brush, more of the same nothingness. But instead, he found soldiers blocking a different section of road.

They were organized as before, with their Todos Altos sign propped up in a pile of rock alongside the road. The two young boys with their automatic rifles were standing by, and a couple more stood leaning against a tree.

The soldier with the scowl and the limp walked alongside his window.

"Whey djew hetting?" he asked, just as he'd done before.

"San Bruno."

"¿Por qué?"

"To visit amigos."

"¿Pasaporte?"

He didn't like the feel of things. These soldiers had not hassled him before, not to this extent, not in this deliberate way. Isaac Po's words about bounty hunters came clearly back to him.

Back among the cactus, well off the road, he could see an old truck and three tents, and the wind was causing the door flaps on the tents to slap around like green laundry on the line. That same wind, now coming out of the east, whipped the baggy uniforms of the other soldiers as they waited and watched.

He handed over the passport. No choice. And in the five minutes it took *el jefe* to study the photo, name, address, walk over to the tent and back, everything changed.

The *jefe* was barking out orders. His voice was sharp and loud, and although Jackson could not understand a word of it, the excitement, the threat, in that voice came through clearly, like the snarling of a dog.

The soldier stuck Jackson's passport into the back pocket of his pants.

"Fuera del coche," the soldier ordered, opening the truck door, stepping back, and waving his hand.

He wants me out. But to get out, to leave the truck and the money in their control, while I stand helplessly by, is beyond consideration, beyond possible.

It brought a bitter, metallic taste to his mouth.

But what can I do, outmanned, outgunned, with no plan, not even a hole to dive into?

He stepped down and felt the prod of a rifle barrel in his back. One of the boy soldiers kept pushing at him, pushing the barrel into his spine, until he'd moved Jackson well away from the truck.

"Acostarse," he said, pointing down at the ground.

Jackson sat down, but the soldier was not satisfied. He held out his arm, palm down, and pushed it toward the ground in a quick angry motion.

Jackson laid face down, head resting on his arms. His heart was pounding wildly in his ears and the back of his neck was hot as a branding iron.

All the while, the *jefe* was still barking comments and orders to the others, and they'd begun to ransack the truck. Everything from behind the seats was thrown to the ground, and one of the soldiers was in the bed of the truck, tossing bags and boxes to the others.

Then the *jefe* began pounding on the toolbox with his fist and yelling at one of the younger men, sending him on the run toward the tents.

He returned with a heavy steel knife, and began to pry at the lid. In less than a minute, Jackson heard the thin metal of the lock break off with a snap.

When he heard the clang of his tools hitting each other on the ground, he tried instinctively to raise himself up, to see what was happening. Then he felt the sharp pain from a rifle butt hitting him in the back again.

"Aqui, aqui, aqui."

The voice was loud and excited, and as Jackson twisted his body around just enough to see the truck, the soldier in charge was holding his plunder in the air.

The canvas moneybag.

A sickening moment of truth twisted Jackson's stomach into knots.

Somehow, they were expecting me.

They knew who they were looking for.

They knew what they were searching for.

But how? How?

One soldier was left on guard. The rest crowded around their jefe, watching him as he pulled bundles of one hundred American dollar bills from the bag, showed them, then put them back again. Then he sent the second boy with a rifle to help stand guard over Jackson, while he and another of the soldiers, maybe his second in command, retreated to the tents.

The rest of the men began throwing his crap back into the truck, and one of the soldiers walked up the road and pulled the *Todos Altos* sign out of the rocks and threw it in the back of the truck as well.

Then Jackson was pulled to his feet and herded off to a spot behind a pile of rocks, well away from the road, and as he walked, he could hear his truck start, run for a short way, then stop.

Jackson sat on a rock and waited. Nearly an hour went by. The two young soldiers said very little to each other, just kept their eyes glued on him and their fingers on the triggers of the rifles.

Other Isaac Po words came back to him: What they want to do

more than anything else in the world is shoot those fucking guns.

The wind felt colder and stronger, but he suspected it was merely fear that chilled him to the bone.

"Listen," Jackson said. "We can work something out. I know where there is even more money." He was thinking of the cash in the box at Obregón. Anything to get himself out of this tightening vise.

But they stared at him with vacant eyes, and he knew they had not understood a single word he'd said.

Finally, just as darkness was setting in and the roadsides were turning into pockets of back shadow, the *jefe* walked around the edge of the boulders, called the two soldiers over, and explained something to them. They said nothing, simply nodded their heads as he talked and pointed off to the east.

Then Jackson was pulled to his feet and herded out past the rocks, further toward the water, further away from the road.

Suddenly, he realized that the sound of walking behind him had stopped. He was walking on alone.

Instinctively, he turned half around and saw that both soldiers had their guns raised to their shoulders and were aiming at his back.

"No," he yelled, and began to run.

He cut around a clump of old and rotting cactus and ran toward a little ridge, hoping to put something, anything between himself and the soldiers. But he lost his footing in the sand and fell, hitting the side of his face on a rusted half-buried can. Without looking back, he tried to get back on his feet and half-crawled, half-ran toward the sandy ridge.

Then came the sound of a shot. And then another, and Jackson felt a sharp and burning pain in the crease of his right shoulder.

Stumbling and half-falling over the little ridge, rolling and tasting sand and fear in his mouth, he somehow got his feet squarely under himself again and ran toward the north, cutting closer and closer to the water's edge, moving faster in the wet and harder sand.

He stumbled again and spun, and for an instant, could see clearly what he was leaving behind. The two boy soldiers had stopped at the margin of the tide and were standing there, dead-still silhouettes, watching him run.

And a thought washed over him that made him want to stop and laugh, made him want to slow his pace and get his wind, and maybe laugh some more: *the two boys, by far the junior members of the roadside brigade, have probably been issued only one bullet apiece.*

And, now that they've missed, or think they have, they can only catch me if they lay down their heavy guns and run as hard as they can.

But they are soldiers, young men of the republic. They can never drop their guns and run.

Jackson walked and trotted on through most of the night, always north, sticking to the water's edge, which was easy to see under a half-moon that rose about two hours after the hard black darkness had set in. And, always, he strained his eyes, trying to see what might be waiting for him along the rocky fingers, behind the rolling dunes.

But there was nothing. And he came to see that once they had his money and his truck, his life or death didn't add up to much, either way.

None of the soldiers, he was certain, would willingly get very far away from the canvas sack and the hundred-dollar bills.

The bullet had gone through the flesh just inside his armpit and below his shoulder bone. It had bled considerably for the first half-hour, but he'd stopped it easily enough with a bandage ripped from a tee shirt he wore under a sweatshirt.

The slug hadn't found enough resistance to cause it to expand, to mushroom, and the damage was far less than it might have been. Still, he'd lost blood. He could sense that loss in confusion, in an emptiness in his head that at times made him want to either cry or laugh, and, at times, his balance left him and he was forced to sit down and stare at something close, at rotten shells, at his dirty hands.

He slept for an hour just before dawn, and just as the sun popped up out of the sea, he found himself on the edge of a small village.

Dogs charged out to challenge him, growling and baring their teeth, driving him back into the water, leaving him in doubt about finding help there. His instincts had told him to stay out of sight, anyway, but the run and loss of blood had left him with a killing thirst. His lips were crusted and cracked and his stomach was in knots, and he knew, dogs or no dogs, he'd come to the end.

Then, a boy came out of one of the huts and began to yell at the animals and to grab tails and necks and jerk them back away from the water's edge, away from the helpless, wild-looking man.

He stood there for a full minute looking at Jackson.

"My name Humberto," he said.

And then Jackson passed out, falling face first into the wet sand.

The Old Wizard

JACKSON CAME AWAKE just as Elder Jackson, *El Brujo*, was changing a bandage on his arm. Jackson said nothing, just looked around and past him, trying to figure out where he was. He was not inside the old trailer, he was not outside under the palapa, and not anywhere near the sea. He was, instead, inside some sort of crumbling old structure with walls half-gone, under an open hard blue sky.

"Welcome to Misión de Parador," the old person said. "I was hoping you'd come around before the sun went down."

Jackson sat up slowly and could see that it was an old Spanish church, set back among a grove of stunted palm trees. Somewhat below, he could see the blue glint of the sea.

"Known only to the fishermen in the village," *El Brujo* said. "But there is water here, an intermittent spring. I sometimes get fresh water here myself."

He paused.

"Protecting it, blessing it, is a large part of my job."

The walls of one chamber were nearly intact, and newer makeshift *vigas* had been laid across the tops of the adobe bricks. Old and rusted pieces of tin provided a roof of sorts.

A battered wooden cot was shoved against the west wall, and a fire ring had been built in the middle of the dirt floor.

"The soldiers burned me out about ten days ago," the old one said. "I thought, after all these years, they understood just how harmless, how insignificant, I really am. But these are not good days to be American."

He'd walked down to the fishing village for food just a couple of hours after Jackson had washed up on the nearby beach. A couple of the villagers had helped carry Jackson to the old mission.

"They were anxious to be rid of you," he said. "The army had already searched their village once, and they will certainly make a return call."

He threw a blanket down on the cot and fetched a canteen of water from the spring.

"Rest," he said, and then left, walking back down toward the road.

For another four hours, Jackson slept.

Right at sunset, Elder Jackson appeared again, this time carrying an iron pot filled with stringy fish and beans, a roll of corn tortillas, bowls and cups, and two bottles of the strong murky liquor that had no name.

The two of them ate almost without words, watching the last of the day's light fade out over the horizon to the west, over water they could barely see. Then, as the air cooled and shadows began to fill the corners of the abandoned church, the old man gathered a pile of scrubby thorny wood and built a small fire in the circle of rocks.

The old one poured each a cupful of the spirits and sat back a way from the fire. For a long while he said nothing and seemed to be waiting for the weakening light to tell him when to speak and what to say.

"I do not track time," he said finally. "One sunset and the following sunrise could all be part of the same day to me, all part of seasons that neither begin nor end. And what are days, anyway, but the scorecard of impending death?

"But three weeks ago, give or take a day or two, a young woman appeared in my little campo just as the sun was sinking into the sea. A Mexican girl, beautiful, someone I think you might know. Lucia Torres."

Jackson said nothing, but he felt hope rising through the pain and fatigue in his soul.

"She was accompanied by your friend, Isaac Po."

Finally, good news.

"We have to get around the military, she told me. Something to that effect. North or south, we have to know. We have to get around."

The snap of the burning wood echoed off the crumbled adobe brick.

"I told them they were not safe there, that the army was swirling like a hot wind. But if they gave me a day or two, I could maybe put together all the mules, all the supplies, they might need."

They had stayed in the mission for two nights while *El Brujo* negotiated for mules and food with the fishermen. Then, with a good map drawn by an old man in the village, with beans and water, they had headed inland, toward the Pacific coast.

The old one poured more of the liquor and passed the bottle to Jackson.

Minutes passed. The only break in the stillness came from the crack of the fire and the whisper of an evening wind. The faint light had left the desert in fading shades of brown and gray.

"Don't be too hopeful," the old one said. "I have no way of knowing whether they made it or not."

"What did they carry?"

"Almost nothing. Whatever it took to keep them alive."

A turkey vulture circled high in the pale sky. Tipping back and forth from wing tip to wing tip as it glided, the bird rode the thermal currents caused by the inland heating of cooler coastal air. For two days, Jackson had watched the ugly bird as it seemed to be watching him, barely straying from the column of bleached air directly over the old mission.

Mostly, though, he just sat and stared at the broken walls of adobe bricks and thought about the broad sweep of sacrifice—time, dreams, money, life—and the small measure of gain. No book, no justice, no Isaac Po.

Still, he felt, some good had to come from it all. As long as he was alive, as long as Quentin Behr's memory was alive, as long as Isaac Po was out there somewhere, perhaps something might yet come together.

The old one and Jackson said their good-byes among the rotting hulls at the end of San Bruno's *malecón*.

"I know a man in town," Elder Jackson had said, "and his name is Karos. An American. He runs a tour bus service between here and San Diego. He can get you across the border."

"I have no passport. They took it."

"Ah, yes, that. Let me explain it this way. Twice in the past ten years, I have had to return to the states, and, well, let's just say my trips were far more precarious, more complicated than yours will ever be."

"What are you telling me?"

"For a hundred dollars, sometimes a little more, the crossing will get done. Complete with paperwork, blurry photographs, if that's what the circumstances demand. He can get you to the bus terminal, if that's where you want to go."

"How soon?"

"He spends Monday, Wednesday, and Friday nights at the Dorado Hotel. Generally, he can be found in the bar, at a table in the corner, and his office hours run late into the night. He will be expecting you."

So the day was Friday, late in the afternoon, and the two Jacksons leaned against the battered hull of one of the old fishing boats. They'd caught a ride into town in a fisherman's rusted ancient pickup, sparing Jackson enough time to buy some clean clothes.

It was an awkward moment, one that he knew ought to be filled with promises he didn't know how to make and gratitude he wasn't certain he could put into words. Jackson was about to try, about to cram the germ of it into a small box and pass it over like a precious and handmade gift.

Instead, Jackson the Elder simply looked down toward the ground for a few seconds, then reached across and took Jackson's hand with the soft loose gesture of their first meeting.

"A rich, strong, shattering death comes to those who fight," he said. "The rest of us simply dry up and blow away."

For the last time, until the next time, dream time, the elder turned and walked off through the shadows cast by the old boats, never looked back, diffused into bones and gauze, and was gone.

Just at dark, before he traveled the ten blocks to the Dorado Hotel, Jackson walked north a block to the small café where the two of them had eaten, and where he had last seen the woman known as Lucia.

I will not go in. I will not take a table and order a dinner I will never be able to eat. I just want to revisit an earlier time, to get closer, to chance another visit from another ghost.

The place was deserted, shades drawn and dirty, weeds and yellowed paper and plastic bags blown up against the front step. A thick padlock hung from a hasp on the door.

A bleached sign in the window said *Cerrado*. Closed.

San Diego.

He found a cheap tavern and drank until he had just enough sense left to stumble back to the bus station and sit on a hard chair and fall asleep. He awoke just as the first gray light of day was creeping through the downtown streets, and a loud, crackling voice was calling for passengers on the first bus to Albuquerque. So he took his place in line behind a thin and bent old woman in a blue parka, with the hood pulled and tied tightly around her face, and behind him, a scowling black man in bib overalls was muttering to himself about Jesus.

He stared off into the future and fought back images from the past. He just wanted to go home.

Deliverance

Months later, rainfall returned to the valley. As winter waned, the warmer season came on with a pent-up constancy, turning the hillsides of cottonwood and aspen into a sea of green. Every creek draining the high Sangre de Cristos ran full, bank-to-bank, turning grassy meadows into shallow verdant ponds.

Jackson healed through the spring, easily under a caring touch, but not as quickly has he'd anticipated. Somehow the fatigue of the long journey, one of miles but also one of thrashing around inside his own soul, had left him slow to mend.

The best he could do, some afternoons, was to sit outside and sip tea and listen to the bluebirds and the doves.

But there would, he prayed, come a day.

On a sun-struck morning, Jackson ventured into town, to the post office, as he did every second or third day. There, he collected a bulky tattered package and knew, before he ever slit it open, what lay in his hands.

It was postmarked Calexico.

Jackson

Notes to Myself II

"Something has changed," El Brujo said to Lucia and Isaac Po. "Something is in the air. The coyotes and owls sense it, and they hunt in silence, move around in the darkness without a sound, even as the moon grows larger each night."

The three of them stood at the water's edge in the twilight of that third day.

"Lucifer is afoot upon the land. Stay here for the night, maybe for another day, even a week. I know a place where you can hide, and where you will be safe."

Most mornings for the past year, I have sat at this grand old table and written everything I saw, heard, and remembered of my time with Isaac Po. Part from the Whitewater years, part from uncountable days in Mexico.

And, here at the end, I can only guess at the details and dialogues of the last days before he was gone again, perhaps for good. These are dreams, not much more than that, but I find that I cannot go on without them.

Midmorning sun casts a warm glow through the south window and across the plank floor of the straw bale room. Although the season is late spring, white caps of snow and ice still cover the peaks on both sides of the valley.

Outside, the clang of a bell and the bellowing complaints of hungry goats come from the pens, and now and then, Noche passes by the window, pushing wheelbarrows full of compost to the garden.

Before fall, we'll begin to rebuild the house—a first step before the long legal battle over the boy can begin.

Through the long winter months, I've had plenty of time to relive those days and nights. And I've had time to read, to study *Adios, Water Dog*, every word, every page of it. It's uneven, obviously the product of two voices, not always in tune, one far more shrill than the other. And I agree with Isaac Po that it is a rare and powerful story, one that should make us all reach for prayer wheels and broadswords. It is sacrifice and passion, insight and lament, and, in the end, worthy of the hard, hard fight.

I will see it into print. I have enough money set aside to put a copy on the desk of every politician and editor in America.

But first, the closing of the circle. Or, perhaps more to the point, managing the lights and shadows so that the circle appears to close itself.

These were, are, the lives of two angry men, real flesh, who ached and bled and drank what we drank and were washed by the same rains. And yet they are not us. They dwarf us. And how that came to be is perhaps the most delicious mystery of all.

So, I will take all that I've written here, and with a stern eye and merciless knife, condense the story of the writing of *Adios, Water Dog* into a forty- or fifty-page introduction to the book. The struggle of the two men, teetering always on the edge of tragedy, must be brought to light.

So must the secret second life of Quentin Behr. Done right, those twin stories will set a spare and fitting stage for the water saga itself.

Probably, I will say more about Isaac Po than about Quentin Behr. About this, I have no choice. I did not share midnight whiskey or blizzards or barroom dreams with the old man. We had no woman in common. I did not even know him when he stood tallest, at his angriest, at his best.

I can only do what I can do.

What happened to Isaac Po?

Anything, everything. *Zopilotes*, maybe. Vultures, rising up from the last bone of a scattered many. Or laughter and music, playing out through the bamboo walls of a little handmade house tucked into the jungles of Belize.

After this story has made it into the common language, perhaps Isaac Po sightings will begin. Sipping tequila at a *cantina* in Loreto. On a mule alongside the highway south of El Rosario. Perhaps even in a jail cell in Jalisco.

Dreams, mostly. Wishful thinking. The human need to find the elusive and the lost.

Another story never meant to end.

Just at dark, movement takes shape in the shadows, and Isaac Po walks into the lantern light. He has a big Mexican sombrero pulled low over his eyes and he's carrying a pair of leather gloves.

"It's time to go," he says, and Lucia hauls four canteens full of water off the floor of the abandoned mission.

"Give us twelve good hours and a decent moon, we're gone. Give us three good nights, they'll never see us again."

The two of them walk to the edge of the lantern light. Then Isaac Po stops and looks back at El Brujo, the old one leaning against one of the crumbling walls.

"When they come," he says, "tell them everything you know. Everything. Tell them we have strong mules, food, water, and bullets. Tell

them we're riding into the desert and we travel at night. Tell them we leave no tracks."

He pauses.

"Tell them all to go to hell."